EX LIBRIS ROBERT CARL
CHA RITAS
& MARION OAK STICHT
1909.

MARION

Brett Martin

Published by Fullers Bookshop Pty Ltd
131 Collins Street Hobart Tasmania 7000
www.fullersbookshop.com.au

Email: brett.martin8@bigpond.com

ISBN 9780994561183

First published 2014
Copyright © Brett Martin, 2016

National Library of Australia Cataloguing-in-Publication entry

Creator: Martin, Brett, author.
Title: Marion / Brett Martin.
ISBN: 9780994561183 (paperback)
Subjects: Historical fiction. Tasmania--Fiction.
Dewey Number: A823.4

Design: Lynda Warner
Production assistance: Tracey Diggins

For Terri

The voice I hear this passing night was heard
In ancient days by emperor and clown:
Perhaps the self-same song that found a path
Through the sad heart of Ruth, when, sick for home,
She stood in tears amid the alien corn;

John Keats – *Ode to a Nightingale*

Municipal Chambers,
Queenstown, Tasmania.
11th January 1923

Dear Mrs Sticht

At tonight's Council Meeting, Warden Lawson reported that it was your desire that no public functions should take place in connection with the departure of yourself and family from this district, with the rise and progress of which, you and your much-loved husband (now at rest) had so much to do.

Members of the Council however, whilst regretting that no such opportunity would be afforded residents generally, unanimously decided that a letter be sent to you expressive of the sentiments of our people to you and yours.

We have therefore a very great pleasure as official representatives of this town, in conveying to you, our keen appreciation of the admirable manner in which you have taken your part in the public and social life of the community, and also of your unpretentious acts of love performed amongst us during your residence here of over a quarter of a century.

That the future may have much that will be cheering to you, that your worthy sons may carve their names on the Roll of Fame with the same brilliancy as their illustrious father and that you may all be spared to each other in loving comradeship for many years to come, is our most sincere and earnest hope and wish.

———

It may from time to time, be your desire to visit us again, and should such a pleasure fall to our lot, we can & do assure you of a warm and heartfelt welcome from each and every section of the place in which you laboured so long and so successfully.

For and on behalf of the people of Queenstown
I am, Dear Mrs Sticht
Yours most sincerely

Archie Douglas

1

21st January, 1923.
Balfour track from Whale's Head Inn,
west coast of Tasmania.

※

I was born in Paris and my father was Napoleon. This is my retreat from Moscow.

A baking northerly off the mainland's desert heart scalds my back through white silk. The sky glares vast and blue over the soggy plain. March flies chivvy my ankles and my ears. I fan them lazily, in time with the plodding horse's swishing tail. Out I roll on wooden rails, carried in a rickety old cart into the summer shimmer, sliding across the sour, button-grass plain, my blasted heath, a sea of wildflowers bobbing in the sunny wind. Bedraggled cargo with my bedraggled train, dragged by a wind-whipped, sullen horse to a wind-whipped, sullen place, my insides full of broken glass. Bleeding again and tired – so very tired, for so very long. Going to ground like a wounded animal, looking for a place to die.

the past alone is true to me

Back home it's winter but surely soon enough to dream of spring: the days drawing out a little, the promise of thaw and rising sap. At the old Stage house in Edgar County, Illinois, Papa's maples – giant when I was yet a child – will start to bud soon and though the bleak wind sweeps off the prairie, the soil will yearn for the plough soon enough. As I once did, a long time ago.

Far away across that prairie ocean, in the high country of Colorado, the crackling winter is never out of mind. In Pueblo, where I grew up, after a fashion, the air is dry as a stick, so clear you can count the leaves on trees ten miles away. The wind howls like a wolf off the icy Rockies and can freeze the words as they fall from your lips; yet even there folk will be planning for the warming.

it is dark and the air feels just like spring

I was born in Paris and my father was Napoleon. Paris, in Edgar County, Illinois, at the end of the Rebellion. Six months before they took Mr Lincoln. My father, Napoleon Bonaparte Stage, hailed from over in Pickaway County, Ohio. Up near Circleville, at Stage's Pond. His Grandfather, Richard Staige, was a Scottish Presbyterian who came out from Edinburgh before the Revolution and settled in Virginia. There was talk his father was a Scottish Lord who threw him out because of his politics but I've heard that story of so many families that I give it credence only in my heart. Richard served in the Revolution and had land as a result, but he was restless and ambitious, and followed opportunity west across the Shenandoah, until eventually he came to the Scioto Valley and settled down. He was 74.

far away, you rolling river

His son William, my Grandfather, was born in West Virginia and spent his childhood on that western odyssey. Maybe that's where my westering comes from. Old Will departed this world just as I was coming into it, so I never knew him. I knew of him well enough, though. A tall and volatile man, Mama said, given to action before thought, even in old

———

age. Maybe I get that from him as well. Lizzie remembered him, though she was only seven when he passed: a kind old gentleman in a black alpaca suit, who smelled of whisky, she used to say, though this was surely based on scant experience. Will changed his name from Staige to Stage but the family paid no mind. He and his brother Richard ran a distillery under both names up in Pickaway. A fine occupation for a Scot but one we rarely mentioned. I suppose he may have smelled of whisky.

Napoleon headed further west as soon as he was old enough. Old Will owned land in Illinois and in 1841 Papa fetched up in Edgar County, in Bloomfield, named after the Staige home back in Pickaway. There he commenced to farming and marrying. He farmed and ran a stage company and like Old Will bought land whenever he could. Did well, mostly, until the railways came. Mother, Sarah Jane Hazelton, was his fifth wife and bore the latter six of his 13 children. I was tenth. Only Lizzie and I reached 21. Charlie died just short, which means he died a child, I guess. Lived and died a child. He was my hero. I never got used to being older than him. It was wrong then and it is still wrong now. Yet he lives, a man-child in my mind and will die with me, directly. There will be not a soul left on earth who knew him. He has been spared much. What would he think to see me now, half a century on, a broken old woman dying in this bleak place? As far away as the moon.

now a funeral procession has gone by towards the cemetery

Mama was from Chester, up in New Hampshire. From a fine old New England family. The Hazeltons trace their line back to 1670 and beyond. I have no idea why. Sarah was one of five girls. She had an education and married late – at 30. I suppose 30 was a good age for a fifth wife.

Papa's mother, Catherine, was a Kile and 30 when she died giving birth to him, which years none of Napoleon's first four wives achieved. Maybe that was part of Sarah Hazelton's attraction – she was already 30. Papa surely thought the risk behind her. So it proved, although the

Hazelton weakness for consumption was always hovering in the wings.

I was a first wife at 30. I had almost given up hope that Robert Carl Henry Sticht would ever feel he had 'control of the ground.' Not that I would have cared too much. I never meant to marry – it seemed, on the evidence, to be a dangerous calling.

There was surely something tragic about the wives of Napoleon Stage: Elizabeth Ann passed over on her first wedding anniversary, the second Elizabeth on her 26th birthday and Matilda on the winter solstice. Louisa was taken by cholera in the same hour as her son.

Childbirth, milk fever, consumption, Indians – the world was a dangerous and temporary place. They are all strangers to me, the dead wives and children of Napoleon Bonaparte Stage, though the children were kin, it must be allowed. Ghost kin. They simply never got going with life, taken before they had time to create a memory. Except poor Kate, who lingered a little while, like the ghost at the banquet, a pale reminder of all that had gone wrong and gone before. Before Mama set things right. Then Kate passed as well. Scarlet fever took her when I was barely conscious of the world. Lizzie said she was a sad child, who seemed – not unreasonably – to live in constant apprehension. So when her end came it was sad but unattended by surprise. Mama's litany kept them all alive, though – women and children she'd never known mingled uncomfortably with her departed kin. And they were many.

we tarried on the bridge and listened to its gurgling – babbling, rushing, dashing music, while I thought of those who had been there before with me and thanked God for the blessed immortality which will again unite my loved ones...

All in Heaven now. The arrangements must be difficult.

Though I was barely ten when we left the house on Brouilletts Creek and rode the rails west across the prairie, to the high country of Colorado, I remember some things as clearly as this morning's sunrise.

———

I remember Mama's greenhouse and her flower garden and Papa's maple trees along the road to the house that passed through a field of nodding flowers in spring. I remember the snow drifting in silent as sleep, blanketing the house and farm and the little bridge over Brouilletts Creek that would wash away from time to time, carried in my imagination all the way to the Mississippi and down to the Gulf of Mexico. In those daydreams I'd float down to the Gulf with Charlie, like Tom and Huck, on a raft of bridge logs.

Papa would rebuild the bridge just the same again, every time. Folk are patient in Edgar County and believe that nature will bend to their will, eventually. Napoleon was surely patient, despite his father's blood. Through four dead wives and seven dead children he kept on marrying and farming and buying land.

They haunted the old house in a genteel way, the dead wives and children of Napoleon Stage. A few things left behind, not much to show for all that graft and grief. There was an old oak sideboard, hand-carved – rather crudely I realise now – that was the first Elizabeth's. She was a Stanfield and Stanfields are thick on the ground in Edgar County. Her folks lived across the South Arm and north a little way, so there was always an echo: the people you met at church and in town or passed the time of day with on a dusty road. There is an awkwardness that such casual encounters engender when you have moved on. What is the etiquette, I wonder? Of course I get most of this from Lizzie. I was too young to notice much more than my own importance.

There was Matilda's table linen, supposedly her mother's but possibly a souvenir of some hotel, according to Mother, who could see embossing where others could not. There was the second Elizabeth's cutlery, her dowry perhaps, the bone handles sallowed and shaped by hands long gone but whose buttery smoothness I can feel to this day, relics of a world already fading and soon to be forgotten. There was a vase or two and some needlework cushions, such as we women waste lifetimes over in order to appear useful. There were some old toys in the attic that we mostly ignored – childhood was brief in those days and often fatal and anyway all outdoors was our playground – and there was the occasional kind and often obscure reminiscence from Papa on the Sunday pilgrimage to the old Wynn Cemetery, to review the wreckage. The past was arcane and archaic. We look forward in America, not back.

Napoleon Bonaparte Stage fought for the survival of the Republic his grandfather fought to create. He was progressive, though a Democrat by happenstance. Support of the Republic was a vexed question in Edgar County, even though Illinois was not a slave state. Slavery divided the state north and south, as it did the Republic, and Edgar County was on the cusp. Papa was elected to the Legislature in 1858 and supported Lincoln against the rebels. He was always quietly proud of that. He was a Presbyterian at heart: hard, proud and brave. A man of principle who never shirked the action principle demands but seldom receives. Quick tempered and tall like his father, it was said, though I never saw anything but patience. He was 45 when he enlisted to fight in the War of the Rebellion. He served two years while Mama fretted after him and ran the farm and the stagecoaches and raised four children, like Marmee March. Women awakened in that war. Half a million dead men creates a vacuum and nature reputedly abhors a vacuum.

Papa was a Quartermaster in the 126th Illinois Infantry. I have little idea what a quartermaster does but I know he was at the siege of Vicksburg, on the Mississippi, and that was known to be a terrible place. Bombs and trenches and terror, random death and madness. Women and children mown down like cattle by their kin, just for living on the river. It was a thing he never talked of but which we knew. The war turned at Vicksburg, Mama taught me later: control of the Mississippi split the Rebels in two, at a cost of 5,000 souls. The town finally fell on the 4th of

July and folk down there do not celebrate Independence Day. Vicksburg spelled the beginning for Grant but the end for Napoleon. Injury overcame his tiring body, a sinewy frame forged by hard work and grief and the wind off the prairie. He came home in the Fall of '63 and I was born a year later, to the day. November 9, 1864, the day after Mr Lincoln was re-elected.

all are of the dust, and all turn to dust again

Napoleon and Sarah prospered steadily after the War, though Mama said later that the man who marched away to war never came back. They did well enough, though, until the railways came and the stagecoach business fell away. They owned land – and land is wealth. After Father passed in '74, Mother sold off some parcels to repay money they had borrowed to invest in a failed railroad scheme. There are always railway schemes to take your money. It is like mining, a game of chance disguised as business.

I bequeath myself to the dirt, to grow from the grass I love

We buried Napoleon Bonaparte Stage in Bloomfield, out in the old Wynn Cemetery, alongside the many wives and children who had gone before. The old Wynn Cemetery, on a fine summer day that burned itself into a nine-year-old girl's mind like a daguerreotype – it is there and then it is not – but when it is, when some scent or sound or pollened breeze rustles it up from the shadows of my mind, it is so real I can smell the summer hay and the horses' restless breath; I can hear the shovels scraping and feet shuffling and the dull thud of clay on wood and I can feel the sweet breeze riffling through the cornfield over west of the cemetery, on the edge of the prairie. The edge of the world. I wondered even then about the other side of oceans.

in my old griefs and with my childhood's faith

The War of the Rebellion left an awful scar on the Nation and the County. Edgar County lost more than 300 men. Not something a child much noticed, mind – all is new in childhood and therefore unremarkable – but even so I knew that Napoleon Stage was respected for what he stood for and how he stood for it. He was admired for the way he carried himself and for how modestly he wore his considerable grief. Good folk from across the County marked his passing. He represented the qualities we Americans cherish: enterprise, independence and endurance. And I guess he believed in Family – God knows he went through hell to get one.

We were all there that day we buried him, the black flock gathered round Mama like a shawl, with Lizzie, Charlie, me and little Emma caught up in its fringes. It was my first tragedy but there were others soon to follow. Charlie and little Emma both joined Papa in the ground within a few years. When Emma died, at eight, Mama buried her over in the Edgar County Cemetery, in Paris, and moved Napoleon and the unnamed child over there as well. A last word of monumental proportions. The four dead wives of Napoleon Stage and their seven dead children had no say in the matter and stayed in the ground at Wynn. Too expensive to move them all, Mother said. I wonder.

She is with them all now, in the Edgar County Cemetery, alongside Papa and the nameless child and Emma and dear Charlie, my reckless hero. In the summer of '81 we three survivors of the 18 Stages, Mama and Lizzie and I, came back across the prairie ocean from Colorado with poor Charlie in the box car, dead of a fall from a horse.

the spring of life seemed to break within me then

Mama's consumption had driven us west after Father and little Emma passed. The weight of running the farm and the business brought on her consumption. The doctors said Illinois would kill her, so we made off to the high, dry air of Colorado, a giant sanatorium back in those days. There was a considerable sum left over to support us after Mama sold off land to pay the banks. We became Capitalists.

Lizzie found a good man, George Barndollar, and married him. It was a happy union, although it never bore fruit. When Charlie died, George and his younger brother Harry became our guardians, three easterner women alone in the Wild West. We lived in their big, old rambling house in town. As the grief of Charlie's loss was assimilated, that old house became a home. It was a busy, happy place. There were always visitors and it seemed always to be full of local children, most of whom I ended up teaching. Mama had a hothouse and a garden, Lizzie ran the house and had her good works and I was studying. George had his shop and Harry tried his hand at a few things but seemed disinclined to settle down. When I came back from Vassar and took up teaching it never occurred to me to live anywhere else.

There were already several consumptive Hazeltons out in Colorado seeking a cure, and there was a distant cousin, the black sheep, Horace Tabor, up in Leadville with his silver mine. Consumption and mining held the state together. And brought Robert and me together. Eventually.

death and distance define my life

We're closer now to Balfour's red hill. Rolling south-east along the wooden rails, burnished by weather and wear, Mt Balfour looming lonely on the right. Further south, along the coast, Mt Hazelton's sleek slopes shimmer in the heat-haze like a beached whale. Named for Mother, a modest mountain as befits a New Englander; from up at Chester, amongst the apple orchards and golden forests.

Having mountains named after oneself would be considered ostentatious by the Hazeltons, but a small mountain on the other side of the world – who will ever know? Only God – and he surely doesn't much care what small mountains are called. A small mountain is a humble choice. 'Mount' Hazelton wouldn't warrant naming in The Rockies.

Papa was from Pickaway, where there are no mountains at all. He was an unlikely match for a woman of Sarah's background, you might think, but she was 30 and had an education and Napoleon Stage stood well in the world. A straight-backed man, with land and energy and a much-tested faith in himself and God. He had a good mind that beheld the world through sad eyes and $50,000 worth of land. It was a combination hard to resist – as many found before Mama.

She came to Bloomfield as a teacher. The schoolhouse was built on Papa's land at Marion's Point, on the other side of Brouilletts Creek from the house. The old Stagehouse – a droll name if ever there was one. Eponymous House, Mother used to call it, to remind us of her learning I suspect.

After Mother married the Squire, her sister Annette came out from Chester to fill the breach and she married Napoleon's man, George Dinsmore, who went out on his own just before the war. Then another sister, Mary, inherited the position. The Hazelton women did well out of that little school. There was only rubble and weeds to show for it when I went back, finally, ten years ago.

all are of the dust, and all turn to dust again

We're coming near the draw now and the long swoop down to the little creek, winding along the bank to its head. Iron rails on the bends. Wood will not bend so exactly to your will.

My name is Mrs Robert Carl Sticht – but I am Marion Oak Stage.

2

There's some relief from the northerly as we snake through the spindly gum trees beside the little creek. Its lazy trickle is the only sound now we have dropped below the ridge. The birds are hiding from the hot wind, the wallabies and Devils are sitting out the heat, waiting for the cool dark. The boys are quiet now as well, wearied by the long journey, apprehensive of the destination, still adjusting to their new circumstances. Our isolation and loss weigh heavily upon them but they are young and have their health and their education is assured. Balfour will be part of their inheritance. It will stay with them long after I am gone. They will remember how to die and that is surely how one should live – knowing how to die.

Across the creek now, past the rickety old sluice and there it is – the mocking mouth of *Copper's Reward*. How perfect the name. I gaze past it to the flank of Mt Frankland as Bob says something about the workings, but he knows I know it is a fool's game. I've had my fill of adits and drives and assays and the elusive vein.

I am the barren promise of the Balfour field. I am Copper's Reward.

but whether there be prophecies they fail

I remember the first time Robert brought me here, in the winter of 1910. Cold, windswept and wet, I was excited as a flea. A new town being born on a hill on a wide sweep of big-skied, buttongrass plain. Robert's discovery, his grand plan for our overdue escape. Our new adventure. The red hill captured our imagination, then, slowly and surely as consumption, it destroyed us.

The red hill in Butte held the richest copper mine in all creation. Robert had been all through that hill like a rabbit. He knew the signs. Balfour would be bigger than Mt Lyell – it needed only an alchemist and capital. The Murrays, poor old Bill and Tom, sought him out and cast the dream before him – the alchemist who made Mt Lyell, the Old Man who created Queenstown and made so many wealthy.

It was a three-day journey up from Queenstown – as it still is. Down to Strahan on the Abt, my railway, then up to Zeehan on the train and on to Burnie for the night. Along to Smithton and through by coach to Marrawah for the second night, then down along the coast to Whale's Head Inn on horseback for the third. The first time I came in there was no rail, wooden or otherwise, from Whale's Head to Balfour. Luke Williams, still lean and sharp as a piner's axe back then, met us at the Inn with horses and we rode in across the button grass swamp, the winter rain and salt-breathed westerly at our backs, the horses up to their girths in mud and water half the time. I always felt safe with Luke.

The wooden rails came later, in the middle of the short boom. A wooden railway set on a man-made ridge pushed up across the swampy plain. Horse-drawn. It was a grand bit of work but not enough to make the place viable. The yields were always too poor and too low.

But the idea took hold. People flocked to the little hill. The Midas touch of Mr Sticht was irresistible, even though Robert counselled caution at every opportunity. He should have taken his own advice but we convinced ourselves that this time things would be different. This time we would be the company; owners, not glorified navvies. This time it would be done our way from the start. Balfour would be a model city, an example of man and nature in dynamic balance, not a Dante nightmare like Queenstown, flayed to its bones, scourged by rain and sulphur.

The hour came, and with it the man. And our capital. Seventy thousand pounds, all we had saved and all we could borrow. All gone. As is the hour. As is the man.

This ramshackle ruin we are trundling through was once our Eldorado. Our stepping-stone to real wealth, a way to do good on a larger scale and grow old in comfort. We would go home and live quietly in righteousness with each other and our memories.

happy is the heart that hath its twilight hour

I saw it straight away back then though, as we sloshed in off the plain, covered in mud and leeches, drenched to the bone. The hill nestled between the mountains and the sea – it felt right, looked right. It looked nothing like Butte, of course, that high, wild place, except for that red hill, so out of place amongst the peat and shale. And the sky, as big as Texas.

I am a sunflower, drawn to light. I grew under vast skies in places where you pray for it to rain, not for it to stop. As the years passed in Queenstown I began to wither in that dank valley of the Queen and to hate what we were doing to it. Stripped of its primeval forest, a graveyard of haggard stumps mourning on the bare slopes.

it is a scene terrifically desolate

A valley filled with fog and fumes and men and always, always rain. 'If you can see Mt Owen it's about to rain and if you can't it's raining.' The joke wore very thin with me after a while. A very short while. West Coasters don't count it rain unless it hurts; they stand bare-headed in the drizzle, as though it were a sunny day. But no-one is there because they like it, however much they might pretend. It is affectation. Everyone is chasing fortune and escape.

where trees lie broken and strewed upon the ground

We had ridden our luck this far – why would we stop now? When luck runs with you it looks like Destiny. That is the gambler's ruin. We were drunk with confidence. The choice was to stay on as servants to Bowes Kelly and the Company, or to fry our own fish. We would be owners, the dividend of our labour would come to us, not to brutes with red noses and ill-fitting suits, snapping their braces in the bar, seeing their luck as Destiny.

The horse is hitched to an old dray. Chet and Hadmar throw our things up behind while Bob tends to the harness and young Ethel helps me up onto the buckboard. The unhappy beast hauls us slowly up the cobbled road, along the ridge from the old railhead to the sad wreckage of the town. Every jolt of every cobble pierces my insides; every prospect pierces my heart. I am bleeding again but there is nothing I can do and we are nearly there. I will deal with it anon. The boys must be spared as much of this humiliation as possible. I hold on to Bob's left arm as he flicks the reins and the horse ignores him. Chet and Hadmar are suddenly alert.

The Three Musketeers, my boys call themselves. Bob, of course, is a man but indulges this little fantasy. Twenty-eight, back from America and the Army four years now and making a name and place for himself in the Company. Hadmar is on the cusp of manhood, 18 and a studious, quietly confident boy, eager to make his mark in the world. He is restless, like his mother, and I sense he will, like me, never truly belong any-where. Chet is the one who will fare the worst from this. He is 15 and just when he needs a father most he is about to be an orphan. Bob will have to replace us. Chet is a bright and charming boy, though, and the handsomest of the three. He is afraid of nothing but inclined to day-dream – a youngest child.

We rattle and creak up along the road towards the burnt-out shell of old Tom Murray's pub, where we stayed in that cold winter of 1910. Back then the town bristled like an anthill with energy and optimism. The men were subdued that night, though, carousing quietly in the back of the pub. Mr Sticht was here with his wife. The Old Man would work his magic and all would prosper. I wonder what they thought of me? I was still lively back then.

We were caught on the hinge of destiny. Robert's contract was about to finish – we had been here 15 years and I had been promised we would be going home. Alice and Lizzie and my country were moving on without me. I sensed that another five year contract meant I would be returning to a foreign country. I would be trapped between two foreign countries. It was a frightening thought, inducing in me a sort of breathless panic. I was becoming a memory.

Balfour offered an irresistible compromise. It would make us rich, enable us to live in both worlds. Once it was established we could move to Melbourne. We would have a house in both places and the chance to return home regularly. It was only three weeks sailing, after all. We could establish a home for our old age in California – on that other west coast. I would be near Alice and Lizzie. I might finally find a home.

The dray swings right, past the ruins of another pub, The Balfour, and we roll down along the gentle eastern slope, the eye drawn south-east across the plain to the winding, tree-hugged river and Mt Frankland. A beautiful prospect, even now. This was where we planned our New Penghana.

We make our way between a few abandoned gardens down to Bob's shack. I remember it being built, from timber hewn on the slopes around. A more modest undertaking than Penghana, our grand house on the hill in Queenstown, to be sure. A little porch facing the track. Two rooms, a brace of small square windows front and back, bare wooden floors and walls; a bathroom out back on the stoop, what passes for a yard – overgrown with bracken and blackberries – and a view south-east over the heath, to the mountain and the vast wilderness beyond. That outlook was to be the focal point of our new house. High up in clean air, with sky to spare.

my poor old heart still clings to these dear old places

There is nobody to greet me, no-one to even notice my arrival. There is no excitement, only relief, and that is temporary. There is nothing new that is not depressing. A dead town picked over by a few mad scavengers. The future is no longer uncertain.

The shack has no tank. Ethel will have to carry water up the long slope from the creek. I am fortunate to have her. Like Hume at his end, I now have to make a very rigid frugality supply my deficiency of fortune.

We had our fortune still to make when we arrived at the shanty town of Penghana, back in 1895, in the rain. I should have been intimidated but I wasn't. If you have lived in Colorado you can live anywhere. The future back then was wonderfully uncertain.

3

I was Miranda, flung upon an alien shore with a wizard and a cast of rogues and angels.

Robert had gone down to Lyell a month earlier, while I waited in Melbourne. He met me at Strahan on a rainy April day. I came down from Devonport on the *Grafton* and counted myself lucky to survive the passage. The west coast in winter is a fearful place to be at sea and the old *Grafton* was only a small ship, a converted paddle-steamer. Even so we struck bottom twice crossing the bar at Hell's Gates – quite normal apparently but frightening nonetheless, the looming wrecks of the *Devon* and the *Pioneer* sufficient to dispel any complacency about the perils of that narrow passage. Robert came to grief there on the same ship, three years later.

From Strahan we set out for the King River on an old stern-wheeler. It rained all day, all the wild way east along Macquarie Harbour, vast and grey and ominous, the wind behind us and the wake of the stern-wheeler a boiling, brown froth, such as I had never seen. We glided across the bar of the King – the gravel of a million years clearly visible in the tea-coloured water. A sense of awe came over me, one that never left me on the King or on the Gordon. It is primeval and it is a privilege.

It rained all the way up to Teepookana, a wharf, pub and railhead clinging to the steep sides of a ravine, looking as though it might be swept away at any moment. Logs perched high up in trees along the gorge testified to the fury of the floods that regularly swept down the King. It was a brutal, manly place, bereft of any conceit of civilization save capital. I had seen many such apparitions in the mountains of Colorado and Montana, seen them begin and boom and bust, but I had never been so far from the comforts of the world.

It rained all the way from there along the cayon on the narrow rails, slowly winding up through the keyhole in the range, along the misty King and then the Queen, wild and pure as unbroken colts back then. Nothing I had seen before prepared me for this rampant wilderness. There were places higher and wilder in the Rockies but there was nothing like this dense forest or these verdant gorges, nothing like this impenetrable profusion of ancient growth, the smell of compost and damp over-whelming me as I fell further and further into the mountains, into Mt Lyell and my future. Into the remainder of my life, as it turned out. What I thought would be a short adventure.

The cog railway was built in sections simultaneously, so I was ferried into Lyell like a parcel, on a series of trolleys and carts. We wound our way up through the rain to Dubbil Barril, then by horse and cart through the mud, through the cloudy, soggy rainforest gorges, down to the forest flats that would soon become Queenstown and on to the muddy camp that was Penghana. 'Meeting of the rivers' in the native dialect, they told me – but that describes almost any given square mile of Tasmania.

We were to share the Manager's house with George Fisher Beardsley, an amiable American metallurgist who had been out here ten years. Robert had crossed paths with him in Colorado, and thought well enough of him. He became our guide to local customs, such as they were, and an unlikely friend and ally. It must not have been easy to give way to Robert when he came but George was a man of intelligence and sense – not a common combination. He was smart enough to see that Robert might change the world. He was the perfect foil to Robert – not afraid to tease him but capable of matching his prodigious work-rate. He is in Big Sur now, with Alice. What a strange world.

The house was directly down the tram line from the smelter, at the top of a squalid gully lined with shacks and tents and lean-tos held together by canvas, tar and fencing wire. Everything emptying into a filthy little creek. That was Penghana. It looked like it had been thrown out of a bucket.

> *is this the region, this the soil, the clime,*
> *that we must change for heaven this mournful gloom?*

And there we were – in a remote and foreign land, cut off from every-thing and everyone we ever knew, with only Robert's theories and our self-belief to call upon. In the rain.

A steady, grey curtain of rain, that continued unabated for a quarter of a century. I own I cannot speak in good conscience of the times I spent away – and while many, those times were not so numerous as I would have wished – but unless my absences were attended by miraculous (and unreported) drought, I can safely say that it rained for the next 28 years. It was raining when I arrived; it rained whenever I was there; it was raining when I left. No doubt it is raining now.

> *for the rain it raineth every day*

Penghana, the old shanty town where Bob was born, was like all the mining towns I had ever seen, back in Colorado and Montana, only worse. Ramshackle buildings, makeshift tents, corrugated iron, canvas, tar and duckboards strewn along a gully that was little more than a crease in the hills. Shacks on stilts to raise them out of the swamp and sewage. Five feet of rain a year. Mud and filth everywhere. Drains and waste emptying into the creek. All cheek by jowl with the smelter, so that the air was a fog of sulphur and smoke.

Penghana had sprung up on The Mt Lyell Company's property, close to the smelter. It was the shortest way to and from work in the rain and mud. From the head of the gully, on the smelter tramline, the Mine Manager's house looked west, down along what passed for the town's street. That meant that the smells and smoke associated with it were driven our way by the westerly that prevails on that coast. The company had a town surveyed downstream a little ways. It was called *Pokana* back then, an aboriginal word for rain, Mr Beattie, the photographer, told me later. A pretty name and a pretty spot, on the flats along the Queen, where the rainforest was being cleared and streets surveyed, all an act of trust in Robert's ability to make their ore viable.

Few saw any point in the mile-long walk to work, uphill in the rain and mud, so Penghana just grew, like Topsy. There was much talk within the Company of forcing the people out, back down to Pokana, but the situation was volatile and alienating your workforce by dispossessing them of their homes did not seem prudent, even to those oafs on the Board. Robert cared little about such things. He had a vision – an obsession, with his smelter and his alchemy. He had waited for this moment most of his life. He would make the ore viable.

19th February 1896

MR ROBERT STICHT whose reputation as a metallurgist competent to devise the most perfect and economical process to treat this ore induced the Mt Lyell directors to secure his services, assumed charge of the department in May last. His initial work was to study the material to be treated, and devise the best means. A great part of the result is before us in this vast reducing plant nearly ready for business and arrival of the crucial moment for the problem. He does not appear to entertain misgivings, from which I gather it has resolved itself thus in his mind: if such and such treatment of x pounds of ore secures certain results, corresponding treatment of x tons must secure proportionately.

In carrying out designs decided upon Mr Sticht has had the able assistance of Messrs G. F. Beardsley, assayer to the company and Mr Shepherd, chief draftsman.

Close attention will be requisite in order to get intelligent hold of the process Mr Sticht has devised for smelting this Mt Lyell ore, the components of which will appear. I am not aware that he has patented it, although in salient features it is unique, therefore highly interesting to professional and lay people, who will pleasurably receive announcement of its successful application very shortly.

Just as Robert was pregnant with his smelter, I fell pregnant almost as soon as we arrived. I did not enjoy the experience. Later I saw whales heaved up on Henty Beach and knew exactly how they felt. Useless, helpless and ugly, who once were poetry in the sea they had abandoned. I carried it through easily enough, though, with a rough doctor and a sound midwife. I had good reason to be afraid but it was straightforward in the end, if rather awkward and humiliating.

I did not succumb – but I lost my life. I became a Mother. When young women become mothers they do not surrender much; having lived so little their characters are not formed. I was 31 and had been my own person half those years. I was suddenly an institution, my identity twice removed: a wife and now a mother. What became of Marion Oak Stage?

Two months before I gave birth to Bob I gave life to Robert's monster. It was a much more pleasant experience. Excitement hung round us like a fog the night I lit the furnace! Anxious faces flared by furnace light and wreathed in clouds of steam, all gathered in the great, gothic hall of the smelter. Tired and bedraggled men, their future hingeing with ours on this alchemy. A bond was forged that night that could never be dissolved and never was – those that were there never forgot Robert Carl Sticht and what he created.

MOUNT LYELL DISTRICT: PENGHANA, as follows: The chief event of the week has undoubtedly been the starting of smelting operations at the Mount Lyell, Mining and Railway Company Ltd. On Thursday evening the furnaces of one of the two 150 ton smelters were lighted.

The actual ceremony of lighting the wood in the smelter was performed by Mrs. Sticht, wife of the popular metallurgist and local manager for the company. Throughout the day active steps were taken to complete the few small matters required to make the running of the plant smooth and successful, and soon after 7 o'clock in the evening the immense concern was started off, having been lighted in four different places. Wood was the first course, and when well started, coke was shot down from the rails above, and soon coke and silica blended with each other in quick succession, with now and again a little ore thrown in.

No official intimation regarding the starting was publicly given, not through any discourtesy to the outside public, with whom the company is on the best possible terms, but with a view of having few persons in the way of the workers when the important part of tapping came on. This act was performed by Mr. Sticht himself, in the presence of a fair sprinkling of the general employees of the company, a few of their lady friends, and, so far as I could see, only one businessman of the district.

The midnight whistle, which brought the second shift of the day to a close and called the third shift to duty, had just died away as the manager tapped the hole at the back of the immense water-jacketed melting pot. After a few well-directed blows, the mouth was opened, and the glowing, burning, glittering stream poured out into the vessels placed beneath to catch the liquid fire.

At 2 o'clock the front gate of the fiery furnace was tapped and opened, the brilliant stream pouring out into the fire-brick-lined iron trucks thrust under the outlet.

I struck a match, the giant stirred like Victor Frankenstein's creature, and all our lives and the lives of all our people changed forever. This strange island, the pregnant nation, these ragtag people, chancers and dreamers, the good and the bad and most of all the noble, faithful, strong and vulnerable women – all changed utterly and forever by the lighting of a flame. Many would die, men and women and children, in mines and homes and hospitals, on the tracks and roads and in the rivers and the harbours and the ocean. Things made of the metal born here would wreak misery and strife on innocent people all around the globe. I know all this.

I had committed deeds of mischief beyond description horrible

But many more would be brought civilisation, wealth and comfort, a measure of happiness and a future for their children and their children's children. Tasmania depends on it still, the wealth it generates spills out across the nation and the wide world. Yet a hundred years from now will anyone remember his name or know about that night? Few will understand the possibility that all that followed might not have come to pass – but for Robert Carl Henry Sticht.

he is dead who called me into being,
and when I shall be no more
the very remembrance of us both will vanish

They could complain later about conditions until they were blue in the face for all I cared – there would have been no mine, no town, no workers and no union without Robert.

Dear old Archie Douglas was there that night. He was there at the station the day I arrived and he was there 28 years later to bid farewell. He was 'there' before 'there' existed, a character who had wandered out of a Dickens novel and couldn't find his way back. A kind and decent man who treated me for a quarter of a century as though I, too, was a character fallen from a book. Treated me like Alice, in fact, and he was not far wide of the mark in that assessment.

Robert tapped the furnace at midnight and the metal poured like liquid fire into the world again, transformed from dirt into something amazing. Later we walked home along the line to the Manager's house with George Beardsley, Archie and the others, wrapped in our Blueys against the drizzle, exhausted and exhilarated. A pregnant woman abroad at such an hour probably caused a scandal.

We neither of us slept – the world was full of promise and our confidence was far too buoyant for sleep to drown. We would happily have never slept again – sleep was for mortals.

There is sleep enough for both of us now.

I am a dream out of a blessed sleep

4

THE MERCURY, HOBART

January 1897

1896 FATALITIES

The list of fatal accidents, suicides, and murders for the
year is long, and includes some most distressing cases.
Among the principal are:

Ernest Webber, *bushman, killed at Penguin by blow
from sapling he was grubbing;*

James Hammond, *miner, killed at Branxholm by falling
tree;*

Henry Davidson Minnis, *architect, Hobart, died suddenly;*

Eather Ribbon, *found drowned at Irish Town;*

James Butler, *woodcutter, found dead at Cascades;*

James Elliott, *elderly man, found dead at Hythe;*

Harry Killalea, *engine driver, crushed by machinery at
Zeehan;*

W. Neighbour, *Hobart, fruit dealer, drowned off Banks Peninsula;*

Ashleigh Lambert, *drowned in Derwent;*

Edward Little, *New Town, killed by fall of earth;*

Jas. Gregory Goddard, *Hobart, committed suicide;*

Harriet Probatt, *suicided in Derwent;*

Bertram Archer, *accidentally shot whilst rabbiting at Cressy;*

Augustus E. Graves, *died from self-administered overdose of chloroform;*

Thos. O'Brien, *crushed by horse at Glenorchy;*

Thos. White, *crushed by falling tree at Huon;*

George Herbert White, *found drowned in Derwent;*

Thos. Oliver Riley, *crushed by fall of earth at Strahan;*

Michael White, *found drowned in Victoria Dock;*

Percy Francis, *died of poison at Hobart;*

Wm. Mead, *mate S.S.Centennial, drowned in Tamar;*

Francis Wm. Jolly, *run over;*

Wm. Barrett, *shot himself at Hagley;*

Fredk. Branchi, *committed suicide, Collins-Street, Hobart;*

Matthew McPhee, *drowned himself in Derwent;*

Duncan Campbell & Wm. Henshaw,*accidentally* drowned in Tamar;

Arthur Young & Arthur Boucher, *accidentally drowned in Derwent;*

Superintendent McCluskey, Sub-inspector Eppingstall, Messrs. McGrath, James Ford, W. Evans, and J. Pyke, *residents of Spring Bay, drowned in boating accident;*

Thomas Brent, *burned in bush fire at Penghana;*

Early one Saturday morning, a fortnight before Christmas 1896, a wall of fire swept down the gully from the hills behind the smelter and in 15 minutes Penghana was no more. We had survived a fire which took the bakery and skittle alley just a few weeks earlier, but there was no containing the monster that roared through the gully on that hot morning.

It was all over by breakfast. A furious northerly gale, uncustomary weeks of hot, dry weather (there, I've admitted that the rain does stop occasionally), and abundant fuel combined to create a firestorm. Two or three buildings somehow survived and stood like tombstones in the smoking ruins. The smelter itself was saved by the efforts of the men, as were the brickworks and the sawmill. There was a choice to be made – save the town or save the smelter. There was no point to Penghana without a smelter.

I watched the conflagration from the front window of the Manager's house, at the top of the gully. There was no time to run, no time to call for help, no time to do anything. I had a three-month-old baby on my hip and only a wooden house to protect me, but the fire turned away from us, raced up the gully then swung south, sucked down along the tramway, razing everything between our house and the scattered shacks of Pokana. When the wind suddenly changed direction and the fury abated, the dense cloud of smoke lifted from the gully that had been Penghana and revealed the sort of smouldering ruination Sherman left behind on his march to the sea.

I had not time to be frightened. In the immediate aftermath it was not possible to comprehend the enormity of what had taken place before my eyes. I left the boy with our girl and made my way along the ruined street in the midst of the smoking wreckage. I helped where I could. There were burns and shock and that strange quiet that prevails as disaster is comprehended. Homes and possessions all gone, except for a few things, such as sewing machines and furniture, thrown into the river by folk further down the tramway.

It was a strange day, attended by a miracle: only one man died in the inferno that morning, Mr Brent, a wood-chopper trapped on a nearby hill, yet a town was razed. Most of the menfolk were at work, where they saved the smelter. There was hardly anyone to defend the town or the scattering of women and children left at home. Mrs Topham and her baby girl were a pitiful sight; caught in the flames as she ran from her house, they had been charred but they survived. Most of the population was reduced to the clothes they stood up in. Many lost not only their belongings, which admittedly were few, but were ruined by their mistrust of banks, their savings hidden in their houses and turned to ashes on the wind. And of course no-one was insured – the town did not exist.

The ground was peaty and already soaked in sulphur from the works. The fire burned deep into the earth for days. Bits of tortured glass and crockery and tinware were strewn among the smoking stumps and twisted iron beds and gaunt chimneys, all mangled by the heat. It was a sad shambles.

It was my first experience of bushfires, as they call them here. Bushfires dogged the hills for years afterwards. A year later, almost to the day, fire swept down the gully again, nearly taking our house up by the smelter – the kitchen caught fire but was saved. Then in '99, in the early hours of Christmas Eve, we almost lost our new Penghana, our grand house on the hill, when yet another fire roared down past the flux quarries and along the west bank of the Queen, taking houses, camps and timber all the way down to Lynchford. Our little mesa had nothing that would burn on its slopes back then and was successfully defended but many on the flats lost everything.

bushfires, notwithstanding their terrors, are hailed as aids
to prospecting

That first fire was also my first experience of a community emerging from chaos. A melting pot of people from around the world, thrown together by ambition, pulled itself up by its charred bootstraps and forged a community. They did not look back. I was always proud to have played a small part in that fusion. I did not fall in love, though, as Robert did. Queenstown was his second child, born that day, three months after the boy.

Penghana was gone and it would not be rebuilt. In truth it had been an ugly and unhealthy place. The Company reasoned that the new site would be free of the smelter's foul fog, but the westerlies trapped the fumes in the bowl of Queenstown instead of clearing them and the whiff of brimstone became part of us.

They had just changed the name of the gazetted town from Pokana to Queenstown, in honour of the old Queen's Jubilee. A pity, I always thought, though one could never say so. Shops and houses had already sprung up and after the fire newly gazetted land along the river flats was bought up quickly. A tent-town sprang up on the Recreation Ground to house the homeless population. Within weeks land had been allotted and buildings erected. Shops and pubs and barracks popped up like mushrooms and in a few months there were streets and gutters and streetlights and a plan and the sense that this might last beyond next week. This town might actually have a future. It was as if Penghana had never existed.

**THE MOUNT LYELL MINING AND RAILWAY CO.
LIMITED.**

15th December 1896

TO THE PUBLIC – As it is desirable that the company
should now reclaim those portions of land on which it
has hitherto good-naturedly tolerated settlements, I make
the following statement:

From this date it is forbidden to erect houses, huts,
tents, camps, or otherwise utilise for living purposes any
portion of the land now known as the company's reserve.

It is well known that no legal rights to residence can be
obtained in this area, and that ejection at any moment is
in the power of the company. The above order is issued
at the present time instead of later at the request of the
local Progress Committee...

By Order ROBT STICHT
Manager Mt Lyell Co.

The only wooden building left standing after the conflagration was a large hut of King Billy pine that the good Reverend Copeland had put up, on a block he had earmarked for a church. The remarkable Reverend would often purchase prime land in new townships in the West, in faith not only that the town would flourish but also that the Church would later reimburse him. He was right more often than not but when he wasn't he bore the cost himself.

The shack had been occupied at the time by a Salvation Army captain and considerable debate ensued on the question of whether God's mercy had been applied on behalf of the Protestants, who owned the building, or the Salvation Army, who occupied it. I understand that a book was run on the outcome and Reverend Copeland asked to adjudicate. He declined, on the grounds that he was hardly a disinterested party and, as far as I know, there the matter lies. But the hut was new, the King Billy was green and the creek was hard by.

Not long after I arrived at Penghana I had been enlisted by the Reverend Copeland. There had been a recent influx of wives and some 20 children into the little village, so I agreed to help him and Archie set up a Sunday School, at which I would be the teacher.

The Reverend created a lovely dry and airy space in the sawmill and advertised widely in the camp. He visited most of the parents, who were all supportive of the idea, but despite their assurances we waited in vain for scholars on that first Sunday morning.

The Reverend was an interesting man, full of dogged Protestant charm. He had a dry, self-deprecating wit and guileless manner that won him many friends among his rough parishioners. He had travelled widely for a youngish man, had served in Gibraltar and had been all through America and Canada. We had places in common, which was uncommon in men of his education. There were many miners who had made the pilgrimage from the mines of Colorado to California and on to the rushes of Australia, but I had little to do with such men.

Reverend Copeland's parish was the whole west coast and he had many adventures and good yarns to spin as a result. He had cut tracks through the wilderness, been lost, almost drowned, fallen off bridges and given sermons in saloons.

So he was not a man to be easily discouraged and at length set off in search of the promised congregation. He found two urchins playing two-up outside the sawmill and pressed them into service. I have to say that they entertained us more than we educated them and I spent most of that first day doubled over, suppressing un-teacherly laughter. After a few weeks, however, the Reverend's boundless energy prevailed, the Sunday School was a success and went from strength to strength when transplanted to Queenstown after the fire.

The heat of the day has lifted on the evening breeze. I sit outside the back door of the shack and watch the long day dying. The softening light accentuates the contours of the treeless hills and Mt Frankland. The cicadas begin to thrum and the occasional March fly disturbs my reverie. Small birds are foraging in the grass – fantails and firetails – inquisitive little creatures, quick as sparks. They seem at home here.

A few summer flowers survive the wreckage. Rhododendrons and foxgloves thrive in exile here, unlike me. They have spread in glorious confusion through the unmade town. I would plant some flowers if I had the energy, organise a garden, pretend there was a future, but I lack faith. Mother planted to the end – her faith was strong and gardening is surely an act of faith. I wonder sometimes if her will to live was stronger than mine. Odd that those who have faith in another world cling so fiercely to this one.

There are extravagant shrubs around the old schoolhouse, abandoned when the last children left a year ago. I managed to walk over there by myself in the evening, yesterday. It is like the Mary Celeste, as though the class has just gone off for an excursion and will be back in an hour. The inkwells are still set in their desks, chalk and dusters sit waiting by the blackboard, on which some basic sums are still visible, and there is that unique classroom smell, a bouquet of chalk and sweat and disinfectant – something sickly sweet I've never understood. I spent much time in such rooms, on opposite sides of the world. I rather liked teaching. I liked the energy and honesty of the children. I liked the idea of making a difference and having my own place in the world. I liked following in the footsteps of my mother and her sisters. I liked believing in the future.

I was raised in the belief that nothing matters more than education. Mama taught me that education would set me free of any oppression, would sustain my soul through any famine and slake my thirst in any drought. There is much truth in it, of course, but there are times when I envy the ignorant their bliss.

I checked the faded sums on the blackboard, ran a stick of chalk across the surface and watched the fine dust float on the light slanting through the dirty windows. The room was imbued with a golden, nostalgic haze. I wrote my initials and the date, like a child in a cave: M.O.S. February 14, 1923. The door creaked shut behind me as I tottered out into the overgrown yard.

The rhododendrons and camellias are still heavy with dead blooms from last spring and faded petals are strewn through the long grass in the playground. Will they still be here a hundred years hence, these alien flowers? Or will the forest close over the red hill like a scab and all traces of Balfour vanish like the heat on this sweet breeze?

The school Papa built on the south fork of Brouilletts Creek has long since vanished. Aunts Annette and Mary were teachers there and they lived with us in turn. Poor Annette died the day before my third birthday, so I have no memory of her. She left George Dinsmore with five children under ten.

I could see our house from the classroom window and though my attention wandered off with every stagecoach and horse that passed across the little bridge, I had a solid grounding. I was quicker than most and precocious. I made friends easily and Charlie always looked out for me.

a boy's will is the wind's will

Charlie tired quickly of book learning, he was so full of life and living. He was a verb. His intelligence was instinctive, his energy infectious. How I still miss him, miss his protection. He died out in Pueblo when I was sixteen and he was twenty, almost a man for ever now, frozen in time. Thrown from a horse and landed on his head. A stupid way to die. I had to go away to Vassar soon after we took him home to Edgar County and I was shattered.

Sneaking up on the roof of the old Bloomfield house with Charlie and making up stories about what was out there beyond the horizon was my favourite thing in all creation – apart from pancakes. We would perch up there and dream about the day we would ride across the prairie to a new world of wonders.

we all begin by singing with the birds and running fast

From the roof of that old house I would look out across a sea of summer wheat, rolling and shimmering to the horizon, the scythe of the wind carving rivers in the wheat. I would be giddy with pleasure and a sense of adventure and the desire to see what was over that horizon. You could see clear across our little world, down to Paris and probably over to Springfield and Abe Lincoln's cabin I bet, if you had a telescope. Of course he never really lived in that cabin – everyone knew that. His family is still scattered thereabouts, though.

In summer the wheat would sweep back to towering black clouds on the horizon, filling the sky, rolling in across the sunlit prairie, every head of wheat, every stalk, every blade and every wisp whipped by the gathering wind with its sweet, earthy scent of summer rain.

Then you would hear the rain, like grain pouring into a silo, building

———

slowly in front of the cracks of thunder and the billowing black curtain sweeping like fate across the golden prairie. And it would begin to fall, each drop a soft drumbeat, building to a million percussions of dust, filling the air with that damp dust smell, the smell of earth reborn, as the storm surged on, irresistible as an avalanche, closing out the world, focussing all of creation into one wild field of majesty and me sitting on the roof with Charlie, straddling the ridgepole, wind in my hair, daring God to strike me.

Vassar Female College

5

be a good girl – do the best you can do for yourself
and all you can do for Jesus

I have taken many long journeys within this one that I will soon com-plete. I have lived my life a stranger in a strange land. After Charlie died and we took him home, I went away to Vassar and became a stranger in my own land. I was 17, a tomboy from well beyond the pale. From Colorado, by God, with no father to support me. I had the rudiments of manners, which I mostly disdained, and little conversation. I had been indulged to think that my opinions were as good as anyone's and that the world was a pretty simple place. As a result my conversation was little more than a series of naïve pronouncements that passed for con-versation in Pueblo but proved embarrassing at Vassar.

and the student should be not merely required to 'learn lessons,'
but trained to discuss subjects and to form and maintain opinions

I became keenly conscious of my shortcomings. Vassar was a fairytale – elegant white dresses wafting across graceful lawns, Greek and art and music and brilliant young women from all across the Union. It was a trial and an honour just to be accepted. Vassar took many young women like me, rough stones cast from anywhere and everywhere, and rubbed us up against a world of taste and education, against girls of privilege, polish and expectation. It set our eyes on a world bigger than we had ever imagined.

I was in the School of Music, but had the whole of Vassar at my fingertips. I saw Matthew Arnold lecture and old Sam Clemens ogle. Twain came to Vassar in my second year. He was a little too avuncular for my taste, a little too pleased to find himself the focus of so many young women. He was amusing, though perhaps a little flippant for the occasion and an audience of earnest young women. Arnold could not be accused of that. He caused a stir, the mournful, mutton-chopped Englishman, stooped raven-like over his notes, dismissing our Emerson as trivial. There was quite a controversy. I adored him and his poetry still haunts me. And I never bothered much with Emerson again.

the end is everywhere art still has truth, take refuge there

I met Maria Mitchell, looked through her telescope to the moon and stars. To Jupiter and Saturn, her favourites. I do not know what was more impressive – the Universe or Maria Mitchell. That a woman, a Quaker from Nantucket, by God, could aspire to and achieve such knowledge and stature suddenly seemed obvious. 'Go to the source', was her motto. Trust no-one's experience but your own. Not very practical, but inspiring at a tender age.

And I made a friend, for life as it has turned out. Alice Kate Wellman, of Oakland, California, had come even further than me to this island in New Jersey. Our first island. A sturdy girl, shorter even than me but a tomboy, just the same. Girls in such circumstances often form close bonds and we were no exception. We were furthest from home of all our class and perhaps the most out of our depth. She was strong and funny and protective. Wiser in the ways of the world than me – San Francisco left little to the imagination, I discovered later. She refused to be intimidated by these eastern girls with their manners and their crinolines and their long, straight backs. Alice Kate Wellman has never taken a backward step in all the years I have known her.

We went up to Chester to the Hazeltons together in the summer and a fine time we had of it, a lazy dream of sun and lawns and reading. On the way back to Vassar, in Boston, we had our portraits taken. Two earnest young women. What became of us?

Then I was ill all through the winter of '82-83. Pneumonia kept me in the school infirmary, too weak to travel, even down to Boston and the Hazeltons. I had never been away from Mother and Lizzie at Christmas. Charlie was gone from me. Alice Kate refused to leave and instead of making the long trip back to California she stayed with me. I was desolate and afraid. All my experience, all 18 years of it, told me I would die in that Infirmary. But Alice was my ministering angel and I survived. I could not tell Mother how ill I was – by the time I could write the crisis had passed. As my health returned I began to feel invincible – I had cheated death. I had not joined the lost tribe of Stage children. It changed the way I saw the world and my place in it. I realised that this place could be home, that I could fit. Being there with Alice and a scattering of winter-stranded girls made me feel that I belonged. I'm not sure why. Perhaps being at rest, the School revealed itself for what it was – an illusion. A noble and kind illusion. And Alice, having saved me, was now responsible for me.

On New Year's Eve there was a masquerade in the school hall. At midnight the skeleton of the old year was carried away by pallbearers dressed in black and the new year paraded in as a golden-haired angel, dressed all in white finery and silver bells. I looked at that bright, shining angel and knew that this time next year they would be carrying its corpse away like Charlie, all dressed in black linen. I resolved that I should grow up.

In my second year I was overtaken by the fates: I decided to go on to the degree with Alice Kate, but having Mother's consent and the world at my dainty feet, the world conspired to trip me up and teach me another lesson. The '83 recession strangled our finances and the dreadful winter that accompanied it nudged Mother close to death. When the time came I could not stay. Even if the money could be found, I could not let Mama die without me.

Dear Marion where are you?

So in the hard winter of '83 I said farewell to Vassar and caught the ferry down the Hudson for the last time. Alice Kate came with me down-river. It was a bittersweet journey. I boarded the train in snow-bound New York, waved goodbye to the best friend I had ever had and steamed on out across the frozen plains, across America to the Rockies once again. I was coming home a woman. I was 19. I had glimpsed a world I dearly wanted to be part of but for now Pueblo would have to do.

Miss Marion C. Stage

Poughkeepsie

— Vassar College —

New York.

6

I can hear the little river rumbling like thunder and the rush of wind up the slope through the trees. Something is stirring. Cotton wool clouds roll eastward, gathering like frightened sheep overhead. The birds are skittish and the smell of wet dirt is in the air. There is serious weather on the way. Mind, there is always serious weather on the way on this battered coast.

I have one last journey left in me and it must be soon. Across Bass Strait again, to Melbourne. The last journey I could not bring myself to take with Robert after he died. I was exhausted and lost. I needed to gather myself for one last effort. It was Bob's turn to play Charon. He will reprise the role directly.

Melbourne is as far north as I will ever get now, but it will be a sunset voyage and there will be no landfall.

I took my first sea voyage in 1887, when I was 23. I climbed the gangway of *The Aller*, down on the Hudson, and dawn broke over a new world in Hoboken.

───────

55

Mama faded so quickly at the end, hollowed out, like an old husk, the last drops of her spirit beading on her pale brow. By the end even the eyes that so beguiled Napoleon Bonaparte Stage were dimmed. Coal where embers once glowed fierce and bright, all through her long decline.

It is tedious to die in middle-age. Neither Keats' tragedy nor Whitman's grandeur attend such awkwardness. You have fulfilled your potential or had none and come up a bit short of your three score and ten – sad, certainly, but neither tragic nor venerable.

It is inconvenient, in fact. A passing difficult to summarise: there are few platitudes to distance oneself from death at 59 – Mother, as always, being the exception. There was both tragedy and majesty in her passing. Fifty-nine was something of a miracle for her. She had been dying so long she seemed much older.

an immortal sickness which kills not

It was a horrible death, drowning in her own frail body, hawking gobs of blood and bits of lung in shattering spasms such that I thought she would surely shake apart in front of us. A dreadful, drawn out slide into oblivion. My decline has at least been more discreet. A miasma has spread through me and while there is blood and constant pain there is nothing epic or romantic in it. No great poets died of a kidney. And I will die alone.

Sarah died with us all around her, Lizzie and me and George and Harry. What a dreadful scene it was. How awful she looked and how horribly she was wracked by the consumption. Her lungs ragged, her mind feverish. She drowned calling for Charlie. Is it worse to lose a son than die?

I was drained and tempered by Mother's long dying and the drawn-out drama that attended her two funerals. She had made dying an opera and the Pueblo funeral was a dress rehearsal. Then followed a hiatus, the long, hot, grief-stricken journey east on the Thunderbolt, from Pueblo to Paris. It was all rather dreamlike, cantering along that ribbon of steel, across the endless, shimmering prairie in the summer sun, towns familiar yet unknown appearing out of nowhere and disappearing forever, slides in a magic lantern show, glimpses of other lives in lamplit windows in the dead of night, Mama in a box in the boxcar and Lizzie and I dressed in black silk.

the land runs past. We saw the iron way, but do not know what it is

There was some relief in both of us that Mama's suffering had ended. We had a sense of mission and a role to play. George was his usual reliable and attentive self. He ushered us across the plains like a eunuch escorting two exotic princesses. Good man – in California now, alone like me but with no children to undermine his confidence. I must allow that he loved Lizzie as much as I did, though I knew her better. We will not see each other again, which is sad but a blessing – what would we say? I liked George. He was true as Troilus and unquestioning, which makes him sound like a pet hound, I suppose. I mean nothing by it for we have a bond: we are the last survivors of our little tragedy. One we might well have staged in the roof of Penghana, though we favoured comedies there. Still, I always thought Macbeth a comedy.

I'll cherish thee, my Marion
In childhood and in youth

We did Sarah Jane Hazelton proud back in Edgar County. She would have noted who was there – and more importantly, who was not. Lizzie had more memories of the town and people than I did.

My memories are not of people but of a golden childhood in a dream-like place, nostalgia enhanced by my returns at times of high emotion. Emma, Charlie, Mother and then, much later, Lizzie, all laid to rest. I could not go back again after that.

and lead thy steps the paths upon
Of happiness and truth

Mama's funeral took me back to another summer, 1874 of course, and as we laid her to rest among the oaks, beside Napoleon and Charlie and little Em, I was suddenly nine again, not a princess from the west dressed in beautiful black silks. I wanted to run down to the fence and ride my horse off across the lake bridge and through the golden fields to Brouilletts Creek and along to the old house and Mama and Papa would be there with Charlie and we would eat pancakes and I would be – what? Safe? Loved? A child again and always, I suppose. Home, perhaps? That is it.

When you keep moving, when you follow dreams or men or adventure or opportunity, you lose the chance to grow old slowly in a place where you note the passing of time in the passing of people and familiar things and mark your own passage against the familiar, not the strange, against trees and hills that mock your trivial years; the chance to note the arrival of newcomers rather than live constantly among strangers; the chance to plant a tree and know you may never see it full grown but know that someone might well remember that you planted it; the chance to be with kin and be kin. I have sacrificed all these things to seek adventure, to follow my heart and opportunity. To better myself and the world. I lacked the courage to return, until it was too late.

and when thy Mother's ta'en from thee
O cherish still her memory

And then just as suddenly I was looking forward into Mama's grave and could see me taking my place beside them all. A stranger who will be unknown to trampers in that cemetery a generation hence. .

The reprise of pain and kindness in Paris was different from the farewell in Pueblo – the platitudes were more familiar; a deeper, sombre memory prevailed, tinged with history and the memory of Father and all his dead wives and children. It was a communal death, with a sense of place, whereas in Colorado everyone was from somewhere else so belonged nowhere. One could not be missed in quite the same way. Back home, in the midst of all those dead Stages, I felt guilty to be still standing. So after all that kindness and futility, with evidence all around me that life was fleeting, I could not go back to Pueblo. I kept running east, driven by the prairie wind, until I fetched up in Europe. A year at the Akadamie in Berlin was mother's dying gift to me. Alice had pleaded with me to join her and mother's death released me.

I felt a mother-want about the world

My Grand Tour! Every time I board a ship or train I can still smell the salt-slicked, oily air and hear the buzz of a thousand excited conversations and ten thousand hungry gulls squawking over Hoboken. I was sick with anticipation and regret as I climbed up onto that magnificent ship and clung to the railing on the promenade deck. I had seen ships from the shore and taken the ferry on the Hudson many times, chugging up to Vassar at Poughkeepsie, but I had been on neither ship nor ocean. I felt faint when *The Aller* finally heaved free of its moorings and slid downriver, past the vast city being born and on past the colossus of Liberty. Brand new, emerging like a shining goddess from the mist as the morning sun burnt off. It was a dream. I felt like a warrior setting forth as we drove on out into the green Atlantic! Sailing to the fabled spiritual home.

go to the source

Across the Atlantic, wide and featureless as the prairie. It is a dream – you move constantly but go nowhere. Then, just as you imagine you might go on like this forever, an impossible continent appears on the horizon – a land only dreamt of. That was a thrill that never waned for me, that first sight of land, though I had the wonder of it many times. I am a country girl but I could happily have spent my life at sea. I was sick, I spoke to strangers, I flirted, I fell in and out of love. I saw things I'd never dreamed of and did things I'd never dreamed of doing. Or would ever dream of telling.

I rode in diligences through foreign lands. I spoke French and German and was occasionally understood. In Paris I joined forces with Alice. We saw the Eiffel Tower being built. We rolled on east to Berlin. The Chicago of Europe, Mr Twain called Berlin back then. He must have seen parts of Chicago I had not.

Living in a foreign city was exhausting and exhilarating. I had some rudimentary German, and I found my way through the world well enough. Alice was quick and prosaic and between us we managed to survive and study our lessons. Alice was always more diligent than I. Being the eldest sister of three gave her some of Lizzie's fierce drive and energy. The younger two, Jean and Em, were precocious and confident beyond their years or station, because Alice paved their way and guarded their flanks, if that is not a mixed metaphor.

Berlin was neither Chicago nor New York, I thought, but I could see what old Sam Clemens meant. There was an irresistible tide flowing from the country to the city, which seemed to be mostly under construction. Berlin had doubled in size in a generation and was well on its way to repeating that in half a generation. It was change that was urgent and unfathomable, especially to a foreigner. A bellicose confidence prevailed but for all its energy and history it was more parochial than I had expected. Bismarck had brought nationalism to the boil.

Bismarck's star was about to fade, though. It was the year of the Three Emperors. Two deaths and two coronations had stirred emotions to a fever. When the liberal Friedrich died after only a few months as Kaiser he was replaced by his son Wilhelm, who seemed to me a character from a comic opera. It pleased me greatly later to be able to say I had witnessed the coronation of Kaiser Bill and to point out that he was Queen Victoria's grandson – sixth in line for the British Crown when he was born. I have never understood the colonial fascination with Royalty, I'm afraid, though that is not something one mentions out here.

There were Americans everywhere in Europe. The best minds and most adventurous spirits of my generation were abroad. I felt a part of something greater than myself. We were the spirit of the New World – young, full of optimism and energy and wonder, trawling the Old World for knowledge and experience and something we thought the Old World knew that we did not. Were we right, I wonder? Or was that an illusion the Old World foisted on the New? I'm not sure I saw much that was forward thinking, until The Exposition, but I saw history. Our shared history. And I found much that spoke of the present and how best to enjoy it.

All those places we had read about in books and magazines – now I walked around and through them, watched them and listened to them and got tired of them and asked myself occasionally whether a cup of coffee or lunch might not serve just as well as another cathedral or museum.

I stood in places where Bach and Beethoven and Mozart had stood and felt a little small – a girl from Pueblo who played not terribly well, and I wondered what I should think or feel about this strange dislocation, apart from a desire to laugh out loud.

At the end of the year the Wellman women came to Europe for their Grand Tour. Alice's family had a very successful business in San Francisco and the education of the four daughters was to be completed with the full Grand Tour. I was invited to accompany them.

My head still spins at the recollection: four earnest and spirited young women, a flighty younger sister and dear Mrs Wellman trying to herd us all along, like a sheepdog herding cats. Alice sent me a copy of Jean's diary and I still treasure it – a relic of a life that might have been among such people.

NATIVE.

№ 1407   ISSUED, *March 29, 1888.*

APPLICANT: *Miss Marion Oak Stage.*

I hereby apply to the Legation of the United States at Berlin for a passport for myself, ~~my wife and minor children, as follows:~~

born at ______ on the ___ day of ______ 18__, and ______

In support of the above application I do solemnly swear that I was born at *Paris Ill.* on or about the *9* day of *Nov.* 18*64*; that my father *was a native* citizen of the United States; that I am a native and loyal citizen of the United States, temporarily residing at *Berlin*; that I left the United States on the *15* day of *Oct.* 18*7*; ~~that I am the bearer of passport No. ______ issued by ______ on the ___ day of ______ 18___~~; and that I desire the passport for the purpose of *Travelling*

(OATH OF ALLEGIANCE.)

Further, I do solemnly swear that I will support, protect and defend the Constitution and Government of the United States against all enemies, whether domestic or foreign; and that I will bear true faith, allegiance and loyalty to the same, any ordinance, resolution, or law of any State, Convention, or Legislature to the contrary notwithstanding; and further, that I do this with a full determination, pledge and purpose, without any mental reservation or evasion whatsoever; and further that I will well an faithfully perform all the duties which may be required of me by law. So help me God.

Marion Oak Stage

LEGATION OF THE UNITED STATES AT BERLIN.

Sworn and subscribed to before me, this *29* day of *March* 18*88*

Fred't W. Crosby,

Secretary of Legation.

DESCRIPTION OF APPLICANT.

AGE: *23* years

STATURE: *5* feet *3½* inches

FOREHEAD: *high*

EYES: *blue*

NOSE: *small*

MOUTH: *medium*

CHIN: *round*

HAIR: *blonde*

COMPLEXION: *fair*

FACE: *oval*

IDENTIFICATION,

I, ______ of ______ hereby declare that I am acquainted with the above named ______ and know ______ to be a native-born citizen of the United States, and that the facts stated in ______ affidavit are true to the best of my knowledge and belief.

*I, the thundering Jean do on this first day of 1889 solemnly
promise myself to keep this journal for every day in 1889,
hoping, by the providence of God to be spared through the
year and to improve every day morally and intellectually.*

It was the most exhausting and inspiring six months of my life. I
never forgave the Kaiser for starting that war and denying my boys the
same experience. Alice and I met her family – Mrs Wellman, Emma, Jean
and little Ray – in Montreaux, then made our way to the coast of France.
From Marseilles we headed east along the coast to Italy, the classic tour.
It was late winter and it was good to be on the coast. For Alice and me,
who had come down from Berlin, it seemed quite balmy.

The towns were full of English and Americans. We seemed to meet
Vassar and Smith girls everywhere. America and Americans were very
popular – Buffalo Bill's Wild West Show was touring Europe with Sitting
Bull and Annie Oakley and causing a great sensation. Annie shot a cigarette
from right out of the new Kaiser's mouth. They say she wrote to him
during the Great War and asked to have a second shot.

There were English hotels, baths (the local versions were usually
disgusting), stores and libraries – a whole economy tuned to the Grand
Tourist. Alice and I got away from all that at every opportunity but nothing
could detract from the sheer wonder of it all.

17th January: Pension Internationale, Nice. France.
Went to races, walked and shopped. Countess Tolstoi, 3 maids,
3 children at Pension.

I love that casual note. A reminder, in case we forgot! 'Countess
Tolstoi'. I saw her several times *en passant*. I was transfixed but tried to be
casual. A sophisticate used to encountering Countesses, not an American
bumpkin abroad. To be so close to legend was disorienting. The line
between reality and mythology seemed to dissolve in the winter sun.

Her party all spoke perfect French, of course, and Em summoned the nerve to engage one of the maids in conversation. The Countess had the youngest three of her eight children with her, escaping the worst of the winter at Polyana for a few weeks. I used to think of her later, when I fled Queenstown in winter. I fancied that if it was good enough for Countess Tolstoi it was good enough for me, even if Deniliquin came up somewhat short of Nice. Later still I found it hard to reconcile the tired, dignified woman I saw sitting quietly in the gardens with the mad shrew portrayed by many at the great man's chaotic end. To think that when I saw her she was in the middle of transcribing The Kreutzer Sonata! Little wonder she needed to escape Polyana. She must surely have known then what the end would be.

Menton, where we stayed in the Hotel d'Italie, was a sanatorium town. Just like Pueblo, I joked to the others. Anything less like Pueblo, with its hard skies and belching smelters pouring filth into the rivers, I could not imagine. Menton was sublime, a hand-coloured postcard come to life. I wondered idly how my life would have unfolded had Mama come to this coast for her consumption, instead of to the Rockies?

We went to a Casino in Genoa, secretly excited behind our scrupulous, Presbyterian faces, but a sad, almost sombre air prevailed within. Nothing like what we had expected, which I suppose was drunken revelry, shady men and exotic women. I admit to being a little disappointed.

30th January: Hotel Grande Bretaque de Chiaga, Naples.
Marion, Alice and Ray go to Rome.

That was a day I could live forever. It had been Jean's 21st the day before. I gave her a beautiful little silver filigreed bonbonniere. Alice and I took young Ray on the train to Rome, winding through the crisp winter landscape, the sun low on the ancient villages and farms. We had a day to explore the most famous city in history and only ourselves to please. Little Ray was charming and energetic and completely uninhibited. We were more discreet, as befitted our ancient years, but men flirted with us with their eyes – we did not speak to an American or English tourist the entire day.

I remember sitting to take coffee in a winter sunlit piazza and wondering suddenly whether I might be in love, though I could not think with what.

We had the strange experience in Rome of seeing the Pope one day and the Chicago White Stockings play the Allstars the next! I had come halfway round the world to see my first (and last) game of baseball.

It is all a pleasant blur now, as though it was a book I read. The significance, the wonder of it all, was lost a little in the excitement. For years after I took as much pleasure, if not more, in the recollection: the Vatican, the Uffizi, the Pitti Palace, St Peter's, concerts, dances, food and more food and the Wellmans shopping always and all of us so earnest and so greedy for it all.

Milliners and dressmakers, deliver me from them...

We took French lessons, German, music lessons; we played our instruments and read Ruskin and the lives of the great artists and always kept our Bibles and our Baedeker close at hand. We played euchre and whist and pretended not to flirt with earnest Englishmen. And then there was Venice.

15th May: Gondola ride in evening.
Floated down canal – three barges with music. Balconies gay
with lights and music. Rows of gaslight detracted from the
scene. Went to cafe for ice and lemonade.

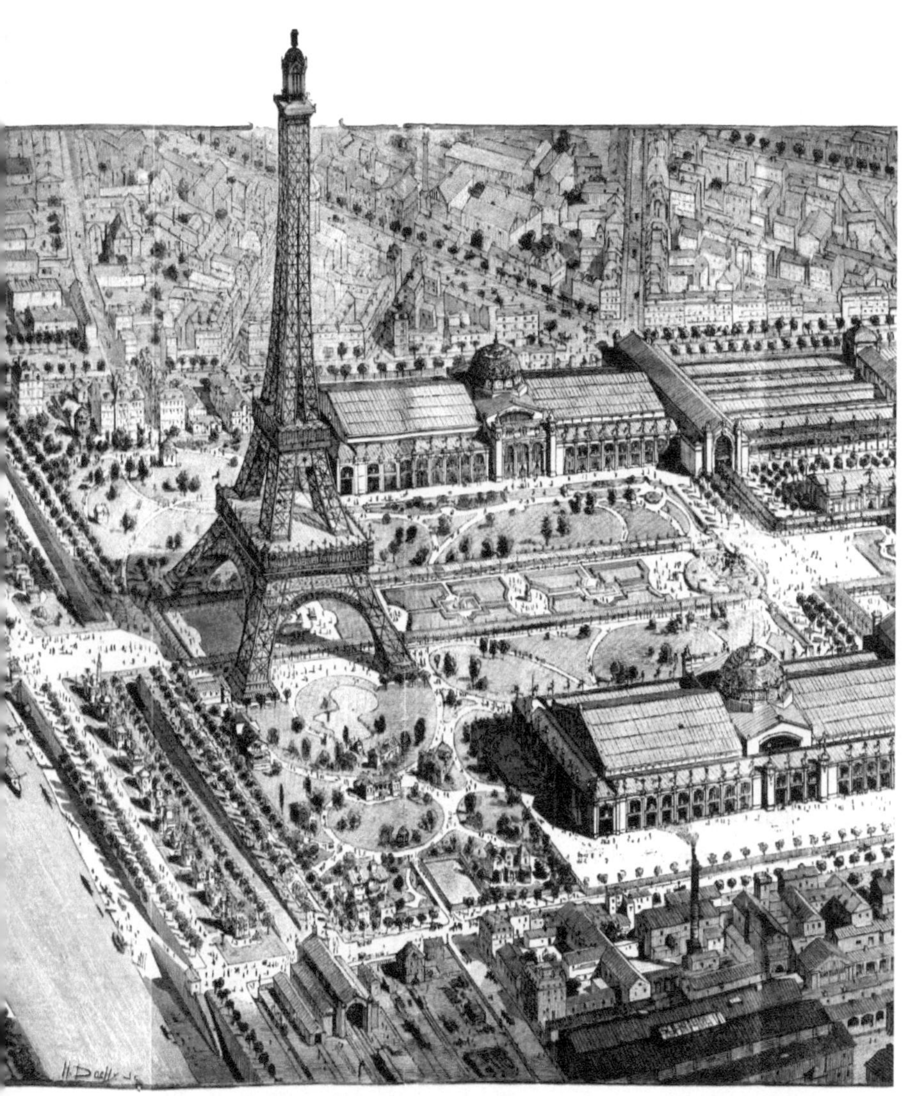

VUE PANORAMIQUE DE L'EXPOSITION UNIVERSELLE DE 1889

We gathered breath at the Grand Hotel in Belligo – so luxuriously
lazy – and then set off to Switzerland and beyond.

After eight months I parted company with the Wellmans in Berlin to
make my long way home, across half the world to Colorado. On the way
I saw The Great Exposition in Paris. Then I felt that I was at the very
centre of creation. Nothing was impossible. I climbed the Eiffel Tower
at night, lit by a million electric lights, the tallest structure in the world.
Still is, as far as I know – 80 storeys high. To think! It took an hour to
climb. When I met Mr Edison, 30 years later, I told him we had climbed
it within a day of each other, all those years ago. I had seen his name in
the book. He was unimpressed but I didn't much care for him anyway.
He had a hard mouth and fidgeted.

I wandered wide-eyed through that wonderland. In the gigantic
Industrial Hall I took childish pride in the prominence of American
invention and industry. Mr Edison was most prominent of all – despite his
fidgeting he was very productive. The world seemed such an exciting place,
full of wonder and goodwill and the spirit of progress. How naïve I was.

I made a little pilgrimage to Vincennes, the birthplace of Pierre Brouillette, the French trader who named my little creek and traded with the Kickapoo along the Wabash, a few miles east of our old place. From Paris to the Wabash – it is a journey to match my own.

I had no idea what I would do back in Pueblo but for the moment I was a pretty enough, intelligent young woman, temporarily of independent means and abroad on her own, with no-one to answer to, a strong sense of righteousness and a desire to show Mr Robert Sticht that I had gumption. I did not give a damn what anyone else thought of me – nobody knew me or where I was from. Or where I was going. I had not much idea on that subject myself but it seemed plain that I should go somewhere. And I did eventually – from the centre of creation to the dark side of the moon – and I never came back.

Our little holiday is over. Bob has taken the boys up to Burnie, to take ship back to school in Melbourne. He will be gone nearly a week. It was an awkward parting. It is possible I will not see Hadmar and Chet again but I think I will last long enough. I will force myself to Melbourne later. There are things that must be tidied, then I can go. Their goodbyes are beyond them anyway.

They may know me better one day, given time to reflect and measure their own lives against mine. They may feel the weight, as I did with poor Mama. Perhaps they will forgive me then for leaving them so soon.

I was a spoiled and wilful child I see now, convinced that I knew best and that my good intentions excused the selfishness I hid even from myself. I thought I knew just exactly what Mama felt and thought. Understood everything perfectly, resented her just a little for her manipulation, her clinging martyrdom to The White Plague. I will not do that to my boys. I was impatient with her illness. I did not understand then that illness is a secret place. It cannot be shared. When you are ill and dying you become an embarrassment – an uncomfortable *memento mori*. Nor did I share Mama's sense of accumulated loss, even though I shared the losing. I was young and going forward and I resented her roll call of the dead – that was the past. I had my life to live and the constant proximity of the too-early gone underscored my sense of urgency. I could sing her litany of loss but I could not understand it. Not then. She had to keep repeating all those names to hold them in her mind. Like Homer's heroes, their immortality depended on her recitation. Now I will take their names, their lives and lies to my grave. There will be no muse to sing us. We will be forgotten.

Won't we be happy when we can be together again?
A few minutes ago snow was falling. Now every cloud has vanished
and the sky is as bright and brilliant as though a cloud had never
swept over its face. 'Such is life.'

I saw the grave of Helen Hunt Jackson once, high up on the mesa above Colorado Springs. It was where she met her husband and he brought her home, I guess. All the way from San Francisco, along the same rails that took me away. I would have liked to meet her – a feisty woman who would not be subdued.

I would like to think to think that I too might one day find my way home; that one day my ashes will lie in the good earth of Edgar County, beside Napoleon and Sarah and Charlie and little Emma. And dear Lizzie.

It will fall to Bob to arrange things but surely the money could be better spent while the boys remain at school. Things will be tight for him.

mastery shows itself, first, in how you cope with restricted circumstances

The light fades and wind chills the air. Autumn is only weeks away but there are no signs of Fall here, no leaves burnish the ground and whisper of winter as you shuffle through them. Only the light mellowing and the ground shrugging off the heat foreshadow a change. And something in the sky.

———

In Europe, as spring cracks, the trees will be a fuzz of green along the grand and hopeful boulevards. In Paris and Berlin the wide streets and splendid parks will stir. The air will be full of ideas and beauty. Promises.

Well, no, not now perhaps, not after their so-called Great War – an ironic name surely? It is still 1889 in the Europe of my mind. Surely the physical wreckage of that late madness will be cleared away by now, if not the spiritual. In my memory Europe will never change. Not now. There's no time left for it to fade. Yesterday it was all brilliant beyond belief. I still smile at the recollection of it, marooned here on the other side of the planet with no hope of rescue and only possums to watch and wonder how I came to this: a woman who climbed the Eiffel Tower and stayed in a hotel with Countess Tolstoi, dying in a ghost town beyond the pale.

a battered, wrecked old woman
thrown on this savage shore, far, far from home

All I have now are memories and my portable museum of letters and photographs, my *Wunderkammer*. Relics I have kept close by me here. Some of my jewellery, which is dear to me: some is mother's, some Lizzie's, most was given me by Robert, who loved to spoil me with such things. He was like a child, cloaking his delight in facts and history. There are Charlie's cuff links, the photographs and Papa's portrait, Mama's letters and the letter books. Not much to show for 58 years, though it is a relief to be free of the Collection. I always liked to travel light.

This final journey requires no luggage. I have put almost everything behind me – sold or sent away, I will never see them again: the Collection, the furniture, the clothes. I have put away childish things. I am suddenly old and what I once spake I no longer understand. I am dissolving.

whither there be knowledge it shall vanish away

I have some clothes suitable for a ghost town and these few precious echoes of my past. Proof that once I was. It is my list, my litany, my catalogue. The bones of my Iliad.

go to the source

I have the letter books, chronicles of my wasted life. I have Mama's letters to me when I first went out into the world, all the way to Poughkeepsie, NY. To Vassar. It seemed the centre of the world to me. Whereas this world I came to has been spun to the outer rim of creation, by nature and by history. We are gravel.

> *my letters*
> *all dead paper*
> *mute and white*
> *and yet they seem alive*
> *and quivering*

Those letters tore at me – I was seventeen, abroad in the wide world, homesick and exhilarated. I knew then, as my sons know now, that I was soon to be an orphan. I sensed, as my sons sense now, that there was much to see and do. I was hungry to be part of something bigger than Edgar County or Pueblo.

I run my fingers over Mama's faded letters in the frail lamplight, as though some miracle will connect us. The tiny words crowd the pages, every inch stuffed greedily with love and longing and faith in the power of the ordinary. So dense my tired eyes can barely make them out in the amber glow of the lamp. But I know them by heart, every syllable, every scratch, every whirl and whorl of ink, every unspoken word and thought. Perhaps I have not put away childish things after all?

good bye little one. Try to realise all you are to your mother and all she wants you to be in the world and in all things be faithful

THE WINDSOR HOTEL.

BUSH, TABOR & CO. PROPRIETORS.

Pueblo Jan. 29th 188_

My Dear ________ I am going to scratch
very few words to you this morning — for
I did not answer some of your questions
in your last letter. Sat. evening Geo.
received a telegram from ______ to
"come down tonight" so he thought best
to go. Harry and I went to meeting as
usual. Sabbath morning we two eat our
breakfast together — just think of your
own little mother all alone with these "strange boys" —
how would you feel? Well we went
to church and the house was full — It
seemed like the old times — for you
must remember that since you old ____
used to go here there have been seven
churches built — in East Pueblo — or ____
on the mesa so that the congregati___

Mother's letters were palimpsests – her spidery hand invaded every available skerrick of space. I had not so much to read them as decode them. They were psychological palimpsests as well – the meaning snaked around and emerged where least expected. The warp of a description of a fire in the outhouse would have as weft unrelated imprecations and advice; serious matters would have salutations from folk hardly remembered creeping in around the edges. They were masterpieces of rhetoric in their own way – I do not believe that any of it was accidental.

I have carried them with me these 40 years since. I can and do recite them, as I can *My Captain*, or *Sonnets from The Portuguese*. I could write a thesis on their inferences. If they were lost I would retain their image in my mind – but the physical contact would be lost. The aura. It is like Robert's fascination with his books and prints and their long histories. I felt I ought to feel as strongly as he did about them – but I never did. Not really. I was too conscious of their weight. They were anchors and I needed sails. They connected him to his history – the world of ideas and science, so his world was always with him; in the same way my little *Wunderkammer* connects me to a more recent and prosaic past – but I could make a case for the profundity of these banalities.

I have some early letters from Robert, from when he was up in Leadville and Helena and Toston and over to Butte; and some from various Hazelton girls that I treasure mostly for their echoes of a life I heard but never had. And from Lizzie of course, towards the end, plain and blunt as always:

Come home! Come home!

I have my medicines and my teeth, some books, writing paper, pen and ink – and I have my Aunt Jemima pancakes. They are not as good as the ones Mama used to make back in Bloomfield, swimming in syrup from Papa's trees, but they still sing to me of Camelot.

it is some dream

———

I have some photographs as well. Here is the daguerreotype of Robert sitting on his father's knee. It is 1858 in Hoboken, six years before I was born. Robert is not more than a year old but he gazes with confident amusement at the future over my left shoulder, while Johan confronts the camera almost petulantly, daring the world to underestimate his prodigy. He is the spitting image of his grandson, who sits across the table from me now, writing yet another report.

I always have 'The History of Edgar County' to hand, with the etching of Papa.

A fine, decent and determined man he looks. I remember his smile, his patience and his stiff-legged limp, the legacy of metal lodged in his back at Vicksburg. He is in his good suit, the one he would have worn over to Charleston to see Mr Lincoln debate Mr Douglas, back in 1858, about the time Robert was being photographed on his father's knee. Emancipation took a strong grip on Papa. He placed himself squarely in the centre of that brawl. There were incidents in Edgar County still talked of when I was a girl – Copperheads and shootings and lynchings – many sins unforgiven to this day.

he was a kind husband and father, and a good neighbor,
cheerfully serving the generation in which he lived.

Like Lincoln, he was a tall, straight-backed man who worked hard his whole life to make something of himself. He was mostly self-educated and not a man to talk much, but when he did he spoke his mind. I consider it to have been a well-ordered mind though I judge mostly on anecdotal evidence. This picture before me – a kindly man with big eyes that look inward more than out – is of a man who, in my memory, will always be taller than he was. Slight of frame, sinewy and strong, he bore sorrow without complaint or self-pity. He was ambitious but not so much he let it sway his sense of right and wrong. You can understand why he admired Mr Lincoln.

Lincoln's people came from just across the County line, over to Springfield. Some of them ran with the Copperheads and would have hung if not for cousin Abraham. He is buried over there. I have seen the grave.

the port is near, the bells I hear

Papa saw him speak twice before the war, in Paris and over in Charleston. That's when Lincoln began to mark himself for fate. An ungainly man, with the strength of a knotty tree, Papa said. He'd bend but never break. An oak.

Papa was a Democrat but he rightly held slavery a mortal sin and fell in with Lincoln's way of thinking on how to end it. He used to say of that debate – and I rely on Mother's word for this – that Mr Douglas was the better speaker but Abraham Lincoln made you want to believe in things higher than yourself. Not like the slick Sunday gospellers, with their practised passion – this was something new. Douglas was a long-term Senator, famous for his oratory and generally expected to be the next President. The debates changed all that. They set Lincoln on the path to the White House and set the Republic on the road to war.

It is dark now. Ethel has something simmering on the stovetop. I do not take much food, I have had no appetite for years and eat mainly to please others. But Bob is a working man and Ethel works hard to do for us. She spends what time she can spare from tending me off in the fields, gathering scraps of tin and metal for the sluice, from which a few shillings might be gleaned.

Misery acquaints a man with strange bedfellows they say – aye, and women too. Only a poor handful of folk is left behind here. A half-dozen sad shacks where once stood hundreds. Weeds overgrow fine gardens that thrived in the rich, red soil. Diffidence prevails where once unbridled optimism held the field. The scratchers scratch but there is neither a sense of purpose nor an air of expectation, just hope, the last refuge of the helpless. It has all been crushed and picked over and the dumb red hill holds its secret fast – if indeed it has one.

there are in nature neither rewards nor punishments –
there are consequences

I have the scrapbook with me – the cuttings from papers, an odd narrative of our life: the balls, the comings and goings, holidays, speeches, openings (I was a dab hand at opening things), receptions, dinners, lunches, teas, bazaars, fetes, picnics and the rest. What does any of it mean?

Mrs Sticht gave a neat speech

Good works, concerts, plays and visitors. It is like looking at a painting through a random set of pinholes, yet that patchwork became the fabric of my life while I waited to go home. My boys went away to school, my friends had gone back to California. I was becoming a reflection.

The morning is almost gone by the time I drag myself out of bed. I have been dozing, aware but not quite conscious. I do not sleep much because the pain seems sharper in the dark. Mornings are often better, there is comfort and distraction in the activity of others. Ethel is cluttering about the place and a south-westerly is buffeting the walls and whistling through the many cracks. I heard Bob go out to the workings earlier. The south-westerly will be cold. Ethel is making my pancakes and I can smell coffee on the stove. I feel a whisper of appetite; I can almost remember what it is to be hungry. I bled again in the night and poor Ethel will have to do the sheets before Bob returns. I have no wish to share such things with him. I remember well the bloody rags soaked in the shreds of Mother's lungs but it is not an edifying memory and I would rather I did not have it. It is harrowing work for Ethel but I pay her more than fairly and she is well out of Queenstown for a while. Anyone is well out of Queenstown for a while.

We might have a visit from old Mrs Mitchell if the wind eases. She is kind, if somewhat eccentric, and visits as often as she can, which is to say too often. She feels uncomfortable because she is no fool and has surely divined our circumstances. She was at a concert at Penghana once, so understands my fall. She takes no pleasure from it though, which is to her credit. Her eccentricity is chiefly manifest in her determination to maintain the illusion that we are living in a functioning town. I indulge this conceit, for it is quite amusing. This place is her albatross as well as mine. Our paths have converged from very different beginnings, although she is a Presbyterian. But she is hardened to her fate and has her health. She is stoic and holds her stern faith close. I sometimes envy her that.

he prayeth best who loveth best

7

I married Prospero by the Purgatory River. *El Rio de Las Animas Perdidas en Purgatorio*, to give it its proper name: The River of Animals in Purgatory.

January 1895. We were suspended in a state of grace on the bank of that river, down south of Pueblo at Trinidad – on the cusp of all that was past and all that could be. You could say that of every moment, I know, but in the long flow of a life few moments present themselves so starkly as turning points. It is a day caught in the sunny amber of my memory. The moment Marion Oak Stage became Mrs Robert Sticht. The day I left behind my past, my kin, my friends and the children and the church and the schools and my music and the sun. I did not know that I was losing the sun. I could not know that I would never return. It was the moment I cleaved myself to that strange alchemist, my Prospero, for better or for worse and forsaking all others and all else. Until death did us part.

all places shall be hell that is not heaven

81

In truth there wasn't all that much to forsake – the only 'others' I forsook were silly boys who'd lost patience anyway. My kin were mostly dead; my friends were few apart from Robert and my future looked depressingly like my past. There was really only Lizzie to leave. I was 30, teaching the brats of Colorado, drifting happily enough into spinsterhood. Motherhood and death were too closely associated in my mind for me to be disappointed in my singularity. Living with Lizzie and George, fending off the few brave boys who tried too hard, visiting the opera and the theatre and mother's old friends and doing my good works. Europe seemed as far away as twenty.

All I had was a good friend, a quick mind and a confidence, that from this draughty cabin in a ghost town half way round the world, seems quite absurd. Charming, but absurd. I wonder what Robert saw in me? I was pretty enough but not uncommonly so. I played the keyboards and read and had opinions. I had been to Germany and had climbed the Eiffel Tower.

if thou would'st love me let it be for nought

We were Adam and Eve and we left the Garden because we could. Such a silly story. Did God really expect them to stay forever in the Garden, to never wonder what might be over yonder? He is a poor judge of human nature if so. We were suitably cursed, anyway, never able to return, only to visit. Those two visits made it clear to me that now I was from everywhere and belonged nowhere.

blown with restless violence round the pendant world

January in Trinidad, beside the Purgatory River – snow on the mountains and a high country chill that could make your head ache but could not dampen the fire in my heart. Poor Lizzie was so happy and afraid. George was George: happy and confused and sweet. The memory is radiant as a Colorado sky. We took a trap down to the old cottonwoods by the river, where the wagon trains heading west once paused to gather strength, before the last surge south into New Mexico.

siste, viator

High country light has printed that day in my mind more surely than a photograph. I see us all there under the frosty cottonwoods, that snow-capped mountain pitched high above us like a tent. So happy and excited and afraid.

We kept going from Trinidad, by train, south to Albuquerque, then swinging west, through Canon Diablo and Mojave and up north along the range, past Fresno and Modesto – delightful name – then west again, always west, for the final run down into San Francisco and the Pacific. It was seven years since I had seen an ocean. It was so unexpectedly blue. And San Francisco – that lost San Francisco! What a riot of activity, what a monstrous and magnificent cauldron of energy and people and sordid life, all poised on the rim of that sublime bay.

I was caught in a pleasant avalanche. I felt much as I did when Mother died. When she finally left us I could not assess my reaction. I felt everything and nothing. I was bereft and free. It was intoxicating. Then I ran east and my momentum carried me across the Atlantic. Now I was free of everyone and everything I'd ever known and my momentum was carrying me west, across the Pacific, to Tasmania – a place I'd barely heard of.

inspirited by this wind of promise

We had little knowledge of Tasmania. Dr Peters, Robert's mentor, had been to the Lyell field and saw it as an opportunity for Robert to make his name. I do not think he expected Robert to take a wife along! There was a metallurgist from South Australia, Mr Hawker, who was, like Robert, a graduate of Clausthal, in the Hartz Mountains of Saxony. He came to visit Robert up at Boulder in the early '90s. He was keen on the Lyell field but Robert had not taken too much notice. Mr Hawker was in

Butte the day they tried to lynch the General Manager of the smelters for fouling the air. At least the unions never went that far at Lyell.

We knew a mining engineer up in Toston who had been to Tasmania. Mr Callow, an educated Englishman who had travelled the world. He had been all around Australia, spoke highly of it and had a collection of boomerangs that claimed Robert's attention. We heard from him about Tasmania's pure white beaches and the bluest water in the world. A place of astonishing beauty and unsullied wilderness; a place of great hopes and temperate climate. A new world of opportunity. So when the chance came for Robert to make his mark in the world, there was something compelling in the juxtaposition of opportunity and geography.

I learned later that when in Tasmania Mr Callow had stayed at Triabunna, a charming little harbour on the east coast of the island, with a view across an azure strait to the looming cliffs of Maria Island. A mild and bountiful climate and a friendly coast. Mt Lyell, on the other hand, is on the west coast. The east and west coasts of Tasmania – were ever two coasts more dramatically different, so metaphorically perfect in their opposition?

The east coast is a long stretch of sweeping white sand beaches, limpid sea and perfect bays, with a temperate climate supporting fertile farms and orchards.

The west coast is a punched face, a whipping post for the Roaring Forties. Wind and wave howl and surge three quarters of the way around the globe to smash down on the stunned coastline and drench the mountains beyond. Five feet of rain a year, dense rainforest and one decent harbour along its entire length – and that a Venus fly trap. Macquarie Harbour – as big as Illinois but with an entrance the size of a parlour and a well-earned reputation for disaster. As Robert discovered on the *Grafton*.

Mt Lyell is a rampart on that wild coast and its mines burrow into steep valleys and hills clad in a profusion of temperate rainforest. When we finally arrived, after a journey that filled me with wonder and apprehension, the miserable little camptown of Penghana, clinging to the mine and smelter, represented the only civilization within three days travel.

It is quiet here. Bush quiet, which means quiet only to city ears. From our house, Penghana, I could hear Queenstown breathing, chewing, snoring and breaking wind. Mining towns run on mechanical shifts, not natural cycles. The shifts finish and the shifts start – three times a day, every day. Three normal town and family cycles every day: the coming and the going, the easing down and the girding up, all oblivious of nature. It lends a timelessness to living that dulls the senses. Nothing begins, nothing ends. Everything strains toward some unknown goal. Capitalism imposes itself on living and something new is born. It is how the world will live one day, Robert said. The Will of Progress demands it and the Will of Progress cannot be denied.

The Will of Progress is tiresome and humourless, it seems to me. If that bleak world is the future, it makes leaving it much easier. We were naïve to believe that change is progress or that evolution is by definition toward a better end, when it is simply adaptation to chaos. What I once thought certainties I see now are defences.

This old shack is elegantly spare. There is no clutter. Nothing adorns the plain, King Billy walls, rough cut like the floorboards. There is a fireplace with a few unrelated armchairs gathered round it. There is a table with four ricketty wooden chairs and an old wood stove with the fire on top. A primitive tool that Ethel handles well, despite her tender years. She is a west coaster. She makes do. My bed is made behind a blanket hung from the ceiling. Bob, another west-coaster, shakes his swag out beside the fire. Ethel has a cot in the little storeroom off the kitchen. When Chet and Hadmar were here, sleeping in swags upon the floor, it was like a campout.

There are a few of Bob's books and charts scattered around. In the lamplight the room glows darkly, like one of Robert's Rembrandts. It is simple but there is nothing to dust or knock over and there is some comfort in that.

I wash myself in a tin bucket in the outdoor bathroom and examine myself in the little mirror Bob has hung on a nail. Even in the soft light my face looks like the hills of Queenstown – exposed and scarified. Reduced to bedrock. Who could know now what smooth luxury this flesh once promised, what heat these withered old thighs once held, what a glow once was kindled here. That fierce young woman in the photograph from Vassar, daring the world, is become this fragile mask, cracked and paper-skinned, hair thin and grey, expression as remote as a stranger's pain. Only the eyes are constant, though now the confusion of a wounded animal lurks behind the old confidence.

I am old without an ageing. Not like Mother. Mama was always dying but by some Faustian trick she never aged. Consumption bequeaths a sheen, that Romantic pallor. And she was always busy, directing her opera from centre stage.

> *I have always been cared for by someone.*
> *I begin to think I am a very selfish mortal*

Yesterday I was lively as a cricket, today I am old and tired and alone and cold. Nothing will ever warm me again. No man, no smile, no idea, no temptation, no glimpse of home, no act of kindness, no scent of childhood. Only pancakes and the whispered memory of sunlight dancing through the golden maples back in Edgar County and I am barefoot, bareheaded and bareback, galloping my pony along the creek and out into the wheat fields, towards the ocean prairie and wondering how far?

> *Good night and bless you with a mother's love*

Sleep seduces me with its vague promise of an end to pain and worry. I bleed for my sins and long for my people. For my country. I keen for them in my mind – it would never do to keen aloud. I yearn for the smell of a dry wind off the high plains. You can get something like it in

Deniliquin but down here the wet westerly howls and drenches and decays. I hid from it as much as I could and never wintered here if I could help it. Now winter has captured me. I feel its chill hand stroke my old bones.

There are no battles to excite me, just my *Wunderkammer*, ephemera of a displaced life. The cold radiates from a space deep inside me that I cannot describe, except to say it is the space where Robert was. I no longer have substance enough to occupy space. I see the smile of my mother and the love of my sons and they are almost one. Soon to be orphans, my boys draw breath, steeling themselves for the rest of their lives. Already remembering me.

The sun I chased all these years no longer warms me. There seems too little of me to accumulate its rays. I am aware of the light but it does not penetrate, no longer eases the dull ache at the back of my neck, the heavy tiredness that presses down in a long, extended sigh through the scrawny muscle and sinew of my arms and sides and bears down heavy on my eyes. It does not lull me into semi-consciousness, I am there already and I am still cold.

and I thought I would much rather go in the spring
when I could see things growing

What once was a garden, full of the thrust and buzz of living, is now barren as the Queen. Poisoned and dying. All that's left is shrivelled up, like the wizened little kidney they took from me. Traitor. They opened me up like a tin of sardines, cleaved the proud white flesh that once was his. Plucked out the dried turd and stitched me up like a bag of spuds, as Luke would say. It still hurts me when I bend or when I breathe too deeply, or laugh, which is not often any more. It still sucks me into the void, that wild space inside me, the shadow of what was me. A toxic wound. Fouled by my own toxic drains, like the Queen, that fallen woman of a river.

How can something so wild die so quickly? What makes it right? What compensation does culture offer such an outrage? My man, my dearest Robert, wrought all this: felled the forest, flayed the hills to their naked ribs, made a sewer of the streams and raped the earth he loved so much.

Did he poison me as well?

for now we see through a glass, darkly

8

Along February evening, the last breath of summer. Light fading over the plain in the foreground, the ranges dark on the horizon. A Renaissance landscape, Robert said once, as we sat on this spot. From here we dreamed the plain populated and cultivated, our grand house looking out over all. A wind-cleansed, open town with room to grow and light for its children and gardens and parks. The river would be pristine in its dark way.

Robert's people were dreamers too. They were 'forty-eighters', part of the flood of German liberals who fled to America in the years after the failed revolutions of 1848. 'Forty-eighters' was a badge they wore proudly. They believed in education, hard work and God, so they fitted in and prospered. They taught their children that they had a duty to be the best person they could possibly be, and they believed that The United States was the best place on Earth to achieve that.

Johan and Augusta were from Bavaria. They spoke an old, northern dialect – Altdeutsche – that has all but disappeared. I have the letter that Robert wrote to his mother from Paris, when he was 14.

Wir aber fuhren über den Kanal so ruhig wie ein
Ferryboat über den Fluß

Johan was a chemist, and Robert's younger brother Ernst followed him into that profession. He and Robert were close. Robert was older by five years and took care of Ernst like a son out west. They often lodged together, all over Colorado and Montana. Two German boys from Brooklyn. Ernst worked as an assayer in the mines and eventually went into business for himself up in Butte. They were sharing a room in a boarding house in East Pueblo, up near the smelter Robert was building, when I first met Robert at the opera.

It is a truth universally acknowledged that a mining town in possession of a good fortune must be in want of an opera house. Cousin Horace built one up in Leadville when he started his wild ride and followed it up with an even grander edifice in Denver. Pueblo was no exception to the rule. Mother and I were subscribers, of course, and went to everything her health would allow. I often noticed a quiet, self-contained young man, short and intense and always immaculately turned out, no matter that his suit was plain and a little the worse for wear. We couldn't help but be introduced eventually and eventually Mother – who took more of a shine than I did to the too-serious young man who spoke German as fluently as English and knew his operas well – invited him to visit.

He brought Ernst along. Dear George teased Robert about that day for years afterwards. He never let him forget how he could not take his eyes off me and how I ignored him and flirted with Ernst, just to annoy him. Ernst was a shy, restless young man, about my age and somewhat in awe of Robert. As was I. As was anyone with any sense.

Ernst was up at Butte for a long time later on. He started his assaying business up there and married Ida Werther, a nice, solid girl from a nice, solid German family. That was at the end of 1889. Robert was up there as well. He moved through all those mining towns, Leadville, Butte, Toston, Golden Sunshine, Helena – building smelters and experimenting.

———

He was obsessed with Pyritic smelting and was making a name for himself. He invited me to Ernst's wedding.

I was just back from the Continent. Lizzie and George and I went up on the train from Denver. I had been away two years and though Robert and I had corresponded some it was quite unnerving to see him again. I had last seen him at Mother's first funeral. Watching him at that wedding up in Butte, I knew.

It was a grand affair – there was a big German community at Butte. There were big communities of any nationality you care to name in Butte at that time. It was a noisy riot of a place, divided into settlements: Irish, Germans, Swedes, British, Italians, Poles and Russians. They all had to work together in the mines, though, and they worked together pretty well. It was America in a bottle. I'd never seen anything like it. Except Leadville perhaps, but that was anarchy, with no future beyond this afternoon or the next pulled cork or loaded gun. Butte did not feel like that. It felt like the tumultuous birth of a new world, not the riotous wake of an old one.

a talent is formed in stillness
a character in the world's torrent

Robert had changed. He was happier. He was living Goethe's *wunder-jahre*, a philosopher-scientist making a name for himself in the big mines of the wild west and now his little brother was getting married to a serious young woman from the old country. He was like a happy father. I saw the real man for perhaps the first time, the man who felt so much but struggled to express it without analysing it or sounding pompous. When he was up at Boulder Valley in '92 and bored with the job at hand, he wrote me this, which I supposed, knowing him as I did, to be a love letter:

...it is all hardly more than child's play and there is a continuous fund of pleasure in the necessity of contact with the rude healthfulness of outdoor roughness, and it has always been a pastime to carry the study of my fellow beings into the remotest corners of human manifestation. No enjoyment is greater than that of producing, and no happiness deeper than that of the inventor.

It has been necessary to go my own path in the design of this little plant, and the delight of seeing the children of one's imagination gradually taking shape is truly fascinating, were tho' thought embody itself in no more ethereal shape than such as are rendered by iron, brick, wood, or stone! It has been the outcome of a much dissatisfied youth to see beyond the material and yet reverence it, too, as the stepping stone to wider utility and profounder impress on the destiny of the race than could ever be accomplished by a life devoted to more artificial ideals.

This conviction is bought only at the expense of many a heart-ache, – the purchase price is well returned by the peace of settled opinion. Briefly, forces of the 'Wander jahre' (curiously enough Goethe also calls him 'Montan' and makes him a devotee of mining) has gradually become the most influential figure in literature to me, and my bosom friend.

Not your conventional love letter. But I was always flattered to be the subject of this strange man. I knew then that if he asked me I could not say no.

Over yonder I can hear someone splitting wood for the evening fire. Like us they will sit outside in the cool while it cooks dinner. Tea, I should say. The axe blows echo around the hill as clearly as the black cockatoos' cracked cackle. There were few birdsongs in the muffled hubbub of the town that reached us through the fog and smoke at Penghana but as the garden grew and flowered they came, fantails and robins and then honey-eaters, wattle birds and the rest.

Ernst and Ida named their boy after Robert and we named our third boy Chester Ernest in return. I was 43 when Chet came along. I had not thought to go through all that again, but there it was and here he is. He is the most like me, I think. A bit of a 'nointer', as they say here, but very quick and his own person already. Robert Jr is just that – a taller version of his father. He is quiet, determined and sees the world as an engineering project. There is no problem that cannot be solved by applying logic and process. Hadmar is an amalgam – he has Robert's intelligence and my wanderlust. He is very bright and very confident.

I hope they will stay close. Robert always regretted the distance that came between the Sticht siblings: Ernst, Gustav, Augusta and himself, spread out across the world.

I suspect Ernst became his true self only after Robert left. His was a shadow hard to grow in. They drifted apart a little then, as we gradually and insensibly drifted apart from everything and everyone we left behind. He moved on from Butte and came to rest up north, in the mountains beyond Spokane. A tiny place called Republic. Remote and beautiful, but not so remote as Queenstown, I used to think. It was still in America.

Was there something in those Sticht men that craved extremes of nature and solitude? Montans in Montana?

Robert was a man torn between what he was and the many things he could have been. He always tried to synthesize his intellect with a passion for the doing. Mind and body, if you will. Then his body betrayed him, as mine has now. Until then he tried to occupy the space between past and future, sensation and experience, being and doing – and he was successful for a while. It is a rare thing in any field, for the petty details of life and work and ageing grind away at your resolve. I doubt it can be maintained for long.

He would sleep only four or five hours a day. Even then he might clamber out of bed at 3am, don his Bluey and trudge up to the smelter to deal with some problem. He had a notch blown in the top of the hill between the house and the smelter so that he could see the stack from Penghana. He had a window put in the north wall of our bedroom from which he could keep an eye on it. He could tell from the colour of the smoke what was going on. Even so, he refused to neglect any side of his being – so no matter how much time his work, his job, demanded, he never spent less time on his 'inner man'.

For my part, as far as the 8 hour system is concerned, I am not sorry particularly that circumstances have imposed an excess of working time on me. What I am sorry for is that they have not allowed me a full share of the 8 hours for recreation – work and sleep have both encroached on the proper allowance for this pleasant function!...

My proud alchemist. He was hungry for knowledge, driven to improve himself and all around him – and the bargain he struck with nature instead of Mephistopheles? Devastation and desolation on all sides. Not a tree for miles around, 1200 tons of trees turned to ashes every week, the river polluted and the air befouled. Forty-two dead men floating inside a mountain and Robert adrift in his den, compiling his catalogue of a moment west of time.

Westering got hold of both of us I guess: Colorado, Montana and then the west coast of the world. As far away as the moon but stranger. Robert needed a challenge – a way to put his science and philosophy to the test. He would never have been happy in an academic position, though it appealed to him in a way and was certainly available later on – when it was too late. Something got inside him though, some German love of wildness and wilderness, the drama of nature perhaps? The theatrical? A desire for a life which was in itself a work of art? Something he recognised in Goethe, something I shared once. But my love of adventure waned with children. Not my courage or my strength, mind – illness took those later, made bed a refuge and my mind a fortress. I first became cautious when I had children. Children, like wives, were transient things, in my experience. I was no longer able to be myself. Risk blossomed into fear. For the first time I had to think of the future as real.

Elvin, Gilmon, Samuel and Nancy,
Mary, Abigail, Annette,
Napoleon, Emma, Charlie and Louise

Robert never had to abandon the alchemy of the furnace. He loved it almost as much as he loved his books and his sons and me: that is what made him unique. He achieved that elusive fusion of mind and nature in the crucible of Queenstown. Of all places. A crucible he cast himself. His private laboratory – not a kingdom, as some have said against him. It was his experiment, the test of his philosophy and he couldn't bear to leave it in the end, not for his books, not for his sons and not for me.

He wanted to be taken seriously as a man as well as a mind. If you had seen him as I have, at three in the morning, wrapped in his Bluey, soaked by rain and sweat, buffeted by the wind, surrounded by navvies and furious activity, framed in the incandescent glow of the fire; if you had seen him in the lamplight, poring over the drawings that led to this scene and seen the pure joy of creation he embodied; then, you would sense as I did, that his knowledge and experience and sweat had been smelted into some rare matter. There is something irresistible, something god-like in that, something adventure or luxury can never give you.

He was a man of optimism, energy and self-discipline – a synthesis of Germany and the New World – but he found himself alone in a culture where these qualities were viewed with suspicion and occasional hostility. He loved Mankind but was never truly comfortable in its company. His tragic gift was his naivety. His faith in men who never understood him. That faith was our tragedy. It brought us undone.

And his love for me? He could not take me back to the world so he tried to bring the world to me. We had Lizzie and George for a while, but mostly he brought all the potential we had left behind: the books and prints and artifacts, echoes of something I never quite understood. But as with everything he started, Robert became obsessed. I knew as much as he did at the start, about art and music at least, but my contribution to the Collection waned as he consumed the lore of accumulation and spent our fortune on ephemera.

Ethel fetches water from the creek – it's a long carry back up the hill and I am too weak to help her. She is a good, simple girl, as uncluttered as this shack and not much older. I sense she will have a long life, untroubled by complexity or choice.

I bathe myself as best I can, outside in the lean-to, sheltered from the westerlies but draughty just the same. Anyone could see me if they had a mind. Bloodied water swirls around me as the evidence of my body's betrayal dissolves in soap and hot water. We heat water on the old stove, which is as draughty as the shed but does its best for us. It has seen many kitchens I suspect, but this will be its last. To move it now would be to invite disaster. It will outlive the shack, though, and has outlived the town already.

<hr>

Ethel cooks my pancakes every morning. Aunt Jemima, the taste of all I left behind. Packets carried halfway round the globe for me – a message from The Lost World of Marion Oak Stage.

9

We had a week in San Francisco to collect ourselves and say goodbye to our homeland. We stayed at an hotel but I spent several days with Alice and the Wellmans as Robert made preparations for the task he was about to undertake. It seemed unlikely that anything much could be had at short notice in Tasmania, so the alchemist's kit bag needed to be complete before we sailed. Alice Kate was as Lizzie had been – happy and bereft at once and just a little envious, I think, of Robert and of my grand adventure. It was a dizzy whirl of days even so – San Francisco before the fire was a maelstrom and we plunged into it, reckless as newlyweds even if we did not feel all that new, or all that wed, for that matter. We were about to set off to the other side of the world. In that giddy state of blind anticipation we sailed out on the Pacific, truly blue, unlike the green Atlantic, and ploughed west for weeks across the vast, undulating belly of the world. When I sailed the Atlantic I knew where I was going, or at least I thought I did. I was going home. Going to the source, of everything I had been taught to value and respect. I had expectations. Few of them were realised, of course, but I sailed with them in my luggage nonetheless.

I had no such luggage when I sailed for Tasmania. How could I? I had barely heard of the place, had no idea where it was until Robert showed me it in an atlas. It seemed almost a joke when he did. You could not get further from where we were than where we were going. It was a dream, not a joke.

The old *Alameda*, all 3,000 tons of her, rolled across the Pacific like a drunken miner, from San Francisco to Hawaii, on to Auckland and then Sydney. There is something seductive about sea travel once you stop vomiting – a detachment from reality. There are no physical landmarks on a sea voyage – the Pacific is immense and empty. You can lose your personal landmarks. It is a flirtation with insensibility and, as long as the ship stays afloat, it is a pleasant one.

and the smile and the tear, the song and the dirge

My daily promenade around the deck used to take me past a small posse of sheep kept in a cage near the stern, under the poop deck, appropriately enough. I watched their numbers dwindle as we ate them. It was a singular relationship, one that even as a farm girl I found somewhat macabre, their sad eyes following me dumbly round the deck on my lurching promenade, killing time until dinner. But it is simply life and death and had I looked around me in the world I would have seen the same thinning and the same dumb gaze of forlorn confusion; the look I saw in the mirror earlier today.

still follow each other like surge upon surge

A ship sings. The vibrato of the giant engine fills every solid and every space like a drone, and the slack, heaving rhythm of the ocean slides across that bass in syncopation. High above in the lines and rigging the wind wails and forms a strange melody.

It fills your body more than your mind, once you hear it. Every moment, waking, sleeping, the ship sings to you. It is the music Beethoven heard when he was deaf.

That creaking old ship carted us to the other side of the planet. Much further than the trip to Europe and with no sense of where I was going. I was caught between travelling away and travelling toward. I went from spring to fall. I only knew the sound inside, the feeling of being half immersed, and the odd sensation of knowing you are moving yet seeing nothing change. One acre of ocean is the same as any other. The ship moves on but you cannot really tell, the wake disappears as quickly as tracks in a snowstorm and you have to trust to reason that you are going somewhere. You could just as easily trust to reason that you are going nowhere. And then magically another continent appears on the horizon and you have to trust to reason that you've girdled half the planet and you have to trust to reason that the world you left behind – forever as it turns out – still exists.

> *then I felt like some watcher of the skies*
> *when a new planet swims into his ken*

I wonder what it would have been like to have lived my life in one place, amongst the same people? To have sung one song, like Homer? What it would be like to know a landscape like the back of my hand? To watch it age like the back of my hand? To count the generations who forged it?

> *...Elvin, Gilmon, Samuel and Nancy,*
> *Abigail and Mary and Annette, Emma,*
> *Charlie, Napoleon, Louise...*

We never 'stuck' out here, perhaps because I was always leaving. Yankees with a German name. 'Mrs Sticks' and so on. They meant no harm but I never made a true friend here, save for Luke, and that was potentially difficult.

Our pretensions were a little grand for this hard-bitten place. It was a great battle though, and I like to think I had some success bringing culture to the wilderness, the way Mama and her ilk brought their learning from the East to Illinois and the adolescent towns of the Rockies – schools and churches and opera houses, libraries and manners and music. Culture and Religion, the two pillars of New England.

Yet I see now how fragile that achievement is – how quickly we are forgotten, how my leaving Queenstown was a little sad for some but mostly a relief. Our time had long since passed. I'll never see any of them again and I do not care much. The only true friends I made were men, and that is altogether too difficult. Dear Archie I will miss, though. Now no-one knows I am a character fallen from the pages of a book. And Luke, of course, whose shadow still falls on Balfour. I feel his presence in the trees and on the breeze. Dear Luke, a man among men. I think my memories of Napoleon are coloured by him – lean and righteous, clever and restless, inquisitive, loyal, strong, querulous and quick to take offence, yet generous and fearless. A true friend and a remorseless enemy. A man who could plant fruit trees in the morning, crack unruly heads in the afternoon and recite Keats in the evening. Robert was a little in awe of him I think. And me? I could never say.

But it is true that I was always leaving. 'I'm just 30 miles away,' I said at the station, but we all knew that to be a brave lie, my equivalent of Robert's 'Tell them the Old Man is holding his own,' the day before he died. A final act of humility and kindness. There was more real love in the unspoken acknowledgement of my lie than there could have been in any speechifying.

A week later I was as good as ten thousand miles away and now no-one thinks of me as anything but gone.

I could say the same about leaving home, of course – quickly forgotten, a little sad for some, the brave lie, the unspoken truth – but that time is frozen in my mind as only childhood can be. The people of my childhood live on, not in Mama's Heaven but in my mind. They never age, they never change.

When we went home to Paris and to Pueblo in 1914 I was in such a state of heightened nostalgia and awareness that I recognised people in the street I realised later were long since gone. Impossible people were everywhere. Everyone and everything seemed so small.

Time is slow in here on the red hill. There are no visits or commitments, no preparations. Neither anticipation nor catharsis, except for pancakes and the fire's warmth. My bed is comfortable enough.

I would have liked to spend more time with my kin, though father's people are scattered all round Illinois and Iowa and I doubt I would have fitted very well up in New Hampshire. The Hazeltons are New England people, a little hard for my taste. Too long in the one place? Is that what happens? Is that what Mama and her sisters fled?

I bequeath myself to the dirt, to grow from the grass I love

We should have liked to retire there, though, to find repose in gentle decline, surrounded by books and gardens and sober refinement in sober New England. We bought some land in the forest up in the mountains. What a dream that was: our long autumnal fading, a quiet denouement in the soft glades. That was to be our reward. Instead we got Murray's Reward, a curse which ruined us and drew me back here to the barren pit, with young Bob still searching for the grail.

I would have liked to spend more time in sunshine and less in rain, wind and clouds of sulphur. I escaped as often as I could, but that just added to the feeling I was *ein wanderleben* – ephemeral, floating, doomed never to belong, to never find a rock to cleave to.

I would have liked to see dear Lizzie one more time before she died. To tell her that she was the special one, not me. That she was the rock, the true holder of the flame, the kindest, most decent, most beautiful of all of us. My only true kin. My other, sensible, half. She had seen them all go on before and knew them better, because she was older: Charlie, Emma, Papa and Mother, Annette and Louise and Abbie and all the others. Now I'm on my way alone and no trace of that lively family will remain.

I would have liked these simple things: a sense of belonging, sunshine and old age, something our family never suffered. But I would change not one thing of my life with Robert – although I might wish him a sager head for money and a more sceptical view of his fellow man – but then he wouldn't have been Robert Carl Henry Sticht.

Wir aber fuhren über den Kanal so ruhig wie ein Ferryboat
über den Fluß

This letter he wrote to his mother from Paris, in 1871, when he was 14. The hand is not as assured as the tone. He is delicately suspended between childhood and reality, as my two youngest are now. It is a prosaic report of his travels – written in the old Bavarian dialect of his parents.

But we travelled over the channel so calmly, it was like a ferryboat
over a river

He must have been an annoying boy, I think. Too serious for childhood and somewhat out of place. Grown up at 12. On this trip with his Father to his homeland they were almost caught in Paris by the Prussians, when the Franco-Prussian War broke out. They were lucky to escape – the Commune would not have been a pleasant place for men with German surnames. They scurried back across the Atlantic to New York. Robert did not get to Germany, his spiritual home, until ten years later.

Our boys are children of this strange island. Will they ever call it home, I wonder? Or will they be out of place everywhere, orphans in so many ways: no parents, no home, no country? What will become of them? Is it a blessing or a curse to be free so early of the weight of expectation?

how soon has time, the subtle thief of youth, stolen on his wing
my three and twentieth year

I was an orphan at 23. I was full of life but Mother's death was a lifetime long and I was in most ways yet a child. I thought like a child, with a child's confidence. I understood like a child. I thought I knew her and everything she thought and felt. I idolised her and loved her but I allowed her very little latitude. None. Now I begin to understand; now that I have put away foolish things like confidence and judgement. Death's constant proximity wears you down like water on rock. Hard or soft, it wears you down. One grain of sand is the same as the next and all the other billions that once were mountains and now are grit.

false chronicle of the stones

I'm too tired to go outside this evening, too weak to lever myself out of this rickety old chair. We've eaten our mutton and potatoes and some greens from Mrs Mitchell's garden. The red soil here is productive and had I prospect of a longer tenure I'd get a few things in the ground, but that thought is just an echo of a lost life.

The lamps will soon be lit. Bob is back from shipping his brothers off to school. It is quiet without their energy and instinctive optimism but while Bob loves them, I am sure he does not miss them at present. He has more than enough to deal with, winding up this tragic comedy, this sad old place and me.

He has brought supplies back in with him. My pancakes from Whale's Head and the newspapers from Burnie. I'm not much interested in the world, though. I am watching from the wings, my character killed off in the second act.

Bob will read to me later, as Harry used to read to Mama, back in Pueblo – it's another sign that I am disappearing. Ethel will sew and listen as Robert reads Scott. *Guy Mannering* again – I read it long ago at Vassar, and thought it hopelessly old-fashioned. It was one of Mother's favourites and I find it comforting these days. I fear Meg Merrilies and company are not to Ethel's taste but she is quiet and comfortable and rounds out our little household rather nicely. Her presence allows Bob and me to avoid the obvious, without the evasion being awkward.

I would like nothing more than to walk down the hill along the Back Track I rode with Luke, to the old bridge over the dark river, feel the darkness quickening and stride back up the long slope with the wonder of this beautiful, strange world coursing through me and the warm knowledge of a comfortable home and my family waiting. Instead I will sit and nod and listen and try to stay awake, and pray to myself that these good people never come to this.

Outside the light holds, pale as Keats' knight at arms. I sit by the tiny window with its four small, grubby panes and despite myself I think of the stained glass and splendid views from Penghana – but that will never do. I will not bemoan my fate.

The small birds have quit the field and the wind has given way to chilly stillness. The lurching of a panicked wallaby through the scrub behind the shack carries indoors. We glance in its direction and then at each other – I have no idea why – it's a form of silent communication I suppose. I'm still here.

the light doth cling reluctant

Almost nine and still the long evening gathers in. From the little windows I feel its softening as much as see it – a gentle dying, unlike my own chaotic dissolution, whose only comfort is sleep, harbinger of what lies beyond our little lives.

such stuff as dreams are made on

I will not be sorry when it comes but I would thunder against death's impatience if I could. I'd fain fade gently as a flower, slowly and gracefully, drooping benignly, watching over gardens and my sons and perhaps their children, teaching them to read and listen, becoming invisible on my own terms, not condemned to this humiliation by a kidney's lack of gumption.

The building of our house, Penghana, was on the grand scale. On a hill looking across the town to Mt Owen, rising stark and steep above it. As first the forest and then the hill were flattened it came to look like an ancient earthwork, the foundation of a Mayan temple in the jungle. Queenstown was still a town in the rainforest then. There was still a struggle to be won.

As the great house took shape, its frail bones set against the majesty of the mountains and the forest, I was bedazzled yet apprehensive. This was Baronial. Feudal. We would see every house and building in the town from our windows, which meant to me that they could all see us. And when I did finally look out from that window the town had become a child's toy, a miniature framed by the copper mountain, impressive at any time but awesome in winter, when snow clad the rocky peak down to the tree line. There was a still a tree line back then, before the forest was burned and the air was filled with sulphur. Back then it was as beautiful a setting for a town as I had ever seen.

In the long evenings I'd stand at the bedroom window and look out over the town, the lights sparkling through my reflection just as the lights of Dodge and Wichita and St Louis shone through me as I crossed America all those times on the Thunderbolt. A girl from the Styx.

In that reflection I could almost see myself as I really am – a woman never quite in focus, through whom time and experience pass, leaving their marks like wind and rain, so that eventually the only trace of that hopeful girl on the Thunderbolt exists here, in my mind. When my mind has ceased to be, all echoes of that young woman – the person I still think I am – will be gone and what memory of Marion Oak Stage survives will be of an old and ailing woman whose husband was once important. I am stranded on the Lethe now, rather than the Styx.

Later, as my body turned on me and I declined, that bed became my world. I watched the town in tired amusement for hours from the window, watched with a growing sense of detachment the pointless business and busy-ness.

The light dies early in Queenstown but it is a long death. A long, melancholy twilight falls on the town. I found it unsettling once things started to go wrong. A hollowness sometimes filled me and I busied myself so as not to fall into sadness. But as I grew ill and became incapable of busying, I had no defence against the dying light. In light I felt connected to the wider world. With its dying came fragility and introspection.

That all is ephemeral cannot be denied in sickness. Decay is our lot. I watched once from the window as another fire took a hundred homes in the town. Lives lost and ruined whilst I watched helpless in safety, a voyeur. Years later a tornado such as I had seen at times back home wreaked havoc in the town, sucked up the valley and tore buildings apart at random. Nature is not happy with what we have done here. Nor with what we thought we had done - tamed her to our petty, human ends. She is not happy.

a mirror scratched reflects no image
and this is the silence of wisdom

The slow morning light revealed the town beneath my window, filled with fog and fumes and wood smoke. In winter it hung over the town all day, so that at times from Penghana it seemed Mt Owen rose from the sea.

The light on Mt Owen, rearing up behind the town, changes constantly. When you can see it, that is. On a winter's day, after a hard frost, if the wind clears the smoke and fumes, the little town will be bathed in golden sunlight. Shadows surge across the face of the mountain as the sun slides along the ridge behind the house. The effect is theatrical.

Later I was glad to see those brutal slopes cloaked in cloud. I have seen photographs of the shattered fields of France from the War – the slopes of Mt Owen were similarly ruined, littered with blackened stumps, the ravaged rock denuded of its soil. Some find the effect a wonder – the sun reflecting off the coppery rocks puts on quite a show – but they have not seen those same slopes clad in dense forest. Magnificent trees, some hundreds of years old, tree ferns, myrtle, Blackwood and King Billy – all gone to feed the monster and stope the mines.

3rd April 1897

THE MOUNT LYELL CO. have had a grand celebration at their mine, entertaining a large party of guests from this and the neighbouring colonies, who were shown the new reduction works, the railway from the King River, and other points of interest to visitors.

The Governor started to attend the festival, but was driven back by stress of weather, and was eventually represented by his Private Secretary, Mr. Rawlinson.

The ceremony of driving the last spike in completion of the Mount Lyell Co.'s railway from Teepookana to the smelting works here took place on Monday afternoon, when Mrs. Sticht, wife of the popular local manager and metallurgist, performed the required act.

The spike, which was of the ordinary size and shape, was specially made of converter copper for the occasion, and this point was a nice one in common with the function. As a pleasing memento of the occasion a presentation 'spike' was handed to Mrs. Sticht, encased in a neat box lined with plush. The 'spike,' which was of the ordinary 'business' shape and size, was made to illustrate the component parts of the metal now being extracted from the mine and the condition in which it is being sent away for final treatment, the head being gold, the shaft copper, and the point silver. The Mount Lyell Co. manage these small matters as nicely as their larger concerns.

A fair sprinkling of those who had been connected with the construction of the line and other works witnessed the ceremony, and success to the line in all its bearings was drunk in bumpers of champagne.

L. S. BARNDOLLAR.
THERMOMETER FOR OVENS.

No. 571,211.　　　　　　　　Patented Nov. 10, 1896.

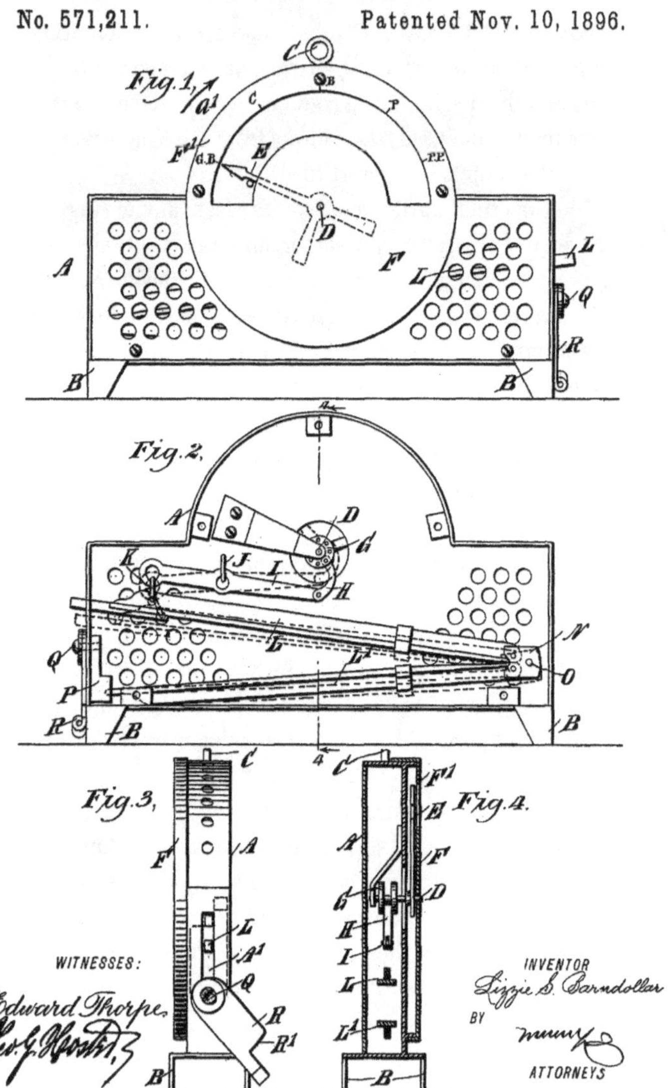

10

The old stove is held together by rust and dirt and the fat of a million mutton stews. It is rather primitive – the fire is made on top and is inefficient as a result. The oven would be slow even in its best condition but its decrepitude makes baking a trial. Ethel manages to get bread and cakes from it somehow. She says she would master it given enough time and then looks sheepish, afraid that she has hurt me. There is no time, of course, and we both know it. She never met Lizzie but they have that practicality and dry fatalism in common.

Lizzie's troubles started with ovens. Lizzie's invention ruined her and George. She had always had a curious mind and a need to express it physically. So she made things: clothes, books, gardens, hats, chicken runs – some made sense only to her but we loved her anyway.

Then when things went bad for George's business after the silver collapse in '93, he thought that Lizzie's idea for an oven thermometer might get them free of their increasingly fragile situation. They had technical drawings made, took out patents and looked for a manufacturer to produce it. Finding none they decided that they should do it themselves. They borrowed money. Less clever ideas have flourished but this was always a desperate gamble, an almost fatal error. Worst of all, they borrowed from Uncle John Hazelton. They failed to find a market for the thermometer. The ramifications were widespread and unpleasant. New Hampshire folk take debt more seriously than death and as the recession worsened, George and Lizzie found themselves with a crippling debt and on the verge of bankruptcy.

Robert knew them pretty well – all those awkward visits to the house as he courted me all those years ago, when we were full of the future. An odd house, it must have seemed to him: three slightly mad women and two very patient men. It was a happy house though. The outhouse caught fire once and but for quick-thinking neighbours would have burnt the house down with it. I don't think Robert had much experience of households where the outhouse could burn down and everyone think it funny.

With the recession showing no sign of abating, George's business gone and the interest on the loan grinding them into poverty, Robert offered George a fresh start out here, as his private secretary. George was capable enough and had been in business all his life. He knew his books and accounts and Robert had such a poor head for money that even a bankrupt was an improvement. Lizzie could turn her hand to anything and often did. Robert knew it would make me happy to have them here and made the offer too good to refuse. So they came, in 1898, just before Robert's adventure on *The Grafton*.

It was a fresh start for them and a deliverance for me. Bobby was by then a three year old and I had little aptitude for mothering, much as I adored him. I was also becoming acutely aware of our isolation. In the midst of all the turmoil and excitement, I was lonely. That is an exquisite form of loneliness.

I was happy. I had a friend and ally and with her I had a context. From my little bedroom verandah I'd see Lizzie coming up those long stairs from the town, her face set as always under her flat hat, her long, stiff skirt straining against her determined stride. I remember her standing in the sun on the lawn below, head thrown back and laughing at 'the lady of the house'. It was not just her company that I needed, it was her history. She alone knew how far I'd come, how proud Mama and Father would have been. I found it easy enough to be 'the Lady of the House'. I had always lived with 'help'. There were some made uncomfortable by the ambiguity and by our foreign-ness. People often thought me English because I spoke well!

I loved to go up in into the roof of Penghana with Lizzie. It stirred memories of me and Charlie on the roof of the prairie house, adventures Lizzie never shared: she was mother's right hand and too busy for such childishness, but she understood.

The attic was a child's world. Access was by stairs fore and aft of the house that let the staff traverse the rooms without disturbing guests, though what they made of the giant possums overhead I never knew.

We would stage plays and games for the children up there in that secret world, its little windows peeking at the sky like portholes on a ship. Lizzie and I and Nanny Westmoreland, our beloved Miss Wissie, would be more childish than the children. Well, Miss Wissie and I would – I rather think Lizzie took a dim view at times. Someone had to be the grown-up I suppose. It was always Lizzie's lot.

There have been many times since, when the weight of our station there threatened to suffocate me, that I'd sneak up into the roof and become a child again, sitting by myself staring out the window, looking for Illinois, listening for Charlie and the prairie wind. Wanting to go home but no longer knowing where that was.

We stayed some summers at Macquarie Heads, a dramatic spot on the south shore of Hell's Gates. From the house we could see the Heads and when Robert was there he liked nothing better than to take the boys down to Hell's Gates in the evening to recount the story of the night he survived the sinking of the *Grafton*.

It was the winter of '98; June 12, just a few weeks after Lizzie and George arrived. Robert was returning from Melbourne on the *Grafton*, its holds filled with new equipment for the Abt railway and machinery for his smelter, 150 tons of it in all. There were eleven passengers below and 300 sheep on deck.

There wasn't much of the *Grafton* – 500 tons and 150 feet or so – just small enough to cross the Macquarie Harbour bar and just big enough to survive the passage across Bass Strait and down that wild coast. She had seen 50 years of service on both sides of the Tasman, so knew all about serious weather. Melbourne to Strahan is about as serious as weather gets.

the coming wind did roar more loud

She arrived at Macquarie Heads late in the afternoon, the weather looming up behind her in the west. With conditions worsening and the swell already high, Captain Morrisby attempted the bar at night, on an ebb tide. This has always struck me as somewhat foolhardy. The Captain of the *Mahinapua* surely thought so. Arriving at the Heads at about the same time, he retreated out to sea to await the tide's turn.

The *Grafton* entered the roads at about 10.30pm. Halfway in she struck a sandbar and Morrisby was forced to fall back out to sea. At first no damage other than to the screws was noticed but soon the engine room began to fill with water, through a crack beneath the boilers. The fires were thus in peril. Steerage would be lost without power and the *Grafton* would be a slave to the wild elements. It must have been a frightening scene: the howling wind, the thundering surf on the sandbanks as they drew closer and the bleating of 300 terrified sheep on deck.

There was near panic at first amongst the other passengers. All eleven had been woken by the impact. On being reassured by the crew that all was well, they had returned to their berths, albeit briefly. Except Robert, of course, who had no intention of missing any detail of the unfolding drama. Around him Captain Morrisby and his crew held calm and firm. With the passing of the years, of course, the situation became more perilous, the seas steeper and the crew's behaviour more stoic.

The *Mahinapua* had been circling out to sea through all of this and had seen the *Grafton*'s distress rockets. She came inshore as close as was prudent and launched boats and buoys to assist.

and the billows frothed like yeast

At about one o'clock in the morning, in heavy seas, Robert and the other passengers got clear of the doomed ship in three lifeboats. It must have been a terrifying ride; the wind and waves on that coast are seldom anything but awesome and the cacophony of wind and thundering surf is unnerving, even in mild weather. Robert and his fellows were soaked to the skin – lashed by wind and spray, frozen to the bone and fearful of their lives.

The transshipment was completed without loss or injury, the crews of both steamers displaying great seamanship. Safely on board the *Mahinapua*, for the first time in his life Robert took a tot of rum, with his fellow survivors and their rescuers. He held that it would have been churlish to refuse and besides he was in danger of freezing to death.

On the *Grafton* the fires were out and the anchors dragging, as the swelling westerly drove the old ship towards the sandbanks and disaster. the *Mahinapua* got a hawser to her but it parted as they tried to haul her out to sea and the end was then inevitable.

it reached the ship it split the bay

The dear old ship foundered soon afterwards, lost in a couple of fathoms near the north side of the bar. You could see the hulk, one of many solemn wrecks, for years afterwards as you steamed into the harbour – a reminder of the danger you were always in when you entered that turbulent gap. All Robert's equipment and 300 sheep were lost. The Captain and his crew stayed on board until forced to abandon her when all was lost. They rowed the last boat through mountainous seas across to the *Mahinapua*, whose own position grew more perilous the longer she stood by.

It is easy to see how sharing an experience so fraught would forge a strong bond between survivors. It was the sort of experience Robert always craved, for balance. A scientist but an outdoor man as well. Robert always spoke admiringly of Captain Morrisby's sang-froid that night. Despite the danger and the knowledge that he was responsible for the disaster, he never wavered from his duty, and never doubted his judgement – though as I say, he might have been wise to do so. Four months later he brought the *Kawatiri* to grief on the same spot.

The bleak and windswept winter morning revealed a scene of desolation at the Heads and along the endless sweep of Henty Beach. The masts of the *Grafton* stood stark as dead trees above the pounding surf, a hundred yards from the flotsam-littered shore. Dead sheep were strewn all along the coast, none lashed to drifting masts but many half-hidden in banks of brown foam and kelp. A few had made it to the shore alive but were beyond saving. There was much mutton to be had cheap that week in Strahan.

I slept through it all, of course. The telegraph that brought news of Robert's peril brought news of his salvation also. My reactions were mixed. There was part of me that envied him the adventure, but I had come close to being a widow without knowing anything about it. I had been as imperilled as Robert in a way, but had no catharsis, no tot of rum, made no lifelong friend. For the first time, I considered my potential situation: a widow with a small child and few means, alone and far from home in a hard and unforgiving place with no kin and no credible retreat.

I was even more grateful to have Lizzie with me.

alone on a wide, wide sea

———

In the morning room at Penghana, when the sky is clear, the sun streams in across the valley, warm and golden. In the foreground mist floats up like steam from my coffee and beyond the ridge, a mile or two away, the smelter stacks spew fumes into the morning sky.

Broad shafts of smoky sunlight fan out across the ridge as the sun climbs higher. I would sit in that lovely morning room, with my back to the sun and Robert looking over my shoulder at the smoke from the smelter up the valley, always eager to get to work. After he went off I would sit a while with my pot of coffee and let the warm sun bathe the back of my neck until I became drowsy.

My beautiful house. Fine rooms and the view from all of them is grand. How strange to think of others living in it. I would have burned it to the ground had I the nerve. Let others build their own dreams, not nest in mine like cuckoos.

To Anna Hazelton,
Chester, New Hampshire.
Queenstown, 30th July 1899

My Anna

It seems such a long time since I have had a good long talk with you. The last letter I sent was cut off before its 'youth and beauty' and yours back to me was woefully short. You have been constantly in my thoughts of late and I do so want to see you. I have been having quite a change in my nice eventful life since I last wrote you. I commenced coughing and had all the appearance of having caught the whooping cough – which Marion, George & the boy have been entertaining all winter. I was determined not to have it and after three or four days ineffectual efforts to rid myself of it I determined to go to Strahan for a few days. George said he would take me down on Sat and stay until Mon. The day before I was to go Marion decided to take the boy and go with me for the day. She also invited Mrs Jasm and Walter – so we went... quite a strong party as usual in one private car. I did enjoy the change and came back the following Thurs quite well and in my right mind. Marion by this time was quite used to the boy at night and I decided to go to Mr & Mrs Clarke for a long talked of visit before taking charge of him again. I wasted a few days and then Marion went with me – to see me safely over the hauling line. I staid from Sat until the following Friday. Had a nice visit. Went to Mrs Emmet for one night – she also lives in Gormanston –

Mrs Clarke came home with me and also her husband's mother who is with us for a week or so. She is a most charming old lady – both intelligent and intellectual. She had a young ladies school in Melbourne for many years and is very dressy...

Yours

Lizzie

MOUNT LYELL RAILWAY EXTENSION

An informal opening of the Mount Lyell railway extension from Teepookana to Regatta Point took place on Wednesday. Shortly after 11 a.m. a launch left the Strahan wharf for the Point with many guests on board, while a much larger number elected to walk quietly round to the scene of the then approaching festivities...

The *S.S. Kawitiri* had early in the morning moored at the company's wharf at Regatta Point, and was there gaily dressed as only men of extended nautical experience can dress a ship. As the Strahan visitors made their way to the company's railway station powerful signal rockets were discharged from the Kawatiri, and this pleasing expression of goodwill on the part of the Union S.S. Co. towards the Mount Lyell M. and R. Co. was continued until the first train from Queenstown, with a large number of guests on board, arrived.

The train in question presented a most holiday like appearance. On the front of the engine was a nicely finished copper shield, bearing the words 'Labor Omnia Vincit.' Underneath the shield was a shovel, upon which, in neat letters, was printed the words 'We find a way, or make it,' and on either side of the shovel was a pick, the whole forming a most attractive and appropriate front to the first passenger engine run on the line from Teepookana to Regatta Point. The mottos employed were truly emblematical of that honest labor which, aided by capital, has brought about the methodical development of one of the world's best mines. In addition to the decorations mentioned, which by right take pride of place, the first train from Queenstown was gaily decorated through out with bunting, ferns, and wild flowers.

Shortly after the arrival of the train from Queenstown

the opening of the line was performed by the driving of
the last spike or 'dog,' which was far too costly to be used
by the thousand on any line of rail way, being composed
chiefly of copper from the great mine. The ceremony
was gracefully performed by Mrs R. C. Sticht, who was
most enthusiastically received.

When the spike was driven Mr Driffield, on behalf of
the officers of the Railway Department of the company,
presented Mrs Sticht with a beautifully made hammer as
a remembrance of the occasion, and in making the
presentation referred briefly but feelingly to the history
of the Mount Lyell Company. He pointed out that while
the hammer Mrs Sticht used in connection with the
opening of the line at Queenstown contained material
from the first block of copper turned out of the converters,
the one then presented was partly made up of the last
block turned out, which was, according to the register,
block No. 159,594. Mr Batchelor then presented Mrs Sticht
with a gold brooch assigned to represent mining and
labor tools, and in doing so made a brief speech.
Mrs Sticht replied, but unfortunately owing to the strong
northerly wind prevailing, the utterances of that lady and
Messrs Driffield and Batchelor were almost inaudible.

The line being duly opened an adjournment was made
to the room which will in future be used as the office of
the railway department of the company. There Mrs. Sticht
stamped the first ticket, and the office was declared open.
This office was tastefully arranged as a refreshment
room, as was also the room adjoining, and the business
of the day having been disposed of the guests were invited
to partake of the many good things provided for their
entertainment. The tables were splendidly decorated
and carried all that could be desired by lovers of a cold
collation. The spread was in every way recherché...

...Later the train took a large number of the guests to
Lette's Point, where fires were speedily lighted and tea,
with cake, were handed round to the ladies by the

gentlemen present, assisted by ladies identified with the company, On returning from Lette's Bay, after spending a pleasant time on the *Kawatiri*, the Strahan contingent of the guests gave their Queenstown friends three hearty cheers as the train moved off for the Copper City, and then returned to their homes by the *Kawatiri*, fully satisfied with the day's outing. From the steamer at night were discharged many fireworks, while red and green light illuminations made her most attractive to the townspeople. Captain Anthony and his genial officers added many names to their list of friends and acquaintances during the day.

Close

11

Then Alice Kate Wellman came back into my life. In 1898, while circling the world, she had come to Queenstown to stay with us and there she met our Mr Beardsley, who was by then Robert's Chief Metallurgist. Alice Kate was 37, George Fisher Beardsley was 45. He was what they call here a 'larrikin', a man of great spirit and energy, who had lived rough, took a drink and fitted in. Alice was – well, Alice was Alice: intelligent, strong-willed and fearless. A less likely match I have never known. The only thing they had in common was California. They were polar opposites and of course they hit it off right from the start. It may have been significant that George was still recovering from a serious injury, having several months before had an ankle crushed while stopping a runaway truck at the smelters. He was something of a hero and in need of assistance – a powerful combination of attractions for any woman. Alice stayed with us through into the New Year and then headed off on her travels. We had a fine time and I missed her sorely when she left but I did not expect what happened next.

In 1900 George took six months leave and went home to California. When he returned he announced that Alice was coming to Tasmania and that they would marry in Melbourne in the new century. A Federation marriage! I was beside myself with joy.

We had our own adventure in the meantime.

Penghana
Sunday, 10th February 1901

Dearest Alice Kate

The joyous anticipation that has filled my heart since learning that George 'hath won the day' and persuaded you to join us here in Purgatory, was tempered last week by the brief possibility that there would be no Queenstown left to welcome you!

On Thursday last our annual bushfire came down again like a wolf on the fold, from the hills beyond the smelter. At first it seemed no worse than the several outbreaks we had dealt with this summer (I confess, after five years I still find it hard to write of summer in February), but in the early afternoon the breeze swung to the North-West and blew like a hurricane. It fanned the fire into an inferno and swept a wall of flame along the tramway towards the town on the east side of the river and down past the lime quarry on the other. Towards us.

A score of houses were lost in a moment at the Piggery and a dozen more south of the quarry. The blaze engulfed the hills around the town. A choking fog of smoke and ash descended on the valley and chaos ruled. Nothing could be seen more than a chain off and the fury was deafening. Most of the men were at work, of course, including Robert and our Georges, and the streets filled with terrified women and children seeking shelter, clutching whatever belongings they could carry. The wind ripped roofs from houses at random, others exploded as though hit by shellfire. At Lynchford a house was flipped over and a woman who had taken to her bed found herself under it – on the ceiling!

125

Up at Penghana we had hardly time to worry. We could see nothing but smoke and the occasional pillar of fire erupting Biblically from the dense cloud that filled the valley below us, as another house was lost. Then the fire was suddenly all around – howling down Raggetty Creek, taking several houses in the little valley and threatening Penghana from the rear.

Lizzie and I rallied the troops – it was unlikely anyone would be sent to help in time. I had already sent the gardener home – the dear man was torn between abandoning us and abandoning his wife. Cook and the girls filled buckets and primed pumps. We patrolled our perimeter as ash and cinders rained down on our little mesa. As you well know, there is little fuel on our hilltop but the house was beset by a storm of embers. I could hardly see at all through my streaming eyes. We wore bandanas over our faces, like outlaws, and must have looked a strange sight, dashing hither and yon with buckets, our white dresses drenched and our hair flying in the wind. I confess that if I had not been required to take charge I might well have panicked, though it was Lizzie, of course who did the lion's share of the work and bossed us all around.

Oh Alice, I do so look forward to you two becoming friends. As you already know, she is not at all like me but has many good qualities and is as true as Troilus.

Just as I was beginning to wonder whether we should abandon the house and save ourselves – if indeed we could – the wind swung suddenly to the north and drove the flames away from us, south along the river, to South Queenstown and down to Lynchford, where still more homes were lost. We took stock of our situation and having caught our breath staggered down into the town, where the fire still *raged on the hills close by and houses were still being consumed by the blaze. It had been dark as night since the middle of the afternoon and now the sky was lit by walls of flame playing on the clouds of smoke, like Plato's cave. We looked for hope in the shadows. Strangest of all, the hills that had been bare for years burned like a scene from Dante. Sulphur from the smelter has saturated the peaty soil and the very earth does burn and burned for days afterwards. There is something unnatural in that which disturbs me. We have wrought something awful here, I fear.*

Alice, do you remember us standing together in the streets of Pompeii, wondering what it must have been like for those poor souls, huddled now forever in the corners of their homes, their world reduced to a cenotaph by a cloud of fire and ash, the very earth alight? It was impossible to imagine, of course, but I think I have some sense of it now. There is a strange calm in such a crisis, when nature dwarfs us so spectacularly. There is an acceptance of one's insignificance; time seems to flow very slowly, divorced from normal human concerns and control. I can remember all sorts of odd and unrelated things – a three-legged dog whose tail had been burnt, a baby whose skin had turned to brown paper, a man in a black hat and no shirt who gave me ice-cream – and silly thoughts crowded my head at random, bereft of any context, Hamlet interrupted by a minstrel show. I did think of Pompeii, though, and you, and wondered at the worst if I might not see you again. Do you know that it was 12 years ago, almost to the day, that we stood together in those ancient streets? It seems a lifetime. We have been busy, have we not?

In the end, as this letter attests, we survived. Your George was perfectly heroic and saved the smelter and the coal stacks. Robert was determined and impractical as ever in a crisis and Mr Barndollar thought it all a fine adventure. The town, as you know, has been forged in adversity. Isolation and disaster seem to bring out the very best in its people. All the petty differences and suspicions disappear, if only for a while. Everyone rallied round and no doubt it will soon seem as though the inferno was little more than a hiccough.

Meanwhile George is 'prettying' the house and we are all agog in anticipation of having you living amongst us. I have many plans and am determined that together we will bring civilization to this benighted place.

I will write again before you set out across the globe to join us. Until then,

I remain your dearest friend

Marion

We all went over to Melbourne on the *Rotomohana* for Alice and George's wedding: Lizzie and George, Robert and me, Missie W and little Bob. It was a splendid time. I had drawn my two best friends across the world to my side. I had Robert and a son, we were becoming wealthy and all I had to put up with was the rain.

Alice and George had the house next to the Mine Administration Building. As Chief Metallurgist now, George was practically living in his office. They were a happy pair, surprised to find themselves in love so late in life. Alice was always busy and George was always amused. I can see him now, lounging in his Mexican hammock while Alice tried to defy nature by making a garden on that bleak ground.

In the meantime I continued to open things and give 'neat' speeches.

THE MERCURY

1st August 1901

QUEENSTOWN, WEDNESDAY
Mrs Robert Sticht formally opened the Queenstown
Public Library and Reading Room this afternoon. The
library and rooms are in the old hospital buildings in
Cutten Street, which the Government granted to the
Town Board for the above purpose.

Apart from giving neat speeches to the same crowd at regular intervals,
I was determined to help get Lizzie and George on their feet again financially. They were resistant to charity, of course, but I made some inroads
of my own and lobbied on their behalf with my Hazelton cousins, whose
father, Uncle John, held the paper. Cousin Anna had become particularly
tiresome since she left the Presbyterian fold and embraced her Christian
Science. I tried to turn her zeal to better purposes.

Penghana

September 1902

Dear Anna

I have sent for a draft to send Gil and when it comes it will be forwarded to him. Out of the money he is to pay Uncle John the balance due him on the note which Geo. & I have been paying. As soon as paid please send the note to George.

Gil will only accept 6% interest for his note. He considers this ample when interest on interest is paid in this manner.

Poor George and Lizzie are struggling nobly to reduce their crushing indebtedness. Have they not had much to endure?

Why not use your Christian Science to help them financially as well as striving to give them happiness along other lines?

Believe me, a liberal adjustment to the money George still owes will do more for Lizzie's happiness than years of treatment. Entreat Uncle John to see it in this light – a word to the wise, a fair thing is a fair thing!

In all love and hoping you may come to the true light

Yours

Marion

The letter had some effect and before long the Barndollars could see the light at the end of the tunnel. Of course I knew that when they were debt-free they would start to look homewards but I was already looking in that direction. It was only a matter of when.

The year after Alice came to Queenstown she fell pregnant. She was almost 40 and a tiny thing but I had such faith in her that it never occured to me that she might be mortal.

When she was eight months gone we went off to Melbourne to celebrate Robert's birthday – not that he cared for such fuss. He knew it would please me, though, so he tore himself away from his smelter and his kingdom. Bowes gave us tickets to Melba's homecoming concert, as a birthday present. We had met at the opera so it seemed fitting.

And so when Alice needed me most I was not there. Alice Ruth Wellman Beardsley was born on 29th September and died three days later.

FIRST MELBA CONCERT – By QUEEN BEE
The audience on the first night of Madame Melba's appearance in her native country was an interesting one. Many people had travelled long distances to hear her, and some had been staying in Melbourne quite a fortnight, the postponement of dates keeping them in town.

The concert was timed to begin at a quarter-past 8 and to conclude at about quarter-past 10, an arrangement that enabled those of us who had been to afternoon functions to dress, have dinner, reach the town hall and take their seats without inconvenience. When Madame Melba, who is exceedingly graceful in movement came on to the platform it was seen how incorrect most descriptions of her had been. She has a charming presence, and she wore only what a woman with a perfect figure could wear, a Princess dress that was a picture in colour. It was of ivy gauze de soie, encrusted with a wonderful and beautiful gold paillette. Near the foot it was slashed open to show the under-dress of rare mellow lace, the slashings being outlined by embroidered garlands of roses in faint pink lining. Melba is as famous for her jewels as she is for her voice. But it was her desire on this occasion that we should see her as much as possible like her old self. Consequently her only ornaments were a rope of pearls and a diamond comb thrust below the coil of softly but very simply dressed hair.

Many in the audience were present at the farewell concert she gave in the same hall sixteen years ago, and some no doubt remembered the dress she wore then as in yellow toning. Even then she was a graceful singer. Now she is reposeful and superb and has a pretty manner of throwing back her head, the voice flowing from her throat like the runs and trills of a nightingale.

The hall presented a wonderful sight, every seat in the big building being occupied. At the same time it was an unusual audience, considering that the booking-fee was the highest ever paid for a concert in Melbourne. The country element was very prominent, therefore blouses and day-time skirts were not uncommon, even hats in some instances being worn...

Among those noticed were Sir Rupert Clarke, Judge Johnston, Lady Fysh, Mr. F. H. Forrest, Mr. and Mrs. Henry O'Hara, Mr. and Mrs. L. C. Mackinnon, the Misses Mackinnon, Mr. L. Mackinnon, Mr. and Mrs. Alec Urquhart, Dr. and Mrs. Dunbar Hooper, Mrs. John Simson, Mrs. Robert Simson, Mr. and Mrs. Cecil N. Hake, Miss Mitchell, Mr. and Mrs. L. L. Lewis, Mr. Molesworth Greene and Miss Greene, Mr. and Mrs. James Hayne, Mr. and Mrs. Everard Browne, Mr. and Mrs. Bowes Kelly,...Mr. and Mrs. Sticht. (Tasmania),...

I sashayed around Melbourne and socialised with strangers while my best and oldest friend lay in torment. Our love had flowered in her vigil at my bedside all those years ago at Vassar. Now my self-indulgence had robbed us both.

I rushed back, of course, as soon as I had word, but little Ruth was already in the cold ground of the Zeehan cemetery and part of Alice was with her there. I never forgave myself and I fear a rift, however slight, opened between us. There was no resentment – Alice is too fine and practical a person for such self-indulgence – but it was something we should have shared. The gods surely willed that we should share this tragedy and now we never could. Our paths diverged.

I hear magpies singing in the trees as I drift through the morning, sleep and pain breaking over me in waves. In my state of half-consciousness the birds' complex melodies seem meaningful. When the burning pain subsides a little and I can focus on something other than my bowels, I try to read a little, or play some Bach or Beethoven in my head. Mostly I fall back on Shakespeare; I know some so well I do not have to read too closely. There is a familiarity that is a privilege to feel. He is a bridge across the ages and the world, a bridge to everything we believe in.

In Pueblo I had been a member of *The Wednesday Morning Club*, a women's group dedicated to cultural progress through education and The Bard. We would read and sometimes perform the plays and had great fun dressing up as favourite characters and listening to visiting academics, actors and producers talk about the man and his work. That the standard of our productions was inevitably clumsy and amateurish mattered little, it felt important and was a great success – I believe it still flourishes. Alice and I decided to start a club in Queenstown. The attic of Penghana was our little theatre and we were soon well established, though a somewhat motley crew.

It seems strange to say now, sitting here in the winter sunlit ghost town, but for the next few years we were a force – Alice and me leading the way but with a wonderful band of supporters, the women of that fierce place. Lizzie and Miss Westmoreland and the company wives were all enthusiastic, as were men like Archie and Carus Driffield. We find a way or make it. We established plans for a Botanical Gardens at Princess Falls, down near Lynchford – a beautiful place with two falls and swimming holes. The Government granted us the land and we began planting. Council appointed a caretaker and the town itself saw something important in the idea. It was, I think, the notion of a future beyond the vagaries of the price of copper.

Alice and I were on the Hospital Board and raised funds. We petitioned the Government to open more schools in the region. We established a branch of the Ministering Children's Fund and we affiliated our Shakespeare Society with the National Council of Women.

no day without a deed to crown it

And I continued to open fetes and fairs and give neat speeches.

Mrs Sticht, in a graceful and appropriate little speech, then declared the bazaar duly opened, and said it gave her great pleasure to accede to the wish of the people of the district by performing the opening ceremony.

7th March 1904

ELECTRIC LIGHT

As applications for 265 lights have been made to the Town Board they are of the opinion that this is more than sufficient to warrant them in at once proceeding with the installation of the electric light according to the scheme already made known, and Mr Robert Sticht, general manager of the Mount Lyell M. and R. Company (from whom the light, so to speak, is to be purchased in wholesale quantities) will be at once informed of the Board's intention, and the Government given all necessary information.

Robert was at the height of his powers. I teased that he had 'let there be light' but it is true that his position was something like a benevolent dictator. He set a standard not just for work but for behaviour – he was living his philosophy. The company and the town all looked to him as a figurehead for Lyell, which was always a separate entity from Tasmania, and he supplied it with modesty and grace.

Robert had brought Lizzie and Alice to me for a while, now he set about bringing the world to Penghana. He had been an apprentice collector since I first knew him, back in Pueblo. Now he had the income to pursue his collecting at a serious level. As with everything Robert did, it became an obsession.

Robert had come to Pueblo to work at the Colorado Smelting Company, the creation of Mr Eilers, who brought him down from the mountains, where he had been serving his apprenticeships in places like Leadville. Anton Eilers was to Pueblo what Robert later became to Queenstown – the creator of its wealth and prosperity. He forged a legacy, not just in the town but in the industry. He set standards of production, responsibility and behaviour and above all he created a generation of disciples, 'Eilers Boys'.

He was 20 years older than Robert, had been born in Germany and, like Robert, educated at Clausthal. As soon as he graduated he came out to NY, just before the War. He was in some ways another 48er, like Robert's parents, with the same self-belief and belief in America as the land of opportunity. He went out west after the war, where he worked with Robert Rossiter on a survey of mining districts. The work they did was the stuff of legend later – often working in areas where the Apaches were still on the warpath. In 1871 they were among the first to explore Yellowstone. They ran into an Indian hunting party up there, led by Sitting Bull, who five years later became the stuff of a much bigger legend.

By 1879 Mr Eilers was up at Leadville, at the start of the boom up there. He built and ran the Arkansas Valley smelter and made his fortune.

―――――

Leadville made him ill, however – a reaction most shared and many did not survive – and he spent some years in Europe convalescing. When he returned he got involved with the Madonna, up at Monarch and, in partnership with its owners, set up the Colorado Smelting Company at Pueblo.

The Pueblo operation was the culmination of his life. He was able to pick the site, build it from the ground up and choose the men to run it. His team of young metallurgists and engineers was known as 'Eiler's Boys' and Robert was one of the first.

The works were famous for their order and a sort of modern beauty. It was a clean and light place, beside a reservoir that looked like a forested lake. It was a civilized place in a world where dark satanic mills were the norm. It attracted the best. Men who served their apprenticeships there became leaders of their industry.

Mr Eilers was everything Robert aspired to. He was an Enlightenment man: a scientist, a humanist, a lover of the arts but also of nature. He was Goethe's *Montan* in the flesh. He and Robert often conversed in German and to Robert he was a mentor, as he was to a generation of young metallurgists out there. He had met Sitting Bull!

And he was a Collector. His library was a legendary place, a sanctuary for Eiler's Boys and others who had the wit to recognise its quality. Mr Eiler collected books on English, German and French literature, Lincoln, Whistler, and of course, mining and metallurgy. He also had a fascinating collection of Daguerreotypes I was privileged to see. His library was a sanctum and a benchmark Robert never let go. The idea of collecting, the contact with history and with immortality, and the construction of your own self-image reflected in that Collection – that seed was sown in Robert at The Colorado Smelting Company, on the heights above the Arkansas, in Pueblo, Colorado.

THE MERCURY

2nd September 1903

NATIONAL COUNCIL OF WOMEN

An executive meeting was held, by permission of the
Mayor, at the Town Hall on Aug 31.

...The Queenstown Shakespearian Society has requested
to be affiliated with the National Council, and will be
represented on the Council by Mrs Beardsley and
Mrs Sticht (Queenstown)...

ZEEHAN & DUNDAS HERALD

5th November 1904

ART AND INDUSTRIAL EXHIBITION

There have been a fair number of visitors to the Academy
of Music to inspect the literary, drawing and painting,
and needlework exhibits, some of which are of a very
high standard. The different articles are all well arranged,
the product of the needle and cotton occupying two long
tables down the centre of the room, and on the left are
the copy books, maps, etc., while the oils and pencils are
well displayed on the wall on the right.

There are several loan exhibitions, the largest and most
interesting being the collection of paintings lent by
Mr Robert Sticht, which are on view in the two anti-rooms
at the entrance to the hall. These include works from the
brushes of such masters as Henri Tebbitt (New South
Wales), R. E. Taylor (Melbourne), John Constable, Geo.
Barrett Wilcock, John C. Horsley, Barend Cornelis,
Willem van Mieris, Frederick de Moucheron, Bierci Boni,
Sir Joshua Reynolds, Joshua Cristall, and Thomas Pyne.

Then suddenly Alice and George were gone. George had an offer from a mine back on the west coast of America, and that was that. He had been out here 20 years and he had been as shattered by the loss of their child as Alice had. Queenstown held too much pain. Why would he refuse?

I was not surprised but it shook me terribly nonetheless. Alice had never quite recovered and could not face the crowd who flocked to their farewell concert, an affair so tinged with sadness that I still shed a quiet tear when thinking of it.

18th November 1903

QUEENSTOWN NOTES

FAREWELL CONCERT

The committee who were responsible for the complimentary farewell concert and presentation to Mr and Mrs G. F. Beardsley, held in the Metropole Theatre on Monday, must have entered into their self-imposed task with whole-hearted earnestness, judging by the admirable arrangements which had been made and the smooth and easy manner in which everything passed off.

The stage was set off with bush shrubbery and flags, the stars and stripes being particularly noticeable on the left proscenium, draped over an easel, and beneath which was hidden away the address to be revealed to the view later on at the proper time. Round the walls and along the ceiling flags were hung, while other spots, bare on most occasions, were made decorative by soft drapings, daintily arranged. Carpeted steps, built temporarily, led up to the stage from the seats occupied by Mr and Mrs Robt. Sticht and party, gathered round whom was a most representative audience.

Everyone of the large number who entered the building were allowed to retain their ticket to serve as something to remind them in time to come of that night's event. A very choice and varied programme of high-class music was submitted, comprising fifteen items by the best local talent, the Queenstown Orchestral Union, and the Queenstown and Reduction Works Band.

The first part of this having been gone through, Mr Sticht was invited upon the stage to perform what was termed the most important part of the programme. He said the honor was an unsolicited one. He had not had the slightest inference of what had happened or what was doing to happen. He knew nothing of what was being arranged till he came back from his recent visit to Melbourne, It was a voluntary token of the goodwill cherished by the entire community for Mr Beardsley. (Applause.) It must have been gratifying indeed to Mr Beardsley to see such a large family gathering – a family gathering they were, for they were harmonious and as one in their admiration for Mr Beardsley's character. He knew Mr Beardsley more intimately than anyone else – Mrs Beardsley was not present – (Laughter.) – and he was sure he could say their guest was pleased with the manner they had met him there, on very near his last day in Queenstown.

Mr Sticht then stepped a little forward, and drew the American flag from over the heavily framed and exquisitely hand-painted address, which he presented to Mr Beardsley. 'This – this' – (and Mr Sticht faltered as he found the word 'address' had slipped from his memory) – this document – (Loud laughter) – leaves little for me to say' He then read the address, which was as follows:

To G. F. Beardsley, Esq. 'On the occasion of your voluntary severance of your long, honorable, and highly successful connection with the Mount Lyell Mining and Railway Company, Limited, we, your fellow employees, desire to assure you of our keen appreciation of the valuable and wholehearted services which you have so energetically and faithfully rendered to the company as metallurgist in charge of the Reduction Works; and we also wish to express our deep regret that you are retiring from a service in which you have displayed such signal ability for nearly a decade. Your characteristic courtesy and goodfellowship, as well as your generous consideration for those associated with you, will ever be kindly remembered by all of us. Controlling large bodies of men, you had necessarily to be a disciplinarian, but though resolute in deed you have always been gentle in manner and of a forgiving disposition; and in all your dealings you have evidently been actuated by honest and rightful motives,

and have thereby earned our sincere esteem and loyalty.
That you have fully merited the success which you have so
admirably striven to achieve is our firm conviction, and
we may be permitted to express the fervent hope that you
will win further laurels in the metallurgical profession.

May health, prosperity, and happiness attend both
Mrs Beardsley and yourself wherever your lot may be
cast, and if the hearty wishes of all who have known you
should be of any avail Joy will surely precede and follow
your footsteps.'

Accompanying the address were over 400 signatures,
bound together with red and blue ribbon.

Continuing, Mr Sticht said he had known Mr Beardsley
for ten years, and it was not everybody who left with
such éclat and distinction as he was. He hoped he would
meet with every success in his future career, and might
some time come back again to Queenstown and find the
bulk of them that were there that night to welcome him
in the same generous way as they were showing their
regret at his departure.

The next thing he (the speaker) had to perform was
something which more concerned Mrs Beardsley, who he
regretted to say could not be present owing to indisposition.
He, therefore, presented Mr Beardsley with a silver tray,
inscribed as follows: 'A parting gift from the Mount Lyell
Company's employees. To Mr and Mrs G. F. Beardsley.'

Mr Beardsley was received with deafening applause, and
addressed them as ladies and gentlemen, fellow-workers
and friends. He hardly knew how to express himself, as
he had never been in the same position before. He felt
deeply grateful for the regard they had shown him and
had expressed in that – that document. (Laughter.)

He did not know how to thank them for it. He knew
something of the sort was in the wind, but that the
expressions of goodwill should be so unanimous
surprised him. When one gained the goodwill of those
under him (and he had always believed in trying to do

so) it was very much easier to get the work required
done. Mr Beardsley next went on to speak of the early
days, telling many of the peculiar characteristics in those
whose names will always be associated with the history of
the West Coast, and as these were mostly all of a humorous
nature, the laughter was frequent and everyone fell into
a good humor. He was sorry Mrs Beardsley could not be
present, but she had begged him to say that she regretted
being absent, and to thank them for their extreme
kindness. He would always look back with kindly feelings
and interest to his life amongst them, and would always
find a deep pleasure in thinking of their lives.

In concluding his remarks, he said he thought it a
splendid thing to be blessed with so much musical talent,
for while they listened to the music there could be no evil
thoughts ; and he also urged them to support their
Technical School and School of Mines and advance
themselves. (Applause.) At a later stage Mr Beardsley
extended his hearty thanks to all those who had taken part.

We saw them off at the station a few days later. It would have been
little Ruth's first birthday.

I would not see Alice again for more than a decade and we lived most
of the remainder of our lives far apart. She will be distraught when she
hears that I am gone but there it is. The world is cruel.

$$12$$

The sudden exodus of my friends and support continued. Fanny Westmoreland, Bob's beloved Miss Wissie, married Mr Millar, moved to Hobart and had a baby girl they named Marion, after me. I was delighted and a little embarrassed. It seemed that Miss W had sensed my longing for a daughter.

Then, in the winter of 1906, Lizzie abandoned me as well. She and George went home, to Long Beach, California and into real estate with dear Harry. The second time we put a world between us was more painful than the first. In a way it was worse than if they had never come. For the first time in my life I was anxious.

I had given birth to our second boy, John Hadmar Hazelton Sticht, born a few days after Christmas. We should have called him 'Bushfire'. He was no more difficult to deliver than the first but I recovered more slowly. I was 41 and the dank climate was never good for my health. I had Lizzie on hand, though, and we were nearing the end of Robert's contract. Lizzie's George had not been well for some time – he had bronchial problems and the climate of sulphurous damp was no more to his liking than mine – he was high country born. Out of the blue Harry wrote and asked him to go into partnership in Los Angeles, where he had moved with his family. George and Lizzie had discharged their debt and had made some savings. The world was opening up for them. It was obvious that they should go and equally obvious to me that we should follow, soon.

Did it occur to me that I might not see her again? I was bereft but that was isolation and, yes, a little envy. We had put them on their feet and they were going home. We had never been off ours yet we were condemned to stay. But not for long, I thought; we were doing well and Robert was famous throughout the mining world. I consoled myself with looking forward. Robert's contract was until 1907 – in a few years we could all be together in California – the Barndollars, the Beardsleys and us, growing old together in the sun. I began to look forward but that is not a healthy way to live. At 41 a Stage should not wish time gone.

what's past is prologue

Lizzie raised me as much as Mama did. Poor Mama was not a practical woman – the weight of mundane mothering was not to her liking. Lizzie was the adult in our family. She raised me and taught me to raise my own boys – I was as one with Mama on the subject of mothering, I must admit, but had not consumption to fall back on as an excuse. I could not be anything but happy for Lizzie, the crippling debt gone and a new life beckoning.

COMPLIMENTARY FAREWELL

Still another one of those gentlemen whose names have come to be considered as inseparably associated with the renowned Mount Lyell Mining and Railway Company as one of its responsible officials has relinquished his post and decided to sojourn elsewhere. This is Mr G. R. Barndollar, who has for about eight years ago acted as confidential secretary to the General Manager (Mr R. C. Sticht), and, of course, in that time has drawn round him, as also has Mrs Barndollar, a large circle of friends.

Mr Barndollar was not by any means an obtrusive man, but at the same time his name and figure were quite familiar to many, who found him in character possessed of a sincerity of purpose that calls for appreciation. What the feelings of the staff of the Mount Lyell M. and R. Co. were towards him is adequately expressed in the address printed below, and therefore it naturally followed that they should tender him a complimentary farewell concert, in which the public, the Queenstown Orchestral Union, and the Queenstown Brass Band took part.

The concert was held in the Metropole Hall on Saturday night while the rain descended in torrents – in fact so much so that a halt had to be called and a shower allowed to pass over before one of the vocalists could proceed. Yet in spite of this most unfavorable and uninviting weather the public were present in large numbers, and none of them appeared to regret the going. The decorations to the interior of the building were really the best seen, and the walls, harmoniously brightened with flags and greenery, made one forget the dreariness of the night outside. The stage, however, was where the most pains, and likewise the most taste, had been expended. Carpeted stairs led up from the front on to the footlights, and all round was

the pretty grass tree glistening in the electric light.
At the back of the stage was an immense Commonwealth
flag, quite as large as any of the drop scenes, and attached
to it was the Stars and Stripes – indicative of the unity
between Australians and Americans. It was altogether a
bright scene and the committee who were responsible
(Messrs T. H. Goode, J. S. Moon, W. H. Wesley, G. E.
Bodycomb, and E. W. U'Ren) are very deservedly to be
congratulated.

The programme opened with the overture, 'New York
Patrol', by the Queenstown Orchestral Union, and the
talented body afforded delight by their playing.
Mr S. O. Prismall gave very pleasantly 'The Anchor's
Weighed'; Mrs A. L. Dean's rendition of 'Kathleen
Mavourneen', with violin obligato by Mr V. B. Mursell,
was a most finished one; a trio, 'The Oars are Plashing',
by Mesdames B. Ricketts, F. Bradshaw, and Miss
Nicholson found high appreciation. Mrs Leo Cronly gave
an artistic interpretation of 'Convien Partir' ('Daughter
of the Regiment'); Mrs B. Ricketts was heard to great
advantage in 'The Beautiful Land of Nod'. Then came
the interval, when Mr A. L. Dean, after a few appropriate
introductory remarks, read the following address, and
presented Mr Barndollar with an elaborate dressing case:

Queenstown. Mount Lyell, Tasmania, Australia, July 28,
1906. To G. R. Barndollar. Esq.
Dear Sir – We, the under signed members of the staff
of the Mount Lyell M. and R. Company, desire to express
to you our sincere regret at the severance of your long
and honorable connection with the Company, and the
departure of Mrs Barndollar and yourself from our
community. Since your arrival in this district on April 1,
1898, you have seen the marvelous growth of the company
in which you have labored so long and so successfully,
and have witnessed the dense forests disappear and give
place to a hive of modern industry, in which your own

labors have contributed no small measure of successful administration. As a colleague we have always found you loyal in all your doings, earnest and attentive in your duty, and sincere in all your friendships, while your uniform and genuine courtesy has endeared you to all grades of officials in every department. We wish it were possible to express adequately in this brief address the esteem and regard in which both your helpmeet and yourself are held by us, and would ask your kind acceptance of the accompanying dressing case as some slight expression of our sincere and cordial feeling towards you. We hope that your departure from these rugged and inclement surroundings, to the sunny shore of your Californian home, will ripen your days to the fall and bring you much happiness, and, in the words of the immortal poet,

> God's benison go with you and with those
> Who would make good of bad, and friends of foes.

And finally we express the present wish that such long and happy associations as ours may be the touchstone whereby the unity of two great nations shall be ultimately consummated and abiding peace to the whole world be realised.

We remain, dear Mr Barndollar, your sincere friends –
[Here follow 40 signatures].

Oh! hast thou forgotten how soon we must sever?

Oh! hast thou forgotten this day we must part,

It may be for years, and it may be forever,

Oh! why art thou silent thou voice of my heart?

It may be for years, and it may be forever,

Then why art thou silent Kathleen mavourneen?

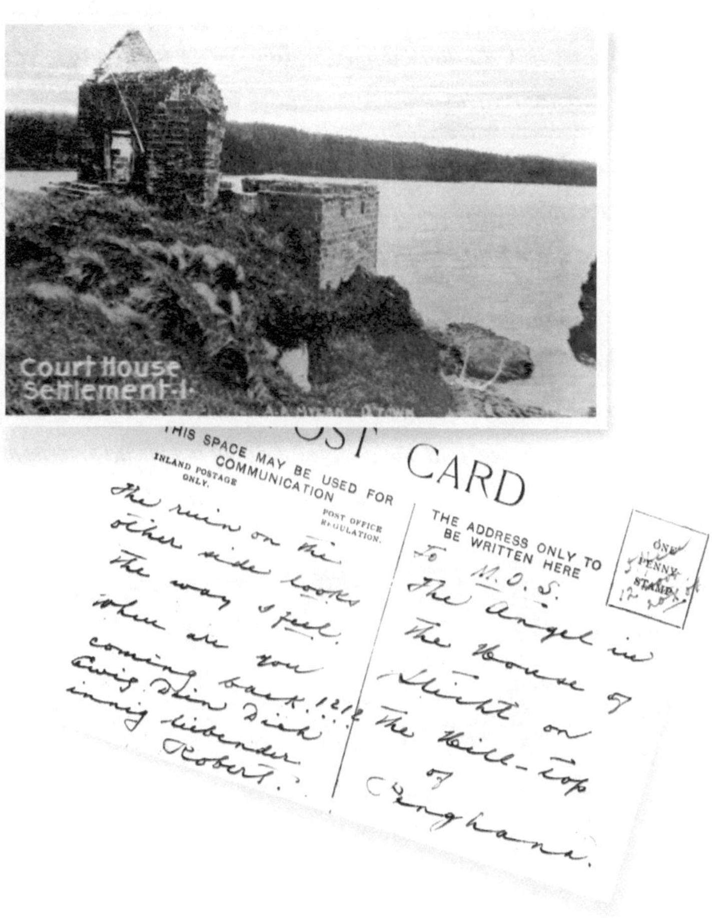

151

Penghana, Queenstown
16th October 1906

My dear Mrs Millar

Your letter was forwarded to Mrs Barndollar at once and you will doubtless hear from her in due time.

You can imagine how hard the separation is for both of us, but Mr Barndollar's health gave us cause for much alarm. So much so in fact that we did not think it wise for him to risk another winter in this damp dreary climate.

Just at this point he had a most tempting offer from his favourite brother to go into partnership with him at Long Beach California. It seemed quite Providential.

Mrs Barndollar writes rapturously of America where she says everyone is 'aggressively young and blooming' and that she is the only one of uncertain age she has seen! Her letters are full of 'Come home, Come home' and she declares she does not intend to write much else until I promise to do so. Someday I am going!!!

Your friend

Marion Oak Sticht

Ethel has heated water for my bath. There is an early chill in the air and the stillness is ominous. A frost tonight, no doubt. Good for the wild gardens flourishing here, amid the ruins. The bulbs will enjoy that.

I started my garden at Penghana not long after we moved in. I would bring the spirit of Sarah Hazelton to Lyell. It was slow going, though. The top of the hill had been flattened for the house, so the thin, rainforest topsoil had been removed or washed away. We imported what we could, built beds and sowed a lawn against the odds. We started a vegetable garden on the north-west slope and planted trees and ferns all around the bare hill and along the stairs and walkway that wound up from the street. It was a slow business – the poor soil, the constant rain and the sulphurous fog were no more suitable for flowers than for folk – except for rhododendrons, of course, which ran amok in the acid soils all along the valley. In the garden our flower beds were regularly filled with hopeful bulbs and seeds that just as regularly came to nought or not much.

But when Lizzie left and Robert began to make it clear that he was going to sign on for another five years, I lost interest in gardens or in anything else much. I went into a deep sulk. I decamped to Regatta Point with Bob and baby Hadmar, to our little cottage, and I swear I did not care to leave.

The cottage suited me perfectly, not all that different from this sparse place, except of course that it was nicely fitted out and had a town at hand, across the inlet. We had the harbour to play on and a little garden I had planted with Luke, who had a green thumb and a house in Strahan.

He was an extraordinary man, self-taught but ravenous in his reading. While lacking Robert's philosophy he was nevertheless all the things Robert strove to be. He was a scientist, a naturalist, a gardener, a writer, an explorer and a horseman. He was a man who would stand beside you to the bitter end if you were his friend.

He had been through much. He came to the West Coast from Bendigo in the early eighties, before there was anything much here at all. In '82 he was on the prospecting expedition south from Macquarie Heads to Point Hibbs, that went badly wrong. The party only survived by bashing through the wilderness all the way down to Port Davey. Starving and exhausted when they arrived there weeks later, they were rescued by piners who ferried them round to Recherche Bay.

Luke knew sadness, having lost his young son in Hobart while he was away in Europe, in 1902. He had a wife and daughter he loved fiercely as a result of that loss. He was our man at Chester and at Balfour for a decade. He believed in Balfour to the bitter end. Robert swore by him and the boys adored him. I adored him. He is down the Huon now, with his pigs and fruit trees. I do miss him.

So I took my time at Regatta Point and made Robert sweat. Bob had a nasty cold and little Hadmar was doing what six-month old babies do – not much but making a great fuss about it. I was tired and lonely and facing another five years here, away from the world. At least at Regatta Point the sun shone quite often and the air was the freshest air on earth. Not a whiff of sulphur.

We went boating and caught fish and walked and walked. Spring flowers were everywhere, the garden was a little jewel. Luke and I planted grapes. We harvested them there years later, something not seen on the West Coast previously. I began to regain my strength, both physical and in my will. I found a way to suppress the panic that had been rising in my gorge – the thought that I might die out here and never go home. I started to understand properly the consequences of decisions I had made a decade earlier. I knew Robert was right, we had to stay a while longer. But I did make him sweat.

I went back to Queenstown, to Penghana and my life of good works, openings, hostess to visiting dignitaries, mother and observer.

LAUNCESTON EXAMINER

16th February 1907

WOMEN'S EXHIBITION BRANCHES FORMED

QUEENSTOWN, Friday – A meeting of ladies interested in the women's work exhibition was held today. An influential committee was appointed, with Mrs. R. Sticht as president, to carry out the necessary arrangements in connection with having Queenstown represented in a practical manner.

THE CLIPPER, HOBART

11th May 1907

WOMEN'S WORK

'Lyell Mary' writes: For some time I have been watching for an interesting item in your Lyell notes re the exhibition of Women's Work promoted by some of Australia's imported titular persons. As an Australian, and a conscientious purchaser of articles produced in the Commonwealth, I was taking quite a keen interest in this exhibition of achievements by my sex but I was startled this week by an announcement in the papers, in which an invitation was extended to the ladies of Queenstown to attend a meeting to meet a lady from Hobart, named Dobson, who was expected to explain a lot about the matter.

That settled the question as far as I was concerned. Did not this name remind me of the lady who takes such a kindly interest in the National Assassination, Employers' Federation, or some other such humbug society in Hobart,

the main object of which is to keep my husband's wages
down to the lowest, and who love the Asiatic so much
that they wish him to come and reside on our shores, to
be a pestilence to us, and a menace to our ideals of
home-purity?

Mr Editor, could a decent minded woman, who always
votes Labor and who eternally believes in white girls for
white men, attend a meeting to hear a person who tries
to make her listeners believe she wishes to promote an
Australian Women's Work Exhibition, when her past
actions show her to be ignorant of all true Australian
ideals; who would allow yellow Asians to mix with the
Australian and cause a mongrel breed to infest the land?
Certainly not. So I let the meeting go. Yet the Chairman of
the Town Board called a meeting of all the ladies (and it is
pretty certain the ratepayers paid for the advertisement),
but the meeting was held at Mr Sticht's private residence.
Was it likely that a smelter man's wife could feel comfortable at the manager's house? More especially when she
saw she would be patronised to her face, like a pug dog
that could do circus tricks, and likewise scorned behind
her back like the same dog!

Therefore, it is safe to say that so far as Queenstown is
concerned the Australian Women's Exhibition is doomed
to failure. The democratic women of this town, many of
whom were driven from good homes in this beautiful
island by the tactics of those who form the Employers'
Federation and such like organisations, now that they are
free to some extent from the trammels of these predatory
parasites who style themselves the nicest people in the
land, all look askance at the proposal, and emissaries from
these bodies, with whatever cry they come, will receive
naught for their pains.

When the proper opportunities are afforded them, the
women of Australia will have achievements to be proud
of, when they can exclaim: 'We are the mothers and wives
and sisters of those men who have determined at all

---

hazards to keep Australia white; and the patriotic
exhibition these our men folk give of their courage in
doing their duty will amply reward our sex for all the pain
and trouble we may have suffered, and be of much more
lasting value than a needlework or painted calico show.'

WOMEN'S WORK EXHIBITION

Mrs Robert Sticht, President of the local committee, who took in hand the representation of the district at the Women's Work Exhibition (Melbourne), has had returned to her the exhibits for distribution:— Mrs F. S. Sanderson, screens; Miss A. O'Connor, crochet work; Miss E. McConnon, point lace work; Mrs Freeman, child's frock; Mrs E. W. U'Ren, ditto; Miss K. Lawson ditto; Miss Maud Griffiths, ditto; Mrs Massey, point lace work; Mrs D. Vance (Gormanston), crochet work; Miss Nellie Hartnett, point lace work; Miss L. E. Nicholson, point lace work; Mrs A. S. Rutter, cushions and point lace work; Mrs Tabart, table cloth. Several of the exhibits were purchased by visitors to the Exhibition.

Penghana
22nd October 1907

Dr E. D. Peters
Professor of Metallurgy
Harvard University

...Personally, I have been too much out of touch with the financial side of mining enterprise to have done well; on the contrary, it is my continual experience to lose, not to gain. So I am 'off' such things, as a rule, and rely on mere salary which, though £5000 annually (since the last 4 years) has not permitted of the accumulation of a fortune.

Needless to remark, I have often had the desire to return to the USA, and my wife is chronically of that disposition. Neither of us is in the least Australianised, nor ever will be. But it has never appeared to us that we would better ourselves by returning. So, insensibly almost, year after year has glided by, and we are still here. More than this, I am on the point of engaging myself for another 5 years, which will see Mt Lyell pretty well out, or, at all events, my participation in it. A special incentive to leave is the lack of suitable schools and colleges, – our older boy is now just past eleven...

Rob't Sticht

Penghana, Queenstown
22nd August 1908

Dear Miss Wissie Mrs Millar

Ever since the dear little book of charming pictures of Baby Marion came I have intended sending you a long letter.

We think the photographs lovely and that you have a charming little girlie. Hadmar says the one in the garden is 'ooful'.

If there is rather a disjointed character about this epistle it is owing to the fact that we are (literally) hourly expecting a visit from the stork!

I have not been at all well until a few days ago – when I suddenly grew very much better – until yesterday. The waiting time must soon be over now. We are so delighted for Hadmar's sake as well as our own. It would do your heart good to see how devoted Robert and Hadmar are to each other.

Hadmar is the joy and life of our home – promises to be as clever as Robert – knows his letters – counts easily to 29 and then will say twenty ten instead of thirty in spite of anything we can do or say. Detests his combinations – calls them 'condemnations' and sounds profane while doing so. He is a perfect picture of happy babyhood with lovely red cheeks, blue blue eyes and yellow hair. His father thinks his two boys quite the finest in the world of course. Robert is at the Melbourne Grammar School and developing into a fine manly boy. He was with us four weeks –mid-winter holidays – lately and was

a perfect joy to me. When you meet with any success in your
photography of the two – do not forget to send it.

You will probably receive a telegram before this reaches you.
With love and a kiss to Marion,

Your friend

Marion Oak Sticht

Chester waited another week after I wrote that letter – a wretched week followed by a long birth. I was almost 43 and it took something from me that I never quite retrieved. I had another boy but I no longer had Miss Wissie or Lizzie to help me deal with it all. It added to my already sharp sense of isolation and a general sense of fatigue. He was a healthy boy, luckily, and an easy one to nurse through those early years but I longed more than ever for a future I could frame my life within.

A TRIBUTE FROM MR. STICHT

During a welcome luncheon to the ex Prime Minister at Queenstown the general manager of the Mt. Lyell M. and R. Co., Mr. Robert Sticht, who presided over a large company, in proposing the health of Mr. Alfred Deakin, said he was one of the best known men in Australia, and the best known Australian outside the Commonwealth. As an American, he could appreciate Mr. Deakin's many qualities perhaps better than most of those present. What his (Mr. Stitch's) politics were no one had yet found out – (laughter) – but if he had any politics he could assure them that they would be those of Mr. Deakin's. (Loud cheers.)

Aside from any such question, Mr. Deakin's presence there was an honor to them, for it was the first time that anyone, apart from a governor, enjoying such distinction had come to show himself amongst them. This was an entirely informal function, and one could not sit along side Mr. Deakin for two minutes without feeling that formalities were out of the question. He was a most charming man. It was not everyone whose oratory would carry him so far as Mr. Deakin's would carry him. He was fully in accord with Mr. Deakin's effort's to create the national feeling of the kind we so want in Australia, and he did not think anything could be better than the work Mr. Deakin was doing in talking to the people. Speaking to them as he was doing was the best way to raise the national spirit that Australia required. (Loud cheers.)

Mr. Deakin, in reply, said that Mr. Sticht was not only a man of great knowledge, but had the gift of using it.

BALL BY MR AND MRS ROBT. STICHT
A BRILLIANT SUCCESS

During their many years' residence in Queenstown the general manager of the Mount Lyell M. and R. Company and his amiable wife can neither be charged with having lived in surroundings of ostentatious display, or appeared to find pleasures in those things which the philosophers tell us are only the hollow shams of life. Instead, Mr and Mrs Sticht have maintained that high, ideal home-life which is exemplary in its contentment, and bespeaking the first and main responsibilities of life. For this, and their many other esteemable attributes, Mr Sticht as one holding a powerful position, and as the foremost citizen has without the seeking earned goodwill and admiration, while Mrs. Sticht by genuine charity and a womanly regard for the welfare of others has endeared herself to many hearts. They have formed round them selves a vast circle of friends, and the mutual attachment has increased with the passing years.

On Monday night Mr and Mrs Robt. Sticht gave a ball at the Metropole Hall, to which numerous invitations had been sent. The function was one worthy of the lady and gentleman who arranged it, and it was an event looked forward to by a great number of people. It was carried through in a very complete manner, with no limitation in the direction of causing it to be long remembered; in a word it was a distinct social triumph.

The vestibule was illuminated by electric lights suspended from the ceiling, and foliage relieved any bareness that would otherwise have been evident. Entering the main building one was entranced with the scene of beauty that presented itself. The interior of the hall was completely transformed as if a magic hand had been at work. Its

immediate effect was to impart a feel ing of tranquility
— the feeling that one has when looking at a canvas
picture of an autumn sunset. Over all there was a soft
warmth, a soothing mellowness. There was no dazzling
brilliancy, nothing garish; it was a subdued whole, an
easy content that filled the very air.

A carpeted way, bordered by majestic ferns, led to the
stage, where Mr and Mrs Sticht received their guests, who
then descended the broad temporary stairway to the hall
below. The stage itself was set out as a drawing room,
and it was arranged with exquisite taste. Here and there
greenery lent additional adornment and electric radiators
gave a cosy warmth. Above the stage and down and
across the hall flags were hung and interwoven over head.
Streamers of rich ribbons supported green-leaved crosses,
from the four corners of which Chinese lanterns hung,
illuminated by electric lamps inside. Along the walls
forest foliage made a back ground of dark green, amid
which colored electric lights glowed pleasantly. Many
mirrors, draped with curtains, reflected the beauty that
was all around, and gave just the required added touch
of sparkle.

At the lower end of the hall the word 'Welcome' was
worked in red electric lights, which were softened down by
being encased in transparent cloth, and the effect was a
warm glow — as if the word itself was speaking its full and
true meaning on behalf of the host and hostess. In one
corner and hidden away behind some shrubbery the
musicians were accommodated, and from here the waltz
and other dance airs came unseen, as it were. Another
corner of the room was built off as a little recess, where the
ladies might obtain refreshments, while for the gentlemen
a large room upstairs was set aside, the stairway leading
to which was carpeted, and bordered with bush growths.

Supper was laid in the Masonic Hall, and to those who
do not know otherwise, it may be explained that this
building is round in Cutten street, and over a hundred

yards away. As the night was wet (like most nights in Queenstown) the full width of Cutten street was canvassed over as a protection from the rain, the street verandahs providing shelter for the remainder of the distance. Dancing began shortly after 9, and in the first set there were Mr E. C. Driffield and Mrs Sticht, Mr Robt. Sticht and Mrs Walpole, Mr R. M. Murray and Miss Wright, Mr G. C. Bernard and Mrs Harris (Zeehan), Mr G. W. Wright and Mrs Driffield, and Mr A. B. Cruikshank and Mrs R. H. Lord. Some very becoming costumes were worn, Mrs Sticht being dressed in cream satin sequin with chiffon over dress, a necklet of well-matched pearls and diamond ornaments. Mr and Mrs Jas. Reed, of the Caledonian Hotel, were responsible for the supper arrangements, and the brightly decorated tables and the rich viands were most eloquent as to artistic taste and ability to cater. At the ball Mr J. H. Keogh was master of ceremonies, and the music was played by Messrs D. Sargeant (piano), A. H. Wesley (violin), and W. Reid (cornet). Mr. R. C. Eyes was chiefly responsible, we understand, for the decorations in the interior of the hall.

My life seems to be little more than a scrap book. Here is a copy of Robert's letter to his brother Ernst, from September 1910, asking whether we could help with young Robert's education, as we had with Gustav's son, Alfred:

I am not by any means as well off as I might be, – in fact, as far as the ability to leave this place for a period of rest, or to execute rapid movements and changes of base, are concerned, I am no better off than at any time in my life. However, having scored the cream compared with the rest of the family, – whatever it amounts to – I have had a natural longing to be of some help to the others, – only, the practical demonstration of it has been kept dormant by the fear of the wolf at my own door, as intimated.

Before anything could be arranged a letter came from Ida, in April of the next year: Ernst had died of pneumonia in March. He died up there in Republic, relatively young at 50. He left Ida and young Robert, whom we had never met. I was so sorry. I liked Ernst very much. He was a good man and he was always kind and courteous to me. I think he was amazed that Robert had a woman!

We helped out Ida and Robert as much as we could, even as things went sour for us. But Ida was no fool – she and Ernst had a property in Spokane that the railway company needed. She knew she had them over a barrel and she stood firm, like a good German. In the end she made a fortune from that little block and went back east.

Robert was confused by Ernst's death, I think. He'd not had as much practice as I had. It was not what he had expected and he struggled to find a context for his grief. He had not seen Ernst for 17 years and that had passed so quickly. That distance in time had more impact than the physical distance. It was the first of the blows that were about to fall on him.

*Letter: Robert to Manager of the Republic Mines Corporation,
3rd June 1911.*

*I know that my brother's pathway in life was not smooth, but, as
you recognised, his soul was above misfortune. To me it is a special
comfort to know that his stirling character was sincerely valued by
his friends, and also that he was surrounded by a host of the latter
of the truest kind. Your notice of him profoundly stirred me in the
reading, and made me homesick for the touch of our Western
American manhood.*

13

The sun is shining. I slept for hours and feel a little stronger today. I cannot manage the walk down to the river but it is a fine autumn day and Robert drives us down the long ridge in the dray. We take a thermos and a rug against the cold. He will return for us this evening. The old wire bridge is still slung across the stream, just as I remember, swinging slowly as a noose over the dark water snaking westward to the sea. I once saw a man who'd been hanged, in Colorado. It was not uncommon for matters to be resolved that way in mining towns.

When Robert first came west he worked up in Leadville, where Mr Eilers had made his name and Mary Hallock Foote had started to write. Leadville was as wild a place as could be imagined – Robert cut his teeth in a place very different from New York and Clausthal. The rule of law was an abstract idea up in those mountains. Claim jumping, shootings, debauchery and lynchings were commonplace. It was a boom town. Its fields were bountiful and made many fortunes, Horace Tabor most of all. He bought the Matchless silver mine with paper from miners who owed him money for supplies. Shopkeepers are the only ones who ever make good livings from a mine, but Horace took that maxim to a level never seen before. He built his first Opera House up there, to show he was deserving of God's grace, and brought Oscar Wilde to town on his American tour, back in 1882.

People there still talk about the dandy who could drink. He had some nerve, addressing a raucous crowd of drunken miners and saloon girls on aesthetics. But while his account of the visit differs in his own favour from that of those few locals sober enough to recall the momentous day, he did go down the Matchless in a bucket with cousin Horace and they did name a vein after him. And he must have gone to Pat Wyman's Golden Nugget Saloon if he saw the *Don't Shoot the Piano Player* sign – though he could have seen that elsewhere – it was something of a Colorado joke, for the benefit of condescending dandies, such as Mr Wilde.

1882 – THE YEAR IN REVIEW

APRIL

On Tuesday, April 4, news was received of the loss of a gold brick, valued at $9,000, between this city and Independence. It was afterwards found near Everett's. The same day saw another fatal shooting on Harrison Avenue in front of the Clarendon Hotel. James Kinney, in self defense, shot John Lukenbill and inflicted injuries which proved fatal.

A brutal beating was administered to Dr. Julius Schaffter by a man named Wescott, at Malta, on the morning of the 5th. Mr. Finn, of Cummings & Finn's Smelter, was thrown from his horse and had two ribs fractured. On the same date, Charles McCullough came in contact with a circular saw in Tennessee park and was seriously injured.

At half past three on the morning of the eighth, the Bennet house, on the corner of Spruce and Elm Streets, was burned and Mike Maddigan met his death in the flames.

John Lukenbill, who was shot by James Kinney, died on the night of the 12th.

On the 15th, Oscar Wilde discoursed to a Leadville audience.

The 17th was the date upon which Billy Nuttall chewed an ear off of Chris Wagner.

On the 19th, an unsuccessful attempt was made by incendiaries to destroy the Rio Grande express office.

It was on the morning of the 21st that General Ward was held up and robbed of $1,700.

On the evening of the 24th, Lulu Sedgwick stabbed Jennie Myers in a house of ill fame on East Sixth Street.

News reached here on the 25th of the killing of Captain John P. Slawson, former manager of the Catalpa Mine, by the Arapahoes in New Mexico.

On the night of the 26th, James Farrell bit off the nose of John McGready in a saloon on Stray Horse Gulch.

The 29th was the day upon which Mrs. Nellie Horen suicided by means of morphine. A case of small pox was discovered in the city. The disease failed to spread.

Mining towns are ephemeral by nature – as elusive as the minerals they pursue. There is no continuity, no history, no real confidence in the future. Not beyond next week. Nothing is embedded, nothing is certain. Puffery and public bombast brandish their blazing faggots at the demons lurking in the dark of every mind, but everyone knows that tomorrow the vein could run out or the price collapse and the town would be pulled apart in a week and dragged over the mountains to the next Eldorado. To Balfour, for example. Where the process will repeat itself. People come to these towns with the idea of moving on firmly rooted in their minds. And most do.

The scrub lining the tea-coloured stream is impenetrable, the banks hidden beneath a tangle of sleek limbs. The first time I was here it was summer, many years ago, before the cholera and the Fall. Doomed, naked children, limbs sleek as trees, threw themselves from the bridge into the brown stream in happy droves, snaking like cormorants beneath the foam for ages, until their slick heads exploded into life downstream. I see metaphors everywhere I look as I grow older. And I once swam naked in the Arkansas.

The Frankland is a stream, not a river. It has not the stark grandeur of the Arkansas or the gravity of the Gordon, that sublime mystery. We went on the Gordon many times and explored its hinterland. The river holds a primeval attraction, or sense of something more profound than our petty lives. It is one thing I would have missed had we gone home. We felt strongly that the river and its surrounds should be preserved. We had followed the development of National Parks back home and saw that this wilderness was even more precious. We had begun to see that we had wrought enough destruction on this innocent wilderness. When it was proposed to set up a sawmill on its banks Robert wrote to the Premier, Sir Elliot Lewis, whom we had met several times.

The local tourist organisation wish me to write you about a proposed desecration of the Gordon River and to enlist your sympathetic interest in the prevention of same. Notwithstanding that a reserve has been placed over the banks of the river, it is feared that a sawmill will be permitted to be erected there. This business enterprise emanates from Strahan, where some of the leading citizens are floating a company for the purpose (Melbourne capital, I understand). Needless to say, if allowed to materialise, the damage to the present beauties of the river which would follow in the wake of sawmilling operations there, would be a greater loss to the state than the very small, and, in any case, uncertain profit, which the enterprise would throw off to the parties themselves. The danger lies chiefly in bushfires.

It is suggested that a bill be put through for the purpose, rendering the Gordon River immune from such harm, and if this should be favoured with your endorsement it would be deeply appreciated.

Very truly yours,

Robt Sticht

And I remember a day not unlike this buoyant day, in the summer of 1911, that I set off on the Gordon and nearly lost a Prime Minister's daughter.

Penghana
20th February 1911

Dearest Alice Kate

*My apologies for writing to you again before receiving your reply
to my last chaotic missive, but I have had the most wonderful adventure
and you will – for once – be sorry you were not here to share it.*

*Robert was away last week in Melbourne, on business (or scouring
the rare bookshops!) and it fell to me to host a disparate party of
visitors at Penghana and then to lead them on a little expedition to
the Gordon, a place you know we hold very dear.*

*It was an interesting party, to say the least. Herbert and Ivy Brookes
are on a speaking tour, rallying the people against some referendum
or other. There is always a referendum to oppose these days and
everybody does. Something to do with Federal power over the states,
as I recall. I suppose it is a more civilised way of settling such things
than marching off to war and slaughtering each other, as we
Americans did.*

*For once I was glad I couldn't vote, though Ivy takes a dim view of
such recalcitrance. I remain strongly of the view that swearing false
allegiance to a distant, inbred monarch is too high a price to pay for
suffrage.*

*Ivy is a delightful woman, at the height of her considerable powers.
She is about 30: tall, angular, quietly confident of mind and body.
She is Alfred Deakin's daughter. You will remember I told you that
we had Mr Deakin at Penghana, back in 1909 and experienced his*

benign eccentricities at first hand. Ivy is of the same inquisitive mind, though being a woman she is by necessity more prosaic than her father and less inclined to idiosyncrasy.

I know you would think as highly of her as I do – she shares our love of music, though she is possessed of a prodigious talent I can only envy. You know that I was only ever competent and what little talent I had has wasted away in motherhood and wifedom and good works and restlessness. Ivy won a singing scholarship as a girl and plays first violin in the notorious Marshall Hall's Orchestra, in Melbourne. It is Mr Marshall who is notorious, by the way, not the Orchestra, which is rather good and has many women amongst its number, which may explain the notoriety. I can not help but envy her access to such opportunities – musical I mean, not notoriety! Orchestras, as you know, are in short supply at Lyell but even such opportunities that arise are forbidden me because of my position. It is one thing for Robert to treat the world to his zither, another altogether for his wife to make a fool of herself in public!

Ivy is strong and lively and has a love of adventure, so nothing would do but that she see the famous Gordon. Herbert is considerably older than her, a widower who had been a friend of her father's. A successful businessman, self-made, landed and politically well-connected – part of the new Australian aristocracy. His brother Norman is good at tennis.

Herbert was the only man in our little party – apart from the crew of the launch – and we tended to be girlish in his company. Miss Arabella Antonia Williams, though, was not in the least bit girlish. She is an imposing, horsey creature in her fifties, I would guess, whose late father had been a Welsh Baronet, whatever that *may be, and whose brother was the Bishop of Bangor, wherever that may be. She is obviously of independent means and mind. She is restless and fearless yet manages somehow to be unlikeable. She has travelled the world for years – has been on safari in Africa with Mrs Jenkins, don't you know? Perhaps her edge is the result of so much travel. A cloak for her inner self. Her inseparable companion on this pilgrimage around the colonies is Miss Childe, or Harold, as Antonia calls her. A poor joke, you will agree.*

Rounding out our little expedition were Mrs Murray and Mrs Driffield, the latter you know well and the former you would not like. Both are well educated but self-conscious.

We set off on a sunny summer's day with only a light easterly in the morning. As you know, easterlies bring what passes for stable weather here, so all the omens were good. We struck out early over the haulage to Linda – still an adventure in itself and one, you will remember, dear Lizzie used to love. She would be over that haulage line to Gormanston on visits at the slightest opportunity.

From Linda we took the Company motor trolley down the North Lyell line, courtesy of Mr Driffield, who is still responsible for such things. We passed in sunshine down the Vale of Chamounix then south, along those stark eastern slopes of Lyell, Owen, Huxley, Jukes and Darwin. In the east the quartz cap of the Frenchman reared up out of the wilderness into an unfamiliar, clear blue sky. We steamed through the ghost towns of Crotty and Darwin – ghost towns you would not recognise since amalgamation made them redundant – and cantered along beside the Bird, through the morning-misted tree ferns, down to Pillinger, a shadow of the port that threatened to outgrow Strahan when you were hereabouts.

I still go down there with Robert every year, to the North Lyell picnic days. They remain remarkable for attracting fine weather and for the fact that every year Robert and Mr Murray and Mr Driffield make exactly the same speeches in response to exactly the same toasts and everyone cheers like mad.

It is still a splendid journey that puts me in mind of the circle line from Pueblo through Royal Gorge up to Leadville, across to Denver and back south along the foothills of the Rockies. When I come home I will take you. The little towns are mostly ruins – Crotty, Darwin, Pillinger – just like the nine-day wonders scattered through The Rockies like confetti.

We took morning tea at the Railway Station and from the long pier opposite we boarded 'The Nellie' – you may recall her – a graceful little launch, low-slung, and built from the timbers of the Gordon. She skims the water like a cormorant, though she has been refitted since you left – caught fire at the wharf in Strahan (there is talk that liquor was involved) and was scuttled to dowse the flames. The re-fit is splendid though, the Grining brothers having a sawmill and the best ship-building timbers in the world on their doorstep. It is all Huon Pine and Celery Top and Blackwood, as you know, my favourite Tasmanian, after my boys – for Tasmanian they are, I must concede, strange as it may seem to she who bore them.

We followed the normal route across a strangely tranquil Macquarie, to Settlement Island, where we took lunch. The old convict station is still a bleak and dismal place of course, the soil is as soaked with suffering as Queenstown's is with sulphur. The sandwiches always seem too dry, as if filled with guilt.

We wandered around the ruins and, as usual, wondered what to think, posing heroically while Antonia Kodaked us. Our dues to sad history paid, we set course for the Gordon. It is a great pity that we were never able to explore it together – it is my favourite place on this benighted island. We glided quietly between the sandbars and the trees which cloak the river mouth, and with a breeze at our backs were quickly enveloped in the wilderness. I recently discovered that in the lower reaches a unique lily grows higher up the slope. I wanted to point it out to Antonia, who knows Miss Jekyll and sends her specimens from her travels, but it was not flowering so impossible to locate from the river.

The marsh quickly gives way to a dense forest of myrtle and tree fern and the occasional Huon pine missed by the piners, whose primitive camps can still be located from smoke-rise on the slopes. We have managed to have the banks preserved as a park – and we will keep pushing until the whole area is protected.

The incomprehensible mass overhanging the banks is reflected so perfectly in the tan water that you lose any sense of horizon, even where the banks become limestone cliffs. But an inquisitive eye soon becomes accustomed to the subtle shades. Behind them mountains clad in untouched forest rise up into the clouds and mist. We should have noticed when those clouds began to crowd the river of blue sky above us but we were all transfixed by the river's beauty. I have seen the effect of the Gordon on many before and I was not disappointed by our little party's response: but it very nearly cost us our lives.

A profound sense of peace possesses you as you slide deeper into the forest. When the water is still – and it often is, as the steep hills gather round – the reflection has the metallic lustre of a daguerrotype. It seems at times more real than the world it reflects.

It can be disorienting. There is little noise – for on the rainforest floor there is little life. Birdsong can be heard from the treetops, though, and black swans shoot past along the banks like arrows, skimming the surface, their white tipped wings heaving silently as angels.

The further you forge on into the wilderness the more serene the picture becomes. Our little launch steamed on to The Limekilns, the furrow of our wake fanned out behind us like a feather, and we took our tea rather late at the Long Reach. The conversation was subdued by the tranquility of our surroundings but Miss Williams and Mrs Brookes were insistent that we push on further, to the Marble Cliffs. My fault, I suppose, for waxing so lyrical about them earlier. As we were independent of any railway timetable we were free to do so and Mr Grining obligingly chugged a few miles further upstream to the first rapids, passing the Marble Cliffs and several tributaries, whose mouths are hidden in the dense thicket. By now we were more than 20 miles along the river and it was after 3 o'clock. High above the mountains the wisps of stratus clouds should have been better heeded.

I sensed trouble as soon as we turned about. A sullen sky glowered in the west as we wound our way back downstream. I more than once caught Mr Grining's eye and sensed his apprehension. He laid on steam and we fairly flew along between the looming banks, running with the river's flow, but by the time we rounded the last bend and headed for the mouth I knew that we were in some difficulty – I could not see Settlement Island! A white mist swept like a ghost across the steely water and fine rain lashed our bows as we split the bar.

We set out upon the harbour and you can imagine my emotions – how many have come to grief in that cold water? The gale had sprung from the north-west and clouds rolled in low over the water, so the sheltering arms of Kelly Basin, only a few miles distant, were invisible. We beat on into the growing storm and white-capped waves and the little craft began to pitch and roll. The Nellie is a slim little launch, with low gunwales and we were taking water as the swell grew steeper. Our course was due north but the wind howled in from the north-west, so we were forced to lurch at an uncomfortable angle across the jagged swell to gain the sanctuary of Kelly Basin. The shrieking wind and the pounding of the surf on the launch's beam saturated my senses. We huddled in the saloon, holding on for dear life as our link to dear life was buffeted by wave and wind and slewed sickeningly from side to side. Rain whipped the decks and I began to truly fear for our survival. I tried to imagine you beside me and drew some courage from the memory of yours. The Nellie seemed suddenly like a toy.

Mr Grining put our nose up into the wind and we ploughed head-on into the surf, due north, away from safety. The blood-red western sky grew more fierce behind the mist and rain as evening came on. We were still only a mile or two from the safety of Kelly Basin's lee shore but it was no good. The gale showed no sign of abating and a night spent beating up into the wind, forty miles to Strahan, was unthinkable. The slightest mischance would have had us in the water and none would have survived. It would be dark by the time we were missed.

Then there was a momentary lull, a few seconds only, yet Mr Grining seized the opportunity and swung us around in a moment – a perilous manoeuvre – and we ran before the wind and rain, in the gathering gloom, back to the shelter of the Gordon. I was never so thankful for the long Tasmanian summer evenings. The twilight afforded us time to find the river mouth – which as you know, is shrouded in foliage – and to negotiate the sandbar. We coasted around the first bend and found an anchorage beneath the wind in the river's arms. Once our pulses had returned to normal we gathered on the deck and sat in wonder as the gale passed overhead, barely disturbing the river's implacable surface.

There is no accommodation to speak of on the Nellie, so we were forced to make do. Mr Brookes bunked down with the captain and his man in the wheelhouse, while we ladies made up makeshift cots in the saloon. In the afterglow of adventure it was a merry evening – we had survived great danger and were warm and fed well enough on the picnic's leavings and cups of tea.

It was like being in the dormitory back at Vassar, Alice! We swapped yarns like schoolgirls telling ghost stories. Miss Williams came into her own – well used to camping out in all manner of odd situations, she regaled us with stories of her safari with Mrs Jenkins. I remember particularly her account of their camp being charged by a rogue elephant, perhaps enraged by the death of five of his family slaughtered earlier by members of the Jenkins party. Mrs Jenkins apparently makes a career of visiting remote and exotic countries and shooting their wildlife. Do you know, when we first went west from Illinois, when I was but ten, people shot buffalo from the train?

I slept like a child in my makeshift cot. The gentle swaying of the boat on its moorings, the creaking of the ropes, the serene silence of the forest broken occasionally by the wind stirring the trees on the ridge above – it was a child's dream.

In the morning we took tea and biscuit on the deck, while Mr Grining steered us slowly downriver, back to the harbour. In no time we were across the now calm waters to Kelly Basin. On dry land at last, we found Mr Driffield, more than a little agitated and bearing news that a land slip had closed the railway. It was evening before we finally steamed back beside the mountains into Linda. We climbed wearily into the ore trucks and were pulled up over the crest on that iron rope. The 700 foot descent – thrilling, as you remember, and 1 in 2 at its steepest – was an experience in tune with the rest of the adventure – a dense fog came up and enveloped our little caravan in a strange world where motion was implied rather than experienced and our arrival at the "terminus" seemed a magical thing, a piece of theatre. It was thus an exhausted but exhilarated party that repaired to Penghana for dinner and an early night.

It was, in retrospect at least, the most fun I have had for years and I am ashamed to say that I did not think of my family once! Are you shocked? I think it is an instinct for survival.

I expect a letter from you at any moment and will write again as soon as I have it. There are other, more mundane matters to discuss and I will write again as a mother and a wife;

And as your friend, always

Marion Oak

I can hear Bob's dray clanking down the hill. It is late – I have drowsed the afternoon away in reverie. I wonder where they are now? Ivy and Herbert and Antonia and Miss Childe? Do they remember their voyage on the Gordon? Or me?

The rain is settling to its winter rhythm, beating in from the coast, across the heath. We huddle indoors around the stove, driven inwards as we brace for winter. Bob seems to revel in it. The more it rains the more he is outside. He is truly a west coaster. There are few here who were born here, and fewer Queenstown born who are older than young Bob. Is it in his blood as Illinois is in mine?

This will be my last winter. As it is Balfour's. We are both dying. The last families have fled, the school closed last year; the few scattered scavengers will find it difficult to hang on as the track deteriorates. Bob is administering the last rites to Murray's Curse. The little red hill will soon be silent and the shacks will decay and moulder in the damp. Trees and bracken will soon bury the dream. A hundred years from now I doubt a trace will remain – except perhaps a few runaway flowers and those pine trees across what was meant to be the street. A passerby – who would in all probability be lost – might find the rubble of an old chimney stack or a few scraps of iron, but all trace of our selves will have vanished, the very air we breathed will have been swept around the world, as I was.

to be imprisoned in the viewless winds

The strength to fight, the will to live, a sense of purpose, the belief in renewal – the natural optimism of my people – all are fatally dimmed. Weakened by isolation.

It seemed that the longer we were away the more Robert tried to bring the world to us, as though the world could be reduced to artifacts, as if all the things of the spirit we were going without could be replaced by relics from that other world. Every square inch of our fortress was bolstered against the world outside, every wall, every corner, every nook and cranny was filled with talismans, deafening, discordant echoes of a civilised world far from this frontier.

The Collection was my rival. *A man's library is his harem.* Emerson had that right.

What is a Collection? What is its purpose? A reflection of the world we believed in but had left behind? Is that all it was? A relic? We lacked Helen's sandal and a piece of the Cross but little else. Mother would have held it all ostentatious but been secretly delighted. Lizzie thought it rather funny but could never say so. George was bemused and continually afraid he would knock over something valuable – but that is George's response to the world in general.

Was it a *memento mori*? Metaphorical dust itself now, dispersed to the winds of commerce and fate. Who could possibly know a generation from now that all those things were once together, an expression of one man's vision of the world? On a hilltop in Queenstown, for heaven's sakes! And what would be made of Robert's sacred catalogue, if it survives a hundred years? What would an educated and interested mind make of that thousand-page record of obsession? Could a pattern be discerned that told something of Robert and me and our brief journey through time? It was my monument as well – whether I liked it or not.

All those things – now gone – were no more than anchors. Did they inspire or comfort us? The latter, I believe. They stopped us floating away. Strange to think of them now, scattered on the winds of time and capital, as am I – floating away on a tide that I can no longer fight. My anchors have well and truly slipped.

What am I without him? What would I want to be? We were a team for so long. It is easy for him – he is dead. So soft he became in his lingering, his skin translucent silk, his momentum slowly spent, in its place a sad knowing and some peace perhaps. Time slowed for him – but not for me. It slid through my fingers all my life like gold dust. Too sick myself to properly understand what was happening to Robert, to rationalise it, to find some resolution or to love him properly. We had so little time. Our great adventure – an insane and reckless ride, one that killed us in the end. And made us, of course, gave us so much, then took it all away. Quickly and cruelly. How very Shakespearian.

14

Letter to Robert Jnr in Melbourne. 26th April 1912

Mother is not at all well...
She is not happy here, as you know, and it would
be better all round if we lived in Melbourne.

Nineteen-hundred and twelve was the year our trajectory reached its zenith. It was the year we lost control of our fate, the year of the disaster, a year too far. It was the year of the *Titanic*; the year hubris met the accountants.

As the scale of the collapse at Balfour became clear we watched in dumb amazement as our future hung on the edge of ruin. It happened so quickly, so noiselessly. The days came and went and I could only hope that things would turn around, that eventually Robert would be proved right – Balfour was another Butte. But I knew it wasn't. I knew that we had lost £70,000. We had 100% of nothing and owed £40,000! Robert and Luke thought it only a matter of time before the mine came good but time had run out as far as I was concerned.

And as this began to unfold, Robert's contract came up yet again. The Company was anxious for him to sign on for another five years. I had agreed reluctantly to the last renewal, back in 1907. Now we had been

15 years in this benighted place and it was time for Bob to go to college. Robert was determined that he should do so back home. It was time to take our leave.

When Balfour came along it had made anything seem possible. We had hoped to segue into that project, freeing us to send Bob back to College in the USA and establish a bridgehead there for ourselves once Balfour was a going concern. Now we were faced with a frightening situation, where our capital was gone and all we had borrowed was at risk. Robert was our only possible saviour but it was clear that even if Balfour became viable, it would be years hence.

The Company offered Robert a General Manager's position, operating out of Melbourne. It made good sense. Mt Lyell now had operations at Port Kembla, Fremantle and Yarraville and was expanding further. He would maintain ultimate control of Queenstown, Balfour, Chester and the rest, but from a distance. It was tempting, as we both liked Melbourne and knew some fine people there. In fact I was deaf to all but the noise in my head another five years created – I was almost 50, dotage for a Stage. I had been gone 17 years. That it seemed the blink of an eye just made me more nervous. But it seemed now that we had no option but to accept, for the moment at least. If Balfour came good we would be on our way again.

So Robert signed on again, with the understanding he would segue into the Melbourne option in the next year or two, leaving Mr Murray to take over officially much of what he was already doing. Poor Russell served a long apprenticeship. Robert would take leave in the transition to go home for a holiday. It seemed better than we had a right to expect, given our circumstances.

But before the ink was dry the sky collapsed on Lyell. A fire's fumes at the North Lyell mine trapped an entire shift at the 700 and below. Forty-two men died, despite a rescue effort of Herculean proportions. Families lost fathers, sons, brothers and breadwinners. The community was shattered. It had survived fires and depressions and the most extreme elements and isolation but it's future now hung in the balance.

It was unthinkable that Robert should leave at such a moment.

The trauma was drawn out over months as the mine was flooded and sealed off. Many bodies were not retrieved and buried for an agonising age, the last three not until eight months later. Every funeral march, every bedecked funeral train and every rendition of Nearer My God reopened awful wounds. It seemed as though it would never end. There were recriminations: about safety, about grudges, about all manner of matters that would drag on and on for years. Scars like that never disappear for some folk, even with the passing of generations. They become a way of life.

Things that happen happen. Who can know what might have been? Forty-two dead men would weigh heavily on any man's conscience. A Company has no conscience but it has responsibility nonetheless, to its own, its kin. Death is with us always but 42 men unburied in the ground is too much for anyone to carry alone.

When they finally drained the mine and brought those poor souls up, they were perfectly preserved by the icy water. They found them huddled against the rough walls of the mine, deep in the earth's heart, clutching their crib or whatever personal relic that was close by in those dreadful last moments. Spectres glowing with pale admonishment, smooth as ivory in their coffins.

The long, sad walk to the cemetery behind the train, with the brass band playing all the way, became a ritual. Dead so long, so long unsung.

nearer my God to thee

That hymn echoed round the sad streets and bare hills of Queenstown ever after. You will hear it now, if you listen well enough.

nearer my God

So many lives changed forever, scattered by the wind of chance, but the mines went on. Men still went down into the damp heat and clinging dust, down into the dark and then out into the fog of sulphur and the whiff of brimstone. I thought the hurt and his strange shame would kill Robert – perhaps it did. The idea that the fire may have been deliberately set played on his mind – to him it was more insulting than the accusations of poor safety. Why would anyone feel the need to embarrass the Company and its men?

I saw no sense in assigning blame for such a catastrophe – would knowing how it started ease the pain? But Robert's was a mind that could not countenance coincidence. Everything is connected, there is always a pattern to be discerned, if you look hard enough. How did Thoreau put it? '*Some circumstantial evidence is very strong, as when you find a trout in the milk*'. That the fire occurred on the day the inspectors were to visit was a trout in the milk, as far as Robert was concerned. There were many who agreed and some who pointed.

Robert Stone's brother, St Clair, had been killed only a week before in a rock fall and he clearly blamed the Company. He was quite aggressive towards Mr Murray and his Caliban, Johnno Pearton, at the Inquiry. Murray had charge of the mines and Pearton was his foreman – a hard, unpleasant little man, inclined to settle trouble with his fists. Robert thought Murray too close to him but they made an effective partnership in the field.

Others pointed at Robert and the Company. The Inspector of Mines, Mr Curtain, considered the mine as safe as any in the land. The Union saw an opportunity to make inroads where they had been unable to before and saw conspiracy and neglect everywhere.

The Union had had Robert in their sights for years and now they thought they would take his creation from him. I'm sure that is how Robert saw it, although he would never admit such unseemly pride. He never begrudged any man a decent wage or fair conditions but he was too much of a philosopher to be a good manager and too American to understand the Unions. He was an enlightened despot, a remnant of another age. He had not a pragmatic bone in his head when it came to people, as Mother used to say. He was a dreamer, the most dangerous of men. The principle of separating the roles of management and Union was one principle he would never bend on, because it was logical '– *and there's an end on't'*.

I thought it all too dangerous. Forty-two dead men in a town the size of Queenstown is shattering enough. There was no room for recrimination. Mining towns are metaphors for the new world – capital, science, ambition and eternal transition. I once thought it exciting but now I find it tiresome. Communities thrive when they can trust in the future. Mining towns always struggle because all is flux: people, the landscape, the future and the past; nothing is safe, nothing means anything, except momentum.

I had had enough. Robert had signed a new contract with the understanding that he would take over operations of the Company's wider interests from a Melbourne base. Bob, Hadmar and Chet would all be at school in Melbourne and I could be close by. There was nothing to keep me in Queenstown any longer.

We were both lonely. Surrounded by activity and people but isolated from the sort of contact that nourishes the soul. It was not that there were no people of quality – far from it – but the nature of our position and the nature of the town meant contact was often awkward and trust at an intimate level hard to develop. Everything was in the context of the Company. We may as well have been in the Army. Robert was no longer a man, he was, like me, an institution.

I had no close friends. No-one I could be myself with. Mrs Driffield and Mrs Murray were fine women and neither one a fool, but we had little in common, save for babies and good works. Even then our different backgrounds and the Company structure had to be negotiated. In ignoring such things a loss is incurred that makes true friendship difficult. I grew resentful and I was already restless.

Then the North Lyell disaster changed everything – Robert felt that leaving would be seen as an admission of a guilt he neither felt nor deserved. Nothing was ever the same afterward. Not Robert, not the town, not the sky, not even the rain. The clouds pressed closer, the fog of yellow fumes hung lower and blotted out the light of optimism. The sun of capital had dimmed and it would never rise again for us. Robert stopped buying – even the Collection could not comfort him as it had before. The tide had turned against us. We were trapped. Comfortable enough, as long as we stayed, but no prisoner would swap freedom for a cosier cell.

We borrowed heavily to invest in Balfour and as the prospect of any return evaporated we were burdened with both debt and interest. We struggled for years without making much impression on it. Robert stopped collecting, we made ends meet, but it slowly became clear to me that no other position would ever pay Robert enough for us to live any sort of life and get clear. Our debt and Robert's salary held us hostage to the Company and Robert's hubris held us hostage to Mt Lyell. So I chose to go to Melbourne alone, at least until Robert's situation at Lyell and with the Company and the Royal Commission was resolved. I would be close by the boys and I had friends there. I would establish a base and Robert would come later. It was not America but neither was it Queenstown.

———

FAREWELL TO MRS STICHT

A LARGE GATHERING. A HANDSOME PRESENT

The Masonic Ball has never, if ever, looked prettier than it did on Tuesday night last. Its interior was most handsomely ornamental with flags, ferns, and shrubbery, and lots more that was pleasing to the eye, and the general aspect was extensively admired by the very large number that was assembled within. The occasion was a farewell evening given to Mrs Robt. Sticht by the Ministering Children's League, of which body she is general president in the Queenstown and Lyell district.

Mrs Sticht is leaving for Melbourne on Saturday next for an indefinite period, and therefore it was fitting that a farewell should be arranged. This was done by the committee of the M.C.L., Queenstown branch, of which Mrs H. Massey is president, and Mrs H. Faull secretary, with Mrs A. E. Lawson as treasurer.

At a suitable interval a presentation was made to Mrs Sticht of a very handsome silver rose bowl, mounted on an ebony stand, and as one admirer described it, it was both rich and pleasing in appearance...

Mrs Sticht, in reply, betrayed that she was deeply conscious of the compliment that had been paid her. She spoke in graceful words of the heartfelt appreciation and full recognition of all that the gathering and the beautiful gift represented. The feelings that possessed her could not be adequately conveyed, in language, and so her kind friends must accept her assurance that she would leave them with the most pleasant memories, which she would retain. She felt that she had played a very small part in the affairs of the Ministering Children's League, for she realised that the greater part of the work – the burden of the day, so to speak – had been borne by the officers and the members

of the committee who had shown love and zeal in their
work, which had brought about such successful results....

Again, she desired to thank them from her heart, for
their good wishes, and say that the night would be one that
would live in her memory. (Loud and prolonged applause).

TO HIS LAST REST

Mr James Robert Park, whose body was found at the
600ft level of the North Mount Lyell mine, was laid to
his last rest in the Queenstown Cemetery last Tuesday
evening. The funeral was a large one, and was attended
chiefly by members of the F.M.E.A., who were headed by
their new president, Mr M. Kean, and the vice-president,
Mr W. E. Treanor, with the secretary, Mr M. Cunningham;
also present, Mr Robt. Sticht general manager of the
Mount Lyell M & R Co; Mr B. Sawyer, the local superintendent; and Mr R. M. Murray, as well as other officials
of the company, attended. The service at the graveside
was conducted by Mr Heny Saw, Presbyterian mission-
ary at Linda, who after the service addressed a few
words of comfort and counsel to the relatives and those
at the graveside. The funeral arrangements were carried
out by the thorough manner demanded.

PERSONAL

It has come as painful news to a great many to read
yesterday that Mr Albert Gadd, who bad been suffering
from the effects of the carbon monoxide gas which he
inhaled during the plucky attempt he made to descend
the North Mount Lyell mine at the time of the disaster,
had found it again necessary to seek a change of climate
in order to regain his health. Only those most intimate
with him were aware that the first trip he had to the
North-West had not fully restored him, and that such is
the case is deeply regretted by a very wide circle of
friends, and their wish is that he will regain his old time
strength and vigor.

THE SHAKESPEARE CLUB
FAREWELL MRS STICHT

Among the members of the Shakespeare Club Thursday last was a most important date. On that day they had arranged a farewell to their President, Mrs Robt. C. Sticht, who took her departure last week for Melbourne, where she has taken up her residence for a little while to come, at least. The function took place at the residence of Mrs H. Massey, in McNamara street, and the assemblage was a large and representative one. The drawing room was nicely decorated, and conspicuous among the flowers were leaves of oak, this being a pretty recognition of one of the Christian names of Mrs Sticht. A programme of items had been arranged, these including a pianoforte duet by Mesdames Dean and Westbrook, as well as some glees that were selected as being part Shakespeare's 'Midsummer Nights Dream', from which readings were given by the assemblage. A pleasing diversion was afforded by a form of guessing competition, in which those present wore any emblem they conceived to be representative of any of the great author's works or characters, and some of these proved to be very cleverly thought out.

During the proceedings a presentation was made to Mrs Sticht of a set of souvenir spoons. The gift was handed over by Miss D'Arcy, who accompanied it with some remarks that were most appropriate to the occasion. She remarked on the fact that the Shakespeare Club had been founded by Mrs Sticht, and as its President she had taken the keenest interest in its welfare and progress. The Club had from its inception been a successful one, and its meeting had afforded many delightful afternoons to its members, and in bringing that about Mrs Sticht had played a most important part. That the members deeply regretted the departure of Mrs Sticht, and with it her absence from future gatherings of the club, went almost without saying, but at the same time they recognised the duty that Mrs Sticht had to fulfil towards her family, and she took with her the very best wishes of each and every member, who trusted to hear from her at intervals and to be made aware that the happiness which she deserved was being enjoyed.

In acknowledgement, Mrs Sticht spoke feelingly and showed that she deeply appreciated all that had been said on behalf of the members. She traced the history of the Club from its first meeting, and spoke of the pleasure its existence had given her, and the many lasting friends she had made as the outcome. The Club had been founded with a distinct object and that object it had achieved, thanks to the very hearty support that had been given her on all sides. Now that the time had come when she must sever her connection, she felt the parting keenly, but there would be many times across the waters when her mind would transport her to Queenstown, and once more she would in fancy be among those taking part in one of their pleasant gatherings.

She could not convey to them by words all that she inwardly felt, but she was conscious that those assembled there that afternoon would accept all that she had said as coming from her heart, and she would conclude by thanking them for their very nice gift, and if only half the good wishes they had extended to her were realised she would be perfectly content.

I liked Melbourne but a woman alone is a socially awkward animal. Couples are the rule, except for young men and women being assessed and matched. I would have liked to be part of Ivy Brookes' circle or Symes', or one something like. I wanted to be pushed and surprised. It should have been possible in Melbourne.

Those last years were something of a masquerade. We mixed with the patricians but we were living on air. Only momentum kept us in the game and when Robert died, the music stopped – we were exposed as frauds. Of course not many could have known, but I knew.

As a woman I could be pitied as a victim of my husband's recklessness, but in faith it was my fault as much as his. If I had been content to be content he would not have taken that risk. Like the Collection, Balfour was for me. He did it to make me happy but I had no intention of being happy here.

So perhaps it was not only Robert's hubris that trapped us – it was ours and our culture's. Maybe it was not our investment in Balfour that ruined us so much as our faith in progress.

I know I should not have resented him so much, but who else was there to blame? He was not alone in his loneliness and I was not sure I could last in Melbourne long without him. But we soon had a new plan, a wonderful plan. Robert negotiated a year's leave and we were going home, to say goodbye properly to Lizzie and Alice and my country.

I was thrilled and immediately set to planning our trip. I was busy in Melbourne and I was going home, if not for good then at least for a good while. I fancied we might yet find a position for Robert once we were there.

Then my world unravelled, even as I was gathering its threads together.

15

It is a curious truth that when two living friends part, they are, as it were, dead to each other until they meet again. Letters may be interchanged, but the present of one is not the presence of the other.

Roberts' Bay View Hotel
Burnie
24th November 1913

My Dear Mrs Millar, Miss Wissie

I was so pleased to receive your letter and heartily echo the wish that we might see each other before we go so far away. However we are coming back again next year – will be home in January 1915.

But the tragedy of it all is that dear Mrs Barndollar passed away at Long Beach California last July the 15th. I was very ill after receiving the news. The blow was indeed crushing – and after all these years we were planning to meet again in America, my own beloved land. God's ways are indeed mysterious. At first I could not be reconciled but time does possess healing power, and I try to look at the blessings with which I am surrounded – My husband and my three boys – and try earnestly not to feel sorry for myself.

M. O. S

The kettle bubbles and fidgets on the hob and we are cast in lamp-light. The westerly howls outside. The chimney does not draw well at the best of times, so a smoky haze imbues the amber glow. We chat of this and that but mostly we just listen to the world.

Bob comes through the front door and the creaking hinge announces him. The scimitar of the moon hangs over his shoulder like an omen.

I see a lily on thy brow

When the telegram came that took Lizzie from me, it cut my last tie to sweet childhood and my country and my kin. I felt much as I did when Old Ben kicked me across the stagehouse barn when I was eight. It knocked the wind out of me, just like that. It knocked me into a new and awful world. Dear, sweet, staunch Lizzie, taken even younger than Mama. I am now the oldest Stage, of twelve children, five wives and a father. I anticipate that 60 is beyond me though. Like Mama, I feel life sucking back across the shingles, on the ebb tide.

Elvin, Gilmon, Samuel and Nancy,
Mary, Abigail, Annette,
Napoleon, Emma, Charlie and Louise.
And Sarah. And Lizzie

These things cannot happen and yet I know that they do.

She should have died hereafter
there would have been a time for such a word

So many gone before. Mother could and would recite the host wait-ing anxiously for her in Heaven while she waited anxiously down here – but I know better. They are all just gone. Now I alone carry them into the future and that is only as far as I can see. Alone in all the world I carry their memory, all that remains of all those lives, all that living and dying. I carry that deadly burden forward into sure oblivion. My boys and Robert kept me going but I cannot carry them much further – I can't remember them forever. I'm so tired of carrying them all. Robert loved everything and everyone that I loved but without him I can no longer see a way. My catalogue of the dead is not so different from his catalogue of dead books – but I hold it in my heart, not on the dry pages of his notebooks.

every thing reminded me of those who 'had been and are not'

Lizzie had been ill from time to time – she used to get a blinding pain behind her eyes that only morphine eased – but she was not one to fuss about it and besides she had such a strong will and so much energy that we all thought of her as indestructible. We worried instead about George – his health was never robust. That is why they went home. A sad irony – he will outlive us all now. He has outlived Lizzie already by a decade and will most likely live another.

They said it was a stroke. She simply dropped down dead in the garden, like Uncle John Hogeland attending to his horses, over in Shelby County. It was quick, they say, as if that is some comfort. Would that it had taken six months. I might have seen her again. In truth we spent those last 8 years impossibly apart and I will never recover from their loss.

Come home! Come home!

When that telegram came I took to my bed. I could neither cry nor speak. When I arose I was a different person, once again: child, orphan, wife, mother – and now the last Stage. I fled back to Queenstown, with my tail between my legs.

Sans teeth, sans eyes, sans taste, sans everything

Robert to Mr Goode, 25th November 1913

*Our troubles at Lyell have apparently come to an end.
We have not found out who set the North Lyell Mine on fire, but the
union is pacific and quiet – even friendly! I am therefore utilizing the
opportunity to take a long cherished holiday to the USA, and will be
sailing with all the family, from Sydney on Jan 12th, by the
S.S. Niagara... The staff and townspeople gave us a splendid sendoff
and bon voyage. Things at Lyell are, of course, generally much the
same as ever, except the weather, which seems to be getting worse!*

Bowes Kelly knew the lie of the land and it suited the Company to
have Robert off the stage for a while as Murray rang the changes. That
many were changes Robert had advocated for a decade was a given but
irrelevant in the emotionally volatile atmosphere after the disaster. It
was Murray Robert had mentored for the task and Murray who had the
energy and ambition to carry it off.

ambition should be made of sterner stuff

He had baggage as well, of course, but he was one of them, not a
bookish Yankee.

So we went. Robert secured free passage on the *Niagara* through his
old friend, the owner of the Union line, Sir James Mills. He wrote to him
and begged a favour. I did not know until later that he had lowered
himself to that degree. He wanted to put things right with me but could
not see that by implicating me in that little embarrassment he made
things worse. I wanted only one thing, however, to go home, and it was
too far to swim. So I let that humiliation pass – it proved good practice
for the others to come. Of more concern to me – and a source of great
delight to Robert – was that his old friend Captain Morrisby of the *Grafton*
was now the Captain of the *Niagara*. I foresaw many a long re-telling of
that famous night at Hell's Gates as we crossed the wide ocean.

————

We left Sydney in midsummer and sailed off to midwinter in our homeland. Captain Morrisby managed to keep us afloat all the way to San Francisco and we maintained the conceit that Robert was considering positions at home. It was nonsense. No offer would come near his salary at Lyell and that, while very generous, was barely enough for us to survive and at the same time service our debt. But we longed to see home and we longed to get away from that dank valley, even for what seemed only a moment.

What we should have longed for was more time. I knew too well how fragile it all is. All gone – Napoleon, Mother, Lizzie, Charlie, Emma, Lizzie and all the rest, long gone and gone young. We needed the still time you sensed in that wild and inhuman bush along the Gordon. Time that is impervious to conceit. Burn and scar and hew it as you might – you will be gone one day like Ozymandias and the forest will close over your memorials like a scab.

I think that I was modern (how odd to talk of oneself so readily in the past tense). I had cause enough to know the fragility of existence; the perilous world of my parents was manifest but so was destiny. I was confident – of myself, America the world and the march of progress – the power of science and art and fine thoughts. Without reason. I am no longer so confident of those things. Progress seems a preposterous idea when so many millions die for nothing and science is an instrument of death. I see only danger and decay and the stench of that stupid war stays with me. To pass through little hamlets, here, on the other side of the world and see the roll call of lost sons and fathers and brothers – dead defending this little lost island from the ravages of Turks and Germans who could not find it on a map if their life depended on it. If North Lyell is a tragedy then what word do we give to this? How can anyone now believe in progress? Or intelligence? Or anything else?

The author of all things watches over me

I was 30 when I left home and turned 50 when I returned. When I finally went home there was no home to go to. Twenty years was a lifetime for most of my kin.

'tis the wink of an eye, 'tis the draught of a breath
From the blossom of health to the paleness of death

My best years were suddenly gone and hardly a soul was left at home to wonder at the return of the prodigal daughter. Twenty years on the dark side of the moon stood for nought. Three sons, a fortune won and lost – and not a soul could I find who knew or cared much.

You can see the ravages of time in the photographs, see my life disappear while I lived in limbo. In 1901 I am 36 and in my prime, more handsome than the perky 18-year-old in the photograph from Boston, on my way back to Vassar with Alice. A tomboy's eyes still. The photograph at 50, with Alice and George in California, shows a woman I do not recognise. Old before her time and a little lost, a little confused, despite her straight back and her head still held high as Mother taught me. I had realised it was too late, that the possibility of living any significant part of my life back home was gone. I was readjusting to that news and wondering what I might salvage from the wreckage.

I wonder what those who knew me at 20 would have made of me at 40, in my finery, in my pomp. Dining with Governors and Prime Ministers and reigning over our little realm, Robert's test tube. Turning a head or two still, even at 40, not that I could ever be seen to acknowledge such a thing and not to say that there were many. But I did – I know that some men found me attractive and a few found me very attractive. I was still young and handsome in my way. Vivacious, some might say; exotic, not something often said of girls from Edgar County. Forever the tomboy, Mother would say, looking for Charlie in me. I was intelligent and spoke my mind – not as often as I wished, mind – and I was adventurous and wealthy and often on my own. Men flirted with me – from a respectful

Lilley
PARIS PA[...]

distance, it is true. But they did flirt.

The light softens to a dull glow in the southern sky beyond Mt Frankland and the blue grows even more exquisite – a pale luminescence that holds my eye like a jewel and sings of a sadness more profound than my own small tragedy – universal sadness that beauty evokes because all beauty is ephemeral. At night above the smoke of Queenstown, the Southern Cross would remind me of how far from home I was. Even the night sky was alien. Here in Balfour the night sky is vast but I see no signs of home. I am still '*head downwards on the cross sticks of the world*'.

From San Francisco we made our way up the coast to George and Harry in Los Angeles and spent time up in Carmel with the Beardsleys. It was all very disorienting. I had a mission to fulfil though, and dear George Barndollar had waited for me.

I set out again across the Nation, across the Rockies and the great Prairie, to bury Lizzie's ashes with Papa and Mother and Charlie and little Emma, back in Paris, Illinois. The last Stage and George reprised that long, hot cortege of 27 years earlier, when he and Lizzie and I took Mother home. The winter landscape we steamed through this time bore no resemblance to that long-gone summer. It was a different country regardless of the weather. Towns had turned to cities and the prairie had turned to farmland. When Mama and Lizzie and Charlie and I first travelled west across the prairie we saw Indians and herds of buffalo from the train. Consigned to the dust of history now, like Lizzie and Charlie and Mama. I had my family with me, this time, though, and never loved them more. It was a pilgrimage – none of my sons had ever been to America, let alone Edgar County.

We fetched up in Paris and laid Lizzie to rest with her kin. There was only a handful of old friends to take note. They were mostly strangers to me by now, of course, but they were kind. A few had been there when we laid Mama to rest all those years ago. George was as staunch as ever, as was Robert, and our boys were strong and well-mannered and did Lizzie proud, though only Bob had known her. The trees in the new cemetery had grown old with the town but I was able to remember the exact spot I stood on the day we buried Papa. I had stood on that same spot when Emma and Charlie and Mother were sent to God. And I stood there again while George and Robert spoke of the world's loss and Lizzie's laugh.

I walked out of that cemetery with the weight of all those lives on my shoulders and the knowledge that when it came my turn there would be no kin to speak over me, save my boys. I showed Bob where to stand, just in case I make it home one day.

we came home through our north pasture and down through our old place – did not stop but crossed the creek

We took a buggy out to the old farm, just as Mama had done while I was at Vassar. To my surprise, it had aged better than I had. Good bones and love will do that for a house, if not always for a woman. We saw the remains of the old school and the bridge waiting to be washed away again and we sat beside Brouillettes Creek for the last time and watched the sunset over the prairie.

I had not been back to to Edgar County since Mother died – a quarter of a century. Longer than Rip Van Winkle slept – or played bowls in some tavern, most likely. The family graves at the cemetery had been tended, though not too often, and people seemed to remember me – but not as well or fondly as I would have liked. My memories of them were intense because they had been suspended in childhood. Their memory of me was part of a long continuum. I was a short episode, long since smelted down and processed. They were a little uneasy and I was a little disoriented. Why had I come back? I struggled to explain feelings I did not understand. The stories associated with every tree and fencepost were someone else's. Robert and the boys indulged me but I felt diminished.

We went on east to Chester and the Hazeltons and that was a happier time. I had not been up there since I came back from Europe in '89. It was coming on summer and it is beautiful country. Not a mine to be seen. I had continuity there, though the shadows of Lizzie's debt and death and the apostasy of cousin Anna still lingered in the autumn haze. It is so beautiful thereabouts, though; the orchards and forests seem in balance. There is a comforting sense of time's impassive passage. The Hazeltons were generous and kind in their New England way and I felt loved. God had smiled on me, it seemed to them. They did not know the price I was paying.

I sometimes wish they were not so dear to me

I was glad to get away. Europe was beckoning, though the talk of war made me nervous. Robert, as always, was sanguine. Reason would prevail over petty Balkan feuds. We travelled down to Washington, where we met the President. Robert was an admirer of Mr Wilson and thought him a great progressive, though I harboured doubts. A southern Presbyterian and the son of slave owners, he was weak on the Negro question and on women's suffrage, though he changed his attitude to the latter when he sniffed the wind of change. His wife Ellen was very ill when we were there and died not long afterwards, of a kidney. If the doctors could not save the President's wife I should not be surprised that they cannot save me.

Later Wilson turned on German immigrants, having joined the dogs of war. It was cynical. Robert was appalled but I was not surprised. Robert had an odd relationship with his Germanic roots and with German history. A child of Forty-eighters, he was fourteen and on his way to Germany with Johan, in 1871, when France and Prussia went to war. The swift rout that followed was the birth of Germany, they say. Robert and Johan had to scurry back across the Atlantic.

He finally got to Germany ten years later. He was up in Clausthal for three years, taking his Masters. Clausthal was the best Metallurgy school in the world, up in Goethe's beloved Hartz Mountains. Robert's soul was forged there, I think. It was his spiritual home and Goethe was his guide.

But Germany had not finished with him. We had crossed America and come to New York, ready and eager to take ship to Europe for the boys' Grand Tour. I had waited 25 years, Robert 30. It was the first week of August, 1914. Once again war intervened.

The outbreak of war changed everything. Copper prices and labour were bound to be affected and Robert saw that the company needed to plan for the effects. He was energised by the challenge. So he sailed back to Lyell, secretly pleased I think, and I had my time in the sun. In California I lived a year in the shoes of my lost life.

everyone is aggressively young and blooming

Robert's plan for Bob to go to MIT fell through because MIT was shifting from Boston up to Cambridge. It was all too difficult but I was not unhappy. We decided on Throop College of Technology in Pasadena and took a bungalow around the corner, in South Marengo Avenue, with the mountains at our back and the Pacific at our feet. George and Harry were a walk away and dear Alice and George were up the coast at Carmel, not across the world. I went to concerts and galleries and met up with those Wellman girls again and stayed at their big house at Fruitvale. There were plays and galleries and there was sunshine. It hardly ever rained. I felt myself emerging from a long hibernation.

We had many visits with George and Harry. The boys heard all the stories from the old days back in Pueblo, some of them true. They heard about Charlie and Lizzie and Mama, about the day the outhouse burned

down and The Adventure of the Cat Burglar. The visit of Thomas Beecher was recounted in pompous detail and, of course, they heard all about the first day Robert Carl Sticht came to call on me on his own. He was as stiff as a board – knocked over a vase! I never thought to see him again but he was not a quitter.

I was drenched in Californian sun. For the first time in what seemed like ages I was not unhappy. I missed Robert but it would not have been the same had he been there. It was my time. It was so different from our life in Tasmania. The boys were at school but not days away, across Bass Strait. We did everything together. We went on day trips to the beach and to the theatres and the cinema – what a revelation! Bob made friends at Throop, he was considered quite exotic. Most folk had never even heard of Tasmania. His young friend Frank Capra had a car and took us several times for drives along the coast.

We visited with George on his birthday. It was a sad occasion but we assumed the mantle of serenity that is the pretence of old age. It is acceptance. George is a man of simple tastes and few words. On my birthday he gave me Charlie's cufflinks, the ones mother gave him back in Pueblo, on his 35th birthday. In 1883, when I was off at Vassar and the world was at my dainty feet.

He had never worn them, for fear of losing them and invoking Mother's wrath from the beyond. They will go to Hadmar, I think, Charlie's brother in spirit.

It was a fine and simple gesture, befitting one of nature's gentlemen. Robert missed him when he left Penghana and would have had him back at any time. He wrote to George much later, to tell him he could finish his days with us in Queenstown, if he wished. How ironic – he will outlive us all.

Queenstown, Tasmania
6th May 1915

Dear Mr Miller

Your letter of the 1st inst conveying the sad announcement of the death of your dear wife, our former beloved "Miss Wissie," has given me pain, and I am sure will also sadden Mrs Sticht. I have written her at once. Her address is 547 Marengo Avenue, Pasadena, California, U.S.A. She remained behind for a few months on account of the children. Robert, Mrs Millar's protege, will be nineteen this year, and it has been arranged that he goes to College in Boston, so his mother naturally wants to stay near him as long as possible. Robert also will be sorry to hear the news of the passing away of one he was much attached to.

To you, dear Mr Millar, I can only offer a handshake of sympathy in silence. You have lost your greatest treasure in life, and we can not understand why these things should be. Fortunate you have little Marion left as a legacy from your loved one, so you are not alone. We will all cherish "Miss Wissie's" memory in love and kindness as long as we live.

Please accept my most heartfelt sympathy, and believe me,

Sincerely yours,

Robt Sticht.

———

Miss Westmoreland, dear Missie Wissie, died while we were away. Bob's beloved nanny and teacher. I got to see her little Marion but once, when I was down to Hobart for yet another session with the doctors. I was not well but it did my heart good to see how happy Wissie was and how bonny was her little Marion. She had the fiercest loyalty to us. I have a photo of her and Lizzie with me and Bob and George, heading up to the Haulage on the little company carriage. Photographs are so cruel.

16

Bob drove me out to Mt Hazelton in the dray today, south along the white quartz track cut into the black peat. At first the carriage jarred me so, I thought I would disgrace myself but I did not. I am a Stage. We do not weaken. Once we left the cobbled road down the ridge, the soft peat of the trail south seemed cushioned and the burning in my insides abated for a while. I enjoyed myself.

my eyes over flowed with tears a good part of the way

It was a huge, blue day and the sky was vast and deep. I am from big sky country. High, dry air, an infinity of blue. The giddy feeling that you could fall upwards into the sky. I felt at home. There was something in me that was young again; just for a few moments, but it was good.

We looked out over that wind-smacked coast – strangely quiet today – and I thought of myself sailing down that coast on the *Grafton* a quarter of a century ago, to Hells Gates and the rest of my life, and in my mind's eye I looked back from out there and saw myself, a broken old woman supported by her son, staring out to sea from a bare mountain in the wilderness. Was there a moment between those two that I would choose for eternity?

Bob understands, I think. He is a good man. I spent so much time worrying about what would become of him that I didn't notice him become a man. It is a comfort to ride in sunshine along an old track in a godforsaken corner of the globe with someone that you trust implicitly, no other human for miles and nothing to do but feel the high sun on the back of your neck, gaze at the broad sweep of the sky and contemplate the mystery of creation and what to have for tea.

Bob, like his father, sees geology.

do you remember the flags which floated from the top of one of the highest bluffs on the right going to the canyon? Well the staff is still there but the flag has been blown away

I was always torn between the comforts of culture and the excitement of the new. Between home and adventure, kin and strangers, learning and leisure. It is what drew Robert to Goethe – balance is what fulfils existence.

Even after Robert Jr was born I did not want to change. I had good people and that helped: Lizzie was a much better mother than I – what irony. Poor Lizzie, who wanted but could never carry children, and her sister, ambivalent but fertile as bottom land and sturdy as a cow, who dropped three perfectly healthy boys in the wilderness, the last at 43, without the slightest problem.

I grew to love them of course, doted on them, but at the beginning, in those first years in the wilderness, I could not help but resent the restrictions they placed on me. By the time Chester came along I was tamed, though. You can see it in the photos – the tomboy segues into the matron, the eyes have learned fear. I have become a mother.

I want to teach my boys that the greatest gift is the ability to know when you are happy. It all goes so quickly and you are always a step behind where you think you want to be.

I think we were happy at times – and knew it and stopped looking a step ahead and just looked around at where we were and what we were doing and how amazing it all was and how much all these decent people liked us. Not loved; you can't love the exotic the way you love kin. But there was a genuine and mutual sense of loyalty, an understanding of our determination to make a better world. There was so much to do, all the time, so much happening, but we always longed for something more, always saw the potential, never appreciated what just was. Or perhaps it was only me that felt that. Perhaps that was what divided us – perhaps Lyell was the only home he wanted?

It is American, I think, to look at what is and see what might be. We find a way or make it. But out here confidence is drained from all but the hardiest and hardest. This is the end of the world. Pride here is mostly a sad reflection of your insecurity.

we had very pleasant calls – more so than usual

It is so quiet here in the old ghost town. The few souls scattered around the desolate hill pass the time of day if encountered but I venture outside rarely and they do not visit. Mama would have been so terribly bored but I find myself light-headed with relief – free of being Mrs Sticht, free of any future and free of my past. It is vertiginous. If I feel this well tomorrow I might walk down to the river.

found everyone at home we called upon and very entertaining

I sleep only fitfully. I bleed in the night and wake to stabbing pain. I lie for hours listening to the busy night. I seldom rise before late morning – I drowse and watch the light wax through the small window, its four squares dividing the sky into a storybook.

Ethel makes my pancakes and chatters, but not too much. She is not demanding company though it might be nice to have some.

I felt well enough to walk down to the cemetery today. Some irony in that. A few hundred yards, a gentle slope down past the old hotel. I had a mind to go to the river but I would have had to be carried back. How I long for just one day when I could be my old, strong, restless self. To go to the river under my own steam and bounce across the footbridge – it's not much to ask.

Instead I tottered around the cemetery. I must have looked as though I was looking for a vacancy. It is a pretty spot above the Frankland, looking out to the north across Looney's Flat. Bracken and saplings are already taking over, as they are the rest of the dead town. There are only a few headstones. The poor, the young and the frail claimed by the fever in 1912, are marked only by little brackened mounds and kerosene-tin markers, rusting away. The painted names are already gone but some live on, their names and dates painstakingly punched into the tin with a nail. I am moved by them. There is more dignity, more history in those nail holes than in flamboyant marble. They will not last much longer, though. There are no families left to tend the graves. Everywhere we walk on bones.

we went to that high bluff just a little south and west of the cemetery

Some died at Balfour but most were killed by it. They are scattered down the slope in no apparent order, most of them victims of the cholera, many of them children. The groundwater drawn from the well was contaminated by the stables or by run-off from the toilets or both. Cholera takes the weak quickly, children and the old especially. It took the doctor early, which did not help things. Here is his stone, poor man:

Dr H. Wadleton

12 June 1912.

Aged 30

He had not been here long – a few weeks only. At thirty he had not the years to have been anywhere long, I guess. But what story is ignored by that paltry epitaph? It is a strange thing to be a doctor, I imagine. The very word is so imbued with hope it is religion. We want miracles but get humanity, if we are lucky. I have been poked and prodded and invaded, opened up, stitched up, lied to and comforted by so many of them I have lost count. They mostly meant well.

There are a few substantial stones, Ozymandias in the bush. Poor Jim Williamson rests under a slab Alma had brought all the way across the water from St Kilda. It is both out of place and unsettling in this profusion of decay and growth - but the sentiment is a fine one:

Jim

Goodnight love

Nay the night is ill

that parts we two

Alma

Ill indeed the night that parted me from Robert. Alone up there in Launceston, so far from home; just we five and our thoughts and our meaningless unspoken goodbyes. He was a true Stoic to the end.

tell them I am holding my own

I would prefer, in retrospect, that the boys had not been there. Dying is an unedifying spectacle. I watched my Mother drown in her own blood. Robert died bravely but it was barely him by then. No funeral, no fuss. It is over – let it be.

his body will be taken to Melbourne for burial

One second he was here and the next he was gone and my world collapsed. Knowing it will happen is no preparation for the shock. The fear. There is no metaphor that serves, no words or thoughts that soothe. Perhaps we invested too much in each other. The price had always to be paid.

———

When they told us he was dying it was like staring into the blackest pit. Thought and feeling disappeared; all was concentrated for a short while on existence. There was neither good nor bad. I said to him that he would never die so long as I drew breath and saw my own mortality reflected in his eyes. He knew that I was not much longer for this world but he loved me so much, we had been through so much and we had believed so much that he acquiesced in the little lie of my survival. My Love.

she tosses her creatures out of nothingness, and tells them not whence
they came, nor whither they go. It is their business to run,
she knows the road

In those long, last Launceston days, he would talk when he had the strength, tell me what to do when he was gone and I would sit staring into the space between his words, searching for a different meaning, a code, a burning bush – some sign that this was not reality but a nightmare.

I felt a tear roll so slowly down my cheek – a glacier of silent sorrow, but I could not feel the pain from which it sprang. I can feel it still, that single tear, the faint tickle of its path down my old face, I can see the wall of the room, the clock that was five minutes slow, I can smell the bleach, hear the silent sound of fear which fills those sterile corridors and rooms – and now I feel the pain of loss as well.

golden boys and girls all must as chimney sweepers come to dust

There were earth tremors in Launceston and Bass Strait during that last week of his life. A portent it was difficult to ignore. Robert thought it wonderful, of course, lectured us on the geology of Bass Strait and tried to explain away the growing sense of awe and loneliness that suffused me through those weeks. But I was unconvinced. The deaths of great men are accompanied by great events. The natural world was saying goodbye to him. I have no doubt of it at all.

Bob took his father across Bass Strait to Melbourne, to Springvale, the only place we can be cremated. I was too ill to undertake yet another long cortege. It will be my destination soon enough. We had settled on cremation long before. The fuss about it amused us. Some argue that the soul cannot survive the flames. Hard lines for all those saints martyred at the stake.

No funeral, no service. He lived and died a Scientific Agnostic, would brook no religion in his life nor sentiment at his passing. There was some discomfort at the fire, I do not doubt, but as Reverend Robinson said, the world would be a finer place if more Christians lived as honestly and kindly and as well. I'm not sure many understood the symbolism of the furnace but it seemed a perfect end to me. His whole life was driven by fire and flux. He is transformed now. Better that than to *lie in cold obstruction and to rot*. What becomes of our ashes I do not care much. That matters only for the survivors. Bob has charge of it. If I cannot be with my kin in Edgar County I would prefer to be scattered to the wind and blown about the globe – some part of me might find its way to Illinois. But Bob is too prosaic for such a gesture. He will keep us close by, I suspect.

the tops of the high ones were white and glistened in the sun

Young men and girls on a weekend excursion crowded the train as we left Western Junction for the long, disjointed journey back to Queenstown, to a house we did not own and must therefore quit, in the midst of our grief.

Penghana was built and paid for by the Company. It is the General Manager's house and the General Manager was dead. Mr Murray would be moving up the hill. I was suddenly in debt, homeless and mortally ill.

Poor old Bill Murray is here in the cemetery too, under a slab so heavy it is already buckling. Marble is a fluid. Bill may have held the gun to his poor old head and pulled the trigger but surely Balfour loaded it. It all seems so long ago, Bill. I wonder would you still be propping up a bar somewhere in Zeehan or in Burnie if Robert had not listened to your story of a bonanza in the north-west? If only he had not been so naïve, such an easy touch for almost every chancer that had the nerve to front him. He could be hard with Company money when he had to be, but had no idea how to look after his own. It slipped through his fingers like mercury. Seventy thousand pounds we put into this place. Now it is young Bob's job to tidy up the mess and move on. We are nearly broken but there should be enough from the Collection and what we have put aside to get Bob through the raising of his brothers.

you can shut your eyes and imagine them all

Now the light fades and the air grows cold and still. It is the hiatus between acts. The flats are dragged away. I can hear the brown river tumbling through the rocks down by the old footbridge. I should like to walk down there again. A lovely spot, surrounded by myrtle forest and with a little bridge the children used to dive from in summer. The same children now buried back up along the hill. Perhaps I will be strong enough tomorrow, or later.

it was the longest walk I have ever taken

I struggle back up along the track, past the old hotel, leaning to rest on my stick every ten yards, bent like a knife. I have gone too far and flirted too long with my fancies. The tiredness in my limbs makes each step a business. My joints ache and my lungs burn as though I were climbing a mountain – and I have climbed many without a thought. How odd to be this tottering old lady. Yesterday I was a young woman who liked nothing better than the wind and sun in her face and needed nothing more from life than a hill to climb and a view of somewhere else. Now, if I fall down, I will have to crawl home.

we found some sweet fragrant flowers

The old cobbles are awkward on the road past the pub but I manage, soaked with perspiration now and late; and then I am on the slope down past the old Balfour and I can see the light set early in the shack and Bob waiting a little anxiously on the step. He smiles like a man as I come near. He remembers me and has been good enough to let me be.

Later, in the lamplight, I go through my little library and find it. Shelley, as I thought:

> *'Good-night?' No, love! The night is ill*
> *Which severs those it should unite;*
> *Let us remain together still, –*
> *Then it will be good night.*

I read it through several times, listening to the cadence, feeling it in my fingers, until the words begin to lose their meaning and become notes that I could play. I think of Robert. I feel his presence and miss it simultaneously. I miss the curve of his short, strong body round mine; a cave, a universe. I think of our grand bedroom at Penghana with its feudal gaze over the town and I wish we had spent more time together in a bare-walled shack like this, reading poetry by lamplight, with no distraction but the state of the fire. It all went so quickly. We rose too quickly and at the end were caught in a quiet avalanche. There was no escape, no time to think. And towards the end an endless round of trains and doctors and hospitals and dwindling, desperate hope fighting against philosophy.

I wonder what chain of circumstance brought Jim and Alma to this place? What story lies behind that grandly futile memorial? I remember them, faintly. I met so many people. But not many who could so adroitly misquote Shelley. I wonder what became of Alma? Where is she tonight? Is she still alive? Does she sit by a fire somewhere tonight reading Shelley?

her book a churchyard tomb

I close my book and slowly make my way to my little bed. How can I call the lone night good?

I will read The Tempest today. I have it here with me in a box of old friends I could not do without. It is the one Shakespeare I've avoided now for years – too close to the bone – shipwrecked as I am on this wild coast. Miranda gone to seed. What would have become of her had she not been rescued? If Prospero had proved fallible? If Caliban was truth? Would she have grown old and frail and useless?

He's tired as well, in that last play. You can feel it. Untidy and promiscuous. Winking at us in the pits; blowing us a long goodbye kiss. Showing off just enough for us to feel the sting of loss.

I'll not see Shakespeare again – not even a brave little effort such as those we undertook up in Penghana's roof. What fun they were, what a strange and magical venue it was. The words rolled impressively around the room, bouncing off the iron roof. When it rained, as it usually did, you had to shout, which spoiled the effect of many passages! But it was always a child's secret world, a place where anything could be imagined – and was. It was my idea and though some thought me foolish, it did work.

I estimate we spread The Bard further from its source than anyone previously. It was a true joy, even if there were many times I was glad we were on the other side of the world, beyond witness. There is no substitute for the sound of Shakespeare, however, even when those sounds fall like so much gravel from the mouths of happy fools such as we were, peeping out over the lights of Queenstown through the little windows.

As I disappear I seem to become heavier. I am slow and am learning to appreciate what is at hand rather than fret about what is over the horizon. To my surprise I find that there is much pleasure in stillness. Sitting in the sun, birds flitting about like an arpeggio, wind stirring up the steepled treetops. If I close my eyes the wind carries me to the distant fringe of things forgotten – a life that now exists only in some recess of my mind. I close my eyes and my mind's eye opens on the past.

After Balfour and the deaths of those poor men at North Lyell and the carnage of the war – the spectacle of his beloved Germany gone mad – Robert was driven into his studies and his study. Like Prospero he neglected worldly ends.

my library is dukedom enough

He was a man of incurable optimism and energy but unworldly in his bookish way. His struggle was to make philosophy real. He loved mankind but was never comfortable in their company. His greatest and fatal gift was his naïvety.

There is some sun still, and shelter from the southerly on what passes for a front porch. Higher up, clouds drive in from the west and form a turmoiled sky. The birds are ominously quiet and only the occasional thump of a wallaby passing by disturbs the evening calm.

As I watch the the wind suddenly springs up from the west and gathers strength as it drives the clouds inshore. Still some sun bathes the hilltop from the west, blessed light falling on me through the whipping trees but I grow colder and the heaviness comes on me again. I might sleep, like Miranda, though 'tis not a good dullness; 'tis defeat.

I would have preferred that my kin had not all gone so early, that something of mother was left to watch over my boys. They are good, intelligent boys, full of energy and wonder. They know what is about to happen. They have watched me wither and tire. The tiredness is the worst part of dying. I wish I could be my old self just once more, for a day, to have that energy and spirit and to have an adventure again with my young men. But I can barely raise the energy to walk to the fence.

I have talked long with Bob. Such a load now falls to him. Head of the family at 28, with two brothers to usher into manhood. But he is very strong and has already achieved so much. I see Napoleon in him some-times but mostly Johan. He has his father's intellect, of course, but he is easier with others. He is more Australian than the rest of us. To see him galloping around the oval playing their strange football, covered in mud and sweat, is a revelation. One his father did not experience, unfortunately. All sport was frivolous. To put oneself at risk of injury in such a pursuit was unthinkable. What was there to be learned? I am afraid that, much as I loved him, Robert was sometimes an awful prig.

I hope we have left Bob better prepared in character than we have in capital. There will be enough to see his brothers through their education but little more.

Mt Frankland and the sinuous hills are sleek curves carved against a Belle Dame winter sky: pale and cold and uncaring of our little lives. Another wallaby galumphs across the wasteland that once was garden – a broken fence, a creaking gate, blackberries and the strappy leaves of flowers gone feral. There are some tree ferns across the track and the pine trees alongside, but the rest of the little plateau is a battleground of broken trees, shattered shacks and decaying dreams.

I was a daydreamer when I was a child. Incorrigible, Aunt Mary said to me once. I had to look it up in Mama's giant dictionary and even then I was not sure whether it was an insult or a compliment. Some days I'd stand out in father's fields, on the vast, skybound plain and stare at the sun until it became a disc. I'd try to imagine what there would be if there was nothing. No Universe. No thing. In what would that nothingness exist? How can there be nothing if there's no thing? I would experience a slightly dizzy calm, a vertigo. Nothing was something I could neither understand nor imagine – how could that be?

I feel distant and relaxed this evening. After the mutton and potatoes and some greens from Mrs Mitchell's garden, we sit around the old tin fireplace and Bob reads to us again. It is pleasant.

If I could survive a few more years and have my health I could tell this story properly.

the story of my life and the particular accidents gone by

The journey Robert promised me back in Colorado was a fusion of art and science – philosophy. It was the expression of everything he believed in and everything I wanted for him. We would thumb our noses at fate and make our own way in the world. We are Americans. We can do. I was 30 and probably stuck in Pueblo for the rest of my life. Robert was 36 and at the height of his powers. What else would we do? How sad it would be to go through life and have never thrown your head back and your hat in the air.

In the end nothing matters much. I have my three fine boys and I lay me down with a will – not the will we would have wished of course, but we have furnished these boys with good minds and manners and there will be enough to see them through their education. It is my greatest sorrow that I will not see them grow into the world. And that they never knew Napoleon and Sarah.

when every third thought will be my grave

A star-dogged moon tonight. Something evil this way comes. Robert would know what star it is, of course, as if naming it explained or made prosaic its stark presence by the incandescent moon. It is a form of nervousness, this obsession with taxonomy, the drive to catalogue and list. It certainly became an obsession with Robert when he saw the writing on the wall.

> *Elvin, Gilmon, Samuel and Nancy,*
> *Mary, Abigail, Annette,*
> *Napoleon, Emma, Charlie and Louise.*

Robert's catalogue was his version of Mother's roll call of the dead. Both lists attempted to smelt high-grade meaning from low-grade ore – the chaos of existence. Both assumed the righteous power of education and self-discipline. They both believed that every person has a duty to make the best of themselves, to find their rightful place in the scheme of things, like atoms. They may have been at odds on the matter of religion but their personal trinity was the same: progress, history and work. They had faith that struggle would be its own reward. And when so much was taken from them, and so many, neither of them ever struggled to reconcile that with their belief. Not like me. Lizzie's death was the tipping point for me. After that I saw religion in purely social terms – it is a glue.

And that was just kin. The supplementary list included many I never knew. The four dead wives of Napoleon and their six dead children. Young men from Chester and Edgar County, slain like cattle in the war. There is in Sarah's list an unspoken acknowledgement of its symbolism, its place in the list of lists. It is an act of defiance in the face of annihilation – this small group, these frail people; I say they matter to me, so they matter.

Robert's catalogue was the same – an act of defiance in the face of chaos. This is what I say matters, so it does. I held these things in my hands. I needed nothing more.

Mother was dying for most of her life – she was genuinely surprised to find herself still here after so many passed before. But her list was also her rock, her stand against chaos.

then the forms of the departed
enter at the open door;
the beloved, the true hearted,
come to visit me once more

She could not countenance the idea that all that pain and suffering was arbitrary, Robert took it as a given.

It all passes so quickly. Nothing dramatic. There are no crescendos, no cadenzas and no time for codas. No one is listening by then. One note segues into another and that note into another still and soon you have a song, or a symphony if you have the stamina and luck. But you notice little in the transition – you construct form as you construct a life – in retrospect.

so, insensibly almost, year after year has glided by, and we are still here

Perhaps the living is between the notes – or in the left hand. I was always listening to the left hand and I became a left hand, I guess. In the background, underneath, not noticed unless it isn't there. Sometimes the left hand leaps across, as in that impossible Beethoven piece, but such flamboyant gestures cannot be sustained without descending into chaos. I could not make a life from gesture. Not once I had children. Not on my own. Not without Lizzie.

What am I, I wonder? A song or an opera? An opera with an act missing, I think – we've come too abruptly to the end – too much seems left unresolved, too many things left undone, too many pretty tunes started but not finished. I still feel like an overture. Our peaceful denouement was taken from us with violence. We just lived flat out and died, is the truth of it. It would make a fine epitaph.

good bye little one

Robert always had two wives: his mind and me. I put up a good fight until the boys came along and Lizzie left and Balfour went bust and we did not go home. I had to fight on too many fronts and I was lost. Lost to Robert. Lost to the Collection. It was our collection once but with time I could not keep up and that went the way of my music. There was never time nor solitude enough to stay in touch and the longer you lose touch the more painful it is to regain. You demand more of yourself than a beginner and every disappointment stings more sharply.

I did not have Robert's capacity for work, nor did I envy it. It was unnatural and depended on the work of others a bit too much for my

New England roots. Of course to him it was never really work, it was the labour of love and always big. He never concerned himself with the daily run of domestic things. He was quite unworldly. Even when he cleaned the Collection it was a ritual, a pleasure he reserved for us and himself, though in truth the boys and I were less than enthusiastic and encouraged him to tackle the task when we were away.

As the boys grew and moved away to school in Melbourne my love lost focus and my fear for them intensified. With Lizzie here I had some sense of my place in the larger world. With her gone I was one of mother's lost atoms.

O Mallie I am so glad that you are well and that you have a wish to do and be something in the world. All of this great big world is made up of atoms like you and me – and if these atoms fit in the places assigned them – all is well – but if they rub and jostle and wear out all the others near them, then there is a vacuum and a sense of unsoundness in society, and a great want is felt.

A want greater and sadder than a mother-want filled me when Lizzie died. I still longed to go home but now I had no home to go to.

my sister, who walks about my imagination like a ghost

It is much cooler today. Autumn. A lovely word and Fall would be redundant here, where no leaves fall. The sun struggles through watery cloud in the east. The cloud will burn off soon enough. I will go outside and read a little if the wind does not get up. If I get up.

Ethel makes my pancakes and I gather myself together and rise and totter out from behind my curtain, making my entrance like a ghost in some dreadful play. Ethel has fetched water in and it is heating it on the old stove. The warmth is welcome this morning. The night was cold and there is a heavy dew. Last night's stillness is stirring into something dark. The wind billows and the old shack shrugs and settles like a boat.

Somewhere down along the gully a sheet of iron flaps in the wind like a broken crow.

Ethel's coffee is wretched as ever but it matters little as she has long since mastered the pancakes. A dear girl, quick but not so bright as to bring trouble on herself. Practical and loyal. We are lucky to have her – there are not many girls who would willingly subject themselves to a ghost town and a dying woman. She is determined – even ambitious, and in her prime. I like that. I wonder what will become of her?

I was a young woman in my prime when I left home and an old woman well past it when I went back. Between those two journeys the world I left grew like a colt who knows only two things – confidence and reckless speed.

I grew old imperceptibly but too quickly. I inhaled too much that was foreign. I learned different ways, different attitudes but I never really felt at home with them. They were things mostly thrust aside as tiresome back home. Back there in 1915, in California, I was astonished by the energy and confidence. At first. Then I began to see that Lizzie had been correct. Everyone seemed young. I had been left behind, grown old without knowing it; I had become irrelevant. I had consigned myself to the outer darkness and it was clearly too late to return to the light.

thrown on this savage shore, far, far from home

And as I came to feel detached from the wide world my own world fell apart; when Robert began to ail and withdrew into the Collection it became obvious that we would never escape. I began to see my life as a *Wunderkammer*. The people in it, the ties and memories and threads, were specimens kept in an attempt to create meaning where none exists. Tolstoy said something about fatalism being the only way for us to explain senseless history. I understand him perfectly now.

every thing reminded me of those who 'had been and are not'

17

I was drawn to this bleak and battered coast. The smell of salt and sea-
weed seemed altogether preferable to the corrosive stench of sulphur.
I loved Macquarie Heads and Henty Beach and Marrawah and all those
wild, windswept beaches. In early summer the muttonbirds swarm in
one long, dark cloud along the coast, up to their Bass Strait nesting
grounds, filling the sky for hours; an astonishing thing to see. I would
often stare out into the wind, west across the ocean, knowing that
thousands of miles of wind and waves were all that stood between me
and South America. From Argentina you could walk to Illinois, if you had
a mind to. And I sometimes thought I had a mind to.

Twenty-seven years after I embarked on my adventure I am stateless,
in decay. This is not my country, these are not my people. I feel no visceral
connection with the landscape or the weather. Dramatic and beautiful
though both undoubtedly are, the novelty wore off years ago. They do
not resound in me, or strike a note of childhood wonder. I floated
through my life here, on a tide I could not stem, anchored by Robert and

my sons against the winds of circumstance, distracted by flattery and good works and a sense of moral righteousness but empty of spirit, once the adventure became a life.

They tell me that when the forlorn remnants of the original Tasmanians were taken to Flinders Island, cast away from mind and care in that wild Strait, they would gather on the southern shore to gaze across the water at the distant blue mountains of their home and weep. I could not see the Rockies or the Great Prairie from Macquarie Heads but I felt the shadow of my home and wept for my lost country and lost people.

the unplumbed salt, estranging sea

The weather is building to something again this afternoon. Dark, rain-heavy clouds are rolling in from the north-west. The birds are skittish, the crickets' friction is building to a constant thrum. Some mad bird screeches and cackles like Lear's Fool in the trees over yonder. It is the last day of autumn.

When I first came to this island it was autumn and I had come from spring. I carried a way of life with me and a sense of destiny – worn down over time, like these old mountains. Like little Mt Hazelton – who can say how high and mighty it once was, this weathered fragment? How appropriate that it will be the only trace left of me and mine on this harsh coast, whereon I spent half my life. How appropriate that no-one will understand the connection. There is a Marionoak Creek over east of here, near Rosebery, but that little joke will surely be forgotten soon.

the clock just struck five and Lizzie has not yet got home

If I were home there would be kin to note my passing and attend to it. It would be their duty and their privilege. There would be among them some understanding of who I was, whence I came, where I stood and what I stood for in the world: they would know what I meant, even if they did not agree.

But here I have only sons and brief acquaintances, most of them embarrassed by my fall if they think of me at all. I have no context, only one that has been shaped for me, as a play is for an actress. I play the part but I no longer know the character I portray.

So at the end of 1915 I came back from California to Lyell and Penghana. Why?

Because I loved him? Because we started this adventure together and it was dishonourable not to finish it together? Because I had nowhere else to go? Because after a year I realised I fitted no better back there than I fitted back here? Because we understood each other?

I came back to stay. Staying imposes a pattern on living that differentiates it from the life of the wanderer. The idea that I could rejoin the old narrative after my long absence was revealed as childish fantasy. Time progresses at different rates for those who travel and those who stay.

how much happier that man is
who believes his native town to be the world

All my life I wanted to go home, yet there came a point in that happy time back in California when I realised I would always be an outsider. I had not paid the price demanded to belong. Not anywhere. I would have to be content with the ephemeral community of mind and with the context of our rootless family. We wanderers.

What if we had gone to Melbourne when that was offered? It was all so complicated – what if North Lyell had never happened and Lizzie hadn't died and we had gone down that more gentle path? I would have been less unhappy there. Murray was ready to take over. Robert had groomed him as his replacement for years and though they often rubbed each other the wrong way, Robert typically saw only his good qualities and groomed him as his obvious successor.

There is much to admire about Mr Murray, though he was difficult to like. I will say he understood Robert better than most, yet he was always of his people. He inhabited difficult terrain for many years with grace and at the end was kind and honourable with me. He had a rough grace, I should say.

Perhaps he understood me – or my position. We were not dissimilar in our circumstance, in thrall to Prospero. There was empathy in his eye as well as ambition.

Murray was a clever man but had no philosophy. He had no understanding of where he stood in relation to the wider world, perhaps because he had little experience of it. It seemed to Robert that he understood neither his potential nor his responsibilities beyond the company and the town.

Murray affected to be one of the men, played so many sides off against each other that he must have been giddy – which would explain his dancing. The Australian versus the Yankee, the worker versus management, the coming man versus the old man – he played all those games fairly skilfully, but time was always his enemy. And beneath his 'common touch' he was always the hardest in pursuit of the owners' aims, because he was ambitious. A lean and hungry man, all the while soaking up everything Robert could and did give him. Because Robert knew no other way, believed in knowledge and its power – its spiritual force, the *Bildung*. What an opportunity Murray was given, to learn from the master. There were many abroad who would have given almost anything for that chance and Murray had it for free.

When he finally got what he was after he acted like a gentleman, with grace and generosity. I think he liked to have me at his mercy but to his credit he never showed it, not for a second. And he went to Melbourne and bore the coffin with old Bowes. I have been a little harsh on him, it seems. Perhaps Robert was right all along, and knowledge made him a better man as well as a better scientist.

In the end it came down to the flotation process. Many thought Robert was old-fashioned and threatened, defending his process – how poorly they understood him. He was a philosopher – not just a scientist, not a manager, and certainly not a capitalist, God knows. He had confidence in his science and believed in progress as the very point of living. But he saw as he grew older that not all change was progress; not all progress could be measured by the dividends. He saw that flotation was probably inevitable if Lyell was to remain viable financially, but he saw also that it would spell Queenstown's end as a social experiment. Once the Queen and King died the town would die as well. He had seen it in Toston and elsewhere – the pristine stream reduced to a toxic sewer, devoid of all life. To accept that was a sign of desperation that would kill the spirit of his town.

The damage we had already wrought upon the landscape weighed heavily on him, called into question the happy confluence of his science and philosophy. They were the same thing once but they remained so only in the mind and soul of Robert Carl Henry Sticht.

So I came home, a stranger now on two continents.

Letter: Robert to Robert Jr at Throop, 15th January 1916

The Xmas holidays passed off as usual, except that they were a good deal damped by the fact that mother was ill during same, and supposed to be confined to her bed and 'resting'. Of course she didn't, notwithstanding that it was something that might have become pretty serious (inflammation of bowels and appendix). There were not too many people up at the house during the holidays (same as always, tree, etc), but there were a few. The weather was truly splendid. Miss McInnes (Mrs Slessor's sister) was staying with us, and helped all she could. Had. and Chet had a good time, and are still having it.

Then my appendix burst. I should have died, the doctors said. I had
the constitution of an ox, they said.

Another traitor. They managed to drive me across the valley to the
hospital but I do not remember much. They filled me full of morphine,
put me on the table Alice had donated and excised the little thing before
it killed me. Somehow I managed to avoid infection but I was weak as
a bled calf. I was there six weeks in winter while they fussed at me. All
the while I could see Penghana from the window, the smoke from the
chimneys, the gardeners and the washing on the line and I fancied I
could see Robert waving from our bedroom verandah. The evening sun
glinting off the windows signalled another wasted day and at night
their warm glow filled me with nostalgic longing.

I was six weeks in the Infirmary at Vassar as well, that cold winter
so long ago. I should have died, the doctors said. I had the constitution
of an ox, they said. Where are they now?

I went home to bed eventually but was never quite the same again.
This time there was no renaissance. Something else inside me had rup-
tured. It was the beginning of a slow and wearisome decline. The beginning of the end.

I have been in love with easeful death

I lost momentum without realising it. The weight of circumstance
and illness dulled my edge. I became cynical where once I had been
sceptical. Where once anything was possible now nothing good seemed
likely. Robert retreated more and more into the Collection. The catalogue
became some sort of metaphor for him, a symbol of all he stood for and
believed, a world made redundant by the War. It was an explanation of
what drove him to this wild shore and why he stayed: a belief in science
and art and man's capacity to improve the world.

The catalogue was the denouement of his Grand Experiment. The
clues to what the Collection and his life were about lay in the catalogue

and its secret codes and hierarchies, as much as in the Collection itself. Six volumes in the end, hand-written in that precise script of his, one hundred and fifty pages each. Every entry coded, graded, provenanced.

Civilisation knows no bounds, it says. Art is still Art in the wilderness. Science is Truth everywhere. Man's first responsibility is to himself, to struggle, to develop his potential through Science and Art and contact with the purifying natural world. In developing himself man fulfils his second responsibility – the development of society; because every man's development enhances his fellow man's development. I had been warned in that 'love letter' all those years ago:

...there is a continuous fund of pleasure in the necessity of contact with the rude healthfulness of outdoor roughness... It has been the outcome of a much dissatisfied youth to see beyond the material and yet reverence it, too, as the stepping stone to wider utility and profounder impress on the destiny of the race than could ever be accomplished by a life devoted to more artificial ideals. This conviction is bought only at the expense of many a heart-ache, – the purchase price is well returned by the peace of settled opinion.

He could be a little pompous, but I know it all too well, heard it many times, knew many a heartache myself while I waited for him, stuck in Pueblo, growing into middle-age while he bounded around the mountains like a happy goat.

Of course the danger with all that steely striving, all that denial and self-development, is that you are fixed always on the future. Where is the 'peace of settled opinion?' I have no idea still, 30 years on. But I have learned that if there is no time for the present you have no time to be happy. That is a gift I lost – the ability to know when I was happy. Is it something we all have as children and lose as we become convinced we need things? I wonder about native people: the Kickapoo who once roamed wide over our bit of Illinois or the Tasmanians, who lost this land to

Progress, or the people I see camped on the fringes of Deniliquin and out along the Murray – they don't seem to understand the value of unhappiness.

What begins in doubt ends in certainty. It is our story, and the story of America and Germany, even though they ended up locked in an unwinnable and destructive war whose consequences could be neither understood nor forgotten. I think the War broke his heart as much as Balfour or the Fire, or me. It undermined the foundations of his world.

among Germans I am completely one

He was never able to return. Germany was his Illinois, I suppose. And that was our bargain in the end. Neither of us could go home again. That he never got to take the boys was perhaps his greatest heartache in later years. The thought that Bob might end up there with a gun was too awful to countenance – and thankfully never looked likely.

Doubt reasserted itself, for there is nothing but doubt, it seems to me now. What begins in certainty ends in doubt. You understand that better as a woman – life's fragility is never out of ken. Robert went back to the Collection in confusion and the catalogue became a pilgrimage, a journey through his learning and belief, a search for certainty or for what went wrong.

It ran to more than a thousand pages in the end. Six volumes on the books and prints alone. And there were supplements. It is coded, a palimpsest of rank and provenance, hidden from the casual observer. Arcane and esoteric, it is a catechism. He must have sensed that he was dying. The catalogue was his argument and his requiem, written for us it seemed, but he must have known that once he was gone and we had neither home nor income, the Collection would be dispersed to pay our debts. He must have known that it was the Collection for a brief few years only. A reflection of himself that would disappear with him. Yet finishing the catalogue became an obsession. It was his cry against the night.

The rain this afternoon was intermittent and gentle and faded with the light. The shack is cosy and quiet, as there is no wind at present. In the amber light of the kerosene lamp I sit and pretend to read. Bob is at the table in his own pool of light, chiaroscuro, writing reports and letters to Ministers – a waste of his time but it is his coming of age: his tribute to his father and the dawning of the realisation that he was human. It will help him raise his brothers.

Dogs bark somewhere off in the stillness. There are always dogs. Their deep, mad rumble rolls around the hilltop. It is a sound reassuring to some but I find it unsettling. There is something primal in my alarm.

I do not hold with pets much, though the children and Robert collected them like stamps. Dogs, birds, wallabies, mice – nothing was safe from domestication at Penghana. I hold with dogs least of all – all that fawning and feigned outrage is too comic to take seriously. They lost whatever made them dogs long ago. Give me a horse – something only ever a split second away from its wild self. Or something useful, a cow or goat; something that has a purpose and therefore dignity.

But we had dogs. And stray, wounded animals: a blind wallaby, a broken parrot. But always dogs. When Hero or Lyell would bark, their barrel-chested baritone booming out above the valley set off an endless chain reaction as every mongrel round the town took its part in turn. Robert would explain that they were alarmed, crying out in stress for their pack. Their instinct drove them to seek kin they'd never known, he said. I would look at him and ask myself: is he deaf to me? Should I stand out on the front lawn and howl for my kin and country? Would he understand me then?

Two days of sunshine – it is a minor miracle. I sit out on the front stoop, as we would call it at home, and doze pleasantly, like someone in an illustration. A short sleep and some broth and I feel stronger. The sun

saturates me. My insides seem settled for the moment – and it is a beautiful moment. No pain, no blood. I feel myself fill with light and could
almost believe that one day I could be well again. It is a pleasant, lazy
thought for a sunny afternoon. I'll to my book.

18

Bob brought in the mail today, from Whale's Head with my pancakes. Letters from Chet and Hadmar and one from Alice. She is well and her life is full of good works and kin. George and the Wellmans send their regards, as always. It is six years or more since I saw them all and I will not see them again, save for a miracle. We had our farewell tour in 1917 but unlike Melba there will be no repeat.

The Company sent Robert over to research new methods for the Rosebery mines and to test a hundred tons of Mt Read ore that went across before us. He toured mining towns all across America, while I reprised my year in California. Alice and George were living in gracious retirement up at Carmel. George was giving lectures on his travels and his collection, Alice was devoted to her nieces and nephews. The Wellmans were as kind as ever but I sensed that I was now seen as somewhat stubborn in my exile. The boys went to school, I paid visits and went to the theatre and to concerts. I spent time with the Barndollars – Harry and his children and George, who was now known universally as Uncle George. It was a happy but meaningless sojourn and I felt strangely restless by its end.

The nation was in the throes of going to war, all that puffery and posing, everyone vying for the moral high ground. I had seen too much to share their enthusiasm. It had been the same in Australia before the lists of dead began to appear and the three-month war became three years, with no end in sight.

The hardest part of going home was leaving Bob behind again. He and young Mr Capra were about to join the army. I prayed the war would be over before he had to go. That was not how we wanted him to see Europe.

Robert was revived by his pilgrimage through his old lairs in the mountains and the contact with his old friends and peers. He was relishing a new challenge and went home full of energy and ideas. I had accepted my fate by then. When we sailed away I knew that I would never return and that this was the most bittersweet farewell. I was not sad, I was resigned. I could tell that I was failing. I was becoming my mother – an invalid with brief resurgences of my old self. I seemed so tired so often. I knew in my bones that we were both ill, both tiring, both losing confidence in ourselves.

We came back. We played our part. The Vice-Regal suite was in use again. The Company's fortunes were on the rise, Robert had new schemes and there was a sense of optimism as the shadow of the war receded. The town, like the nation, was emerging from that shadow, knowing it had changed but not sure how or why. The loss of so many young men would be felt for years, I knew, just as it had been at home after the War between the States. And there would be the unseen damage, to the survivors in the field and the survivors left at home. Bob, a Lieutenant now, was planning his return and I looked forward to having my family in one place.

Letter: Robert to Luke Williams, 18th November 1918

…The signing of the armistice was communicated to us while at dinner at Govt House, but the first news, though from Washington, was premature, and evidently due to the anticipation of some newspaper. However, the gunner fired off his guns and the populations started rejoicing. An hour or so later the ADC had to report that the news was not official, and on His Exc. remarking about the guns the ADC explained 'The gunman lost his head, Sir, – he could not wait any longer…'

The eleventh of the eleventh. It was a memorable night and yet I remember very little, save my sense of relief that it was finally over and that Bob was safe. I took a glass, as did Robert. It would have been churlish to refuse.

Letter: Robert to Robert Jr, 28th October 1918

Do not think of a position, after absolving your military obligations, but come straight out here, and help me to put that mine on its feet. Not one son in many hundreds has such a chance… it is on account of the chemistry that I want you, and your general good sense. I want you for many other untechnical reasons also, for your companionship, now that you are a man, – we have had nothing of each other while you were a boy. Intellectually I am a lonely man and am just getting old enough now to feel that I need a male to express myself to of my own persuasion. My sister Augusta died 26 Sept. It is the second death among us children. We have been widely separated, and my opinion is that this is not good. May my own children stick closer together.

Robert and Bob demanded so much of each other in the past that they never listened with anything other than their hearts. Now Bob had proved himself and Robert knew that he would soon have responsibility for the mess he was leaving behind. For my part, I was determined that Balfour would not ruin another life.

Robert was hard on his sons in his expectations, but he loved them more than life itself and never forgave himself for the legacy he wasted. It humbled him and he withdrew a little. Men become their fathers, they say, and while I only met Johan twice, I knew enough of him from Robert and Ernst to see him in Robert's raising of his sons. He loved and admired his father and saw him as the source of all he was. He dearly wanted to be that man for his own sons.

To have three sons is a blessing and a burden and though I dearly would have loved a daughter to play tomboy to my Sarah, it was not to be. I had Chet when I was 43, which was dangerous enough. The burden of direction fell on Robert – sons look to their mothers for faith, not approval.

ACTIVITIES AT LYELL

INTERVIEW WITH MR. ROBERT STICHT

'We have 1600 men employed at the mine when we should have 2000,' remarked Mr. Robert Sticht to *The Advocate* yesterday on his arrival at Burnie from Balfour.

Mr. Sticht remarked that he had spent a fortnight in the far North-West. The trip was purely a pleasure outing, spent with his wife and family, who accompanied him yesterday on the homeward tour.

The party put in some six days at Balfour, the rest of the time being spent in travelling. Though they struck some very bad weather, the trip was on the whole an enjoyable one...

As to the possibilities of the Balfour field for copper, he was not prepared to say. The mining at Balfour at present was tin 'scratching', and as the tin miners were scattered it was difficult to say how many were eking out a living. The slump in copper, following on the cessation of the war and the decision of the Imperial Government not to continue making purchases, had caused, or assisted to cause, the shutting down of every copper mine in Australia except the Mt. Lyell mine. The position at Lyell was very stable, the only trouble being that they could not secure sufficient miners.

Are not returned soldiers returning to the mine?

'They are coming back almost every day', was the reply. 'It was through enlistments that we lost many men, but if other occupations are available they do not care about mining. For one thing, the weather conditions at Lyell are far from pleasant'.

Mr. and Mrs. Sticht and members of their family continued their journey to the West Coast in the afternoon by rail motor.

BALFOUR COPPER

Mr. Robert C. Sticht, jnr., son of Mr. R. C. Sticht, general manager of the Mount Lyell Mine and Railway Co., who has been specialising in the oil flotation treatment of copper ore in U.S.A, has gone to Balfour to install a flotation plant at the Copper Reward mine. The necessary machinery has already been purchased in Melbourne, and will arrive at Stanley very shortly. From there it will be taken to Whale's Head (Temma) by ketch, and from the last-named place by tramway to the mine, which it is expected to reach by the end of the year. The Balfour-Temma tramway which had got badly out of repair, is now being reconstructed in readiness to carry this plant and the subsequent output of ore at the mine.

Mr. Luke Williams, who for the past six years has been general manager of the Copper Reward mine, has now relinquished that position, and handed over the control to Mr. Sticht, jun. Mr. Williams returned to his home at Moonah on Wednesday and will reside there. But although he has resigned from active management, he will continue to act as consulting engineer and agent for the mine.

Robert clung to Balfour as he did to Goethe and Humanism and faith in progress. Its failure insulted him. He had not been wrong before – at least not on such a scale. He kept increasing our investment – emotional, if not financial – like a bad gambler, until Bob came home and took charge. And here we are, three years on, closing down the old ruination.

19

THE MERCURY

12th July 1919

HOW TO GET TO BALFOUR

Our Balfour correspondent writes – 'Mr and Mrs Sticht and their sons arrived here last Saturday, 28th June, and have seen some of our worst weather. They travelled from Queenstown to Smithton by rail and road on Wednesday, then by train to Marrrawah, 27 miles. The ten mile ride in the horse tram (open trucks), being in the rain, was not pleasant, at 2 1/2 miles an hour. The journey from Marrawah to Temma, 24 miles, was by coach and from Temma (Whale's Head) to Balfour by road (16 miles), on horseback. The party of six enjoyed the various forms of travelling, notwithstanding the bad weather'.

The journey in to Balfour was a part of its attraction for me – it was always something of an adventure. By trains from Queenstown to Burnie, on to Smithton by road and then the next day the little train and tram, twenty-seven miles down through the green hills to Marrawah. The last ten miles was in an old horse tram – I could walk faster and sometimes did, rather than suffer the indignities of the open truck. Five hours and particularly uncomfortable in the wet, which was mostly. The prospect, however, was splendid as you wound your way down to the shore through lush pastures. In spring the wildflowers blanket the countryside for miles and miles. Marrawah is on a wild and beautiful coast with a splendid beach. I walked its length to the headland several times and rambled through the high dunes with my boys – when I was well, of course. There are aboriginal carvings on the headland, who knows how old?

A coach takes you on to Whale's Head – or Temma as it seems now to be called. The old Whale's Head Inn once sat beside the harbour at Kelly Basin, built there by the Cartledge brothers when Edgar won Tattersalls. They were huge men, the Cartledges. They had been teamsters and that is a business for big men. When Pillinger's fortunes began to wane they picked up their hotel, put it on a ship and took it up to Whale's Head. It was always a welcome sight at the end of that 25 mile ride along the dunes, sand-whipped and spray-soaked. There were several little bridges across creeks which could become rivers in a moment and often washed out the timber crossings.

The last 16 miles in to Balfour across the buttongrass plain was by horse tram in the boom years, but that fell into disrepair until Bob had it fixed when he took over. That was the last time we came in together as a family, back in 1919, when Bob came home from the Army and Robert asked him to take on Balfour. We rode horses in from Whale's Head, across the buttongrass plain. It was winter and a fine but exhausting ride it was, the horses often up to their girths in the swamp. I have that image of us in my mind now – the five of us on horseback, hunched

before a cold wind and drizzle, riding across wild country. It was perhaps the last time we were happy.

Two years later I came in with Hadmar and Chet. I met the boys off
the ship at Devonport, back from school in Melbourne. Robert was already
in at Balfour with Bob. Bad weather dogged us all the way. At Marrawah
we discovered that the rains had washed out the bridges between the
Arthur River and Sundown Creek, on the track south to Whale's Head. I
was determined to press on, however, and the three of us set off on
horses along the coast, thinking to ford the streams at their mouths,
where they are usually shallow and fanned out across the sands.

There was a curtain of grey cloud on the ocean horizon as we set off.
After an hour it turned an ominous black and began to advance, filling
the western sky. Ahead of it a westerly heaved and grew and began to
whip the waves across the beach, to the foot of the dunes. When the
westerly howls across that southern ocean, unchecked for thousands of
miles, it lashes the west coast and creates a thick wall of brown foam
that surges irresistibly across the broad sands. The beach is quickly buried
as it piles against the steep dunes. It is quick and terrible and difficult
to escape, as the dunes are sheer for miles. Cattle have been known to
drown in it and we were suddenly confronted with that same possibility.

We were in line, me leading, leaning sideways into the wind, foam
surging high around the horses' flanks and clinging to our clothes, so
that we looked like strange dolls mounted on some legless creatures of
the sea. At first I pressed in hard against the dunes, for there was some
easing of the wind there, as we sought a breach in the wall by which to
make our escape. But that was the worst place to be. The foam banked
deeper there and cloaked the pile of branches, logs and kelp. The horses
were on the edge of panic – the wind unnerved them and their footing
became unsure in the wet sand. There is quicksand all along that coast.
The foam had piled so high in places that if I had tried to lead them on
foot I would have disappeared beneath the wall of froth. We were on

the point of abandoning the horses to their fate and scrambling for our lives up the steep sand walls, when we came at last upon a small creek and the wall opened up. We took to our feet and stumbled with the horses along the creek, until we could take shelter in the lee of the wind-lashed dunes.

The boys' natural confidence had been badly shaken but with the resilience of children they were quickly pretending it was all a marvelous adventure. I remained concerned though, aware that we were still exposed – ten miles from Whale's Head, with no way forward or back that did not involve considerable difficulty and some danger. We were stuck inland now and whichever way we went, we would have to ford the creeks along the track where the bridges were out. The rain now drenching us meant those creeks would soon be swollen beyond their banks and probably impassable.

I reckoned we were closer to Whale's Head than Marrrawah and so struck on south, more in hope than confidence. The Inn was expecting us today and there was a chance someone might come out to meet us. Otherwise we faced the possibility of a cold, wet and unsheltered winter's night behind the dunes.

An hour later we had forded the first small stream with difficulty – the creek was rising but it was only twenty yards across and I could still pick a way on foot, leading the boys in their saddles. I was soaked anyway and the horses' sure-footedness had to be trusted. But I knew there were two more creeks and I knew they would be harder. And then, just as our prospects looked the dimmest, old Mr Dixon appeared along the track, carrying ropes and trailing fresh mounts. The dear man had come out from Balfour to meet us at Whale's Head and come on from there when the weather blew up and he realised we might be in difficulties.

He took charge immediately. An hour later we were across those rising streams and sitting snugly before the fire in the Whale's Head Inn. I had no dry clothes, our luggage having been as soaked as we were, so

I had to make do with men's breeches, a flannel shirt and a Bluey. I never felt so comfortable or so warm. Men have no idea what indignities and discomfort our clothes inflict upon us.

I picked up a pebble from the creek that saved us from the beach that day. I have it with me still. Smoothed and rounded by ten thousand years of polishing, it sits cool in the palm of my hand as my fingers add their oils to its burnished surface. There is comfort in it – I know not why. Maybe because it is whole and perfect in its solidity or because it is of the earth, as we all are? Because its age belittles our trivial concerns? Its form is the result of a million random influences. I was always a great one for bringing home stones. Robert would tell me what they were but I did not care. I cared about how they felt, not how they were formed. It was a difference between us that we never bridged. Robert never heard anything from a rock.

a stone falls to ground for its love of it

Letter: Robert to George, 30th April 1920

...Socially the place is much improved. The company has started spending a lot of money on what is called welfare work, ie., work-men's houses, clubs, YMCA, butchers shops, stores, etc, etc. They wages are now 50% higher than when you left. Everybody has a garden now, both vegetables and flowers, though the hills are barer than ever. People have found out what will grow. At my house the garden some years is rather fine – nothing like California – but it has a distinctive air about it. The garden is Marion's particular hobby... Marion still makes use of the cottage at Regatta Point...

Marion has not been too well this last few years. She is as active as ever, but can not, of course, get about as she used to, though she still wants to. Just now the people in Queenstown are in the whole perhaps nicer than ever, but there is at present no woman there she can make a real friend of, and that makes it bad for her.

In contrast with this wild bush and standing on a huge rock above the town, is the magnificent home of the late Robt. Sticht, who was general manager for the Mount Lyell Company. Contained in this home is the largest private library in Australasia. It is comprised of works produced in the 14th century, original manuscripts of books written by famous authors Bibles written on vellum before printing was invented, and almost, every known book written on geology. This collection of books is now being packed in cases made specially for the purpose, numbering 200, and weighing 10 tons, to be sold in Melbourne. It seems strange that this library, valued at £10,000, should come from the heart of this great forest, where the railway line forms the only means of communication.

19

16th January 1923

GARDEN' PARTY AT 'PENGHANA'

FAREWELL TO MRS STICHT.

A large number of people assembled at 'Penghana', the residence of Mrs R. Sticht, on Saturday afternoon for the purpose of saying good-by on her approaching departure from the district. The gathering took the form of a garden party, and was attended by representatives of all parts of the field and of Strahan.

The function was organised by a committee of ladies to provide an opportunity of saying good-by to a large circle of Mrs. Sticht's friends, and also for the purpose of making a presentation. It was the wish of the townspeople to have given Mrs. Sticht a public farewell in the town, but the state of Mrs. Sticht's health prevented her from

acceding to these very kind wishes. The garden party,
though ostensibly of a semi-private nature, was open to
all who desired to bid farewell to the guest of the afternoon.

During the afternoon Mr R. M. Murray, general manager,
in a short speech, referred to the long residence of
Mrs. Sticht amongst us, about 28 years, and to the many
good qualities she had shown us. Our reputation for
hospitality originated from the example shown from the
start by the late general manager and Mrs. Sticht. We
were all very sorry to lose her. He sympathetically referred
to the long long battle against ill-health which she had
fought during the past few years. He assured Mrs. Sticht
that those present were very grateful for being allowed
the opportunity of being there that afternoon. There were
people of many years' residence present there, and he
felt incapable of finding words to suitably express the
thoughts and wishes of those present that afternoon.
He had very great pleasure in presenting Mrs. Sticht, on
behalf of her many friends, with a small token of the
great esteem in which she was held by all who knew her.

Mrs Sticht, in a very appropriate little speech, acknowledged the gift with very great pleasure, and said she felt
all in attendance were her true friends all through the
years. She reminded them that she would not be far away,
her home would be only about 30 miles distant. Words
could not express all she felt, and she thanked them all for
their handsome present and for all their kindness to her.

During the afternoon The 'Occasional Orchestra' rendered
some delightful items which were very much appreciated.

The committee provided a recherche afternoon tea,
and altogether a very pleasant afternoon was spent.

The old house was naked when I left. I heard the train whistle and my heart sank.

some day I am going

I had heard that whistle so many times before and longed to be aboard, going home, or anywhere. I steeled myself to walk down the front steps, through my garden, knowing I would never see it again. I turned my back on my beautiful house and my life in it and I did not look back.

We were the house and it was one of us. We are all still there, ghosts in the walls, caught in the dust, caught in the light streaming through the stained glass, our skin-dust hidden in every edge and corner and gap of every room. Our hands shaped and polished the Blackwood banister. Our sweat is in the floorboards, our music vibrates deep inside the ballroom walls and its floor still echoes to the stamp of our gay feet. Our breath and tears and laughter imbue the very walls. We will never leave. We will always be there.

We walked slowly to the station in the summer sun, Bob on my arm and the boys with their heads held high. People watched from their windows. Many came out and waved or called a greeting. I might have been going to the shop. We crossed the footbridge, staring up at Mt Owen, trailing clouds. Archie was waiting at the station with a small band of '95ers, the few remaining souls of these who were there when I came up the line in a dray, 28 years earlier.

Of course I cried when I left the house but I had composed myself by the time we walked onto that old platform I saw built half a lifetime ago. The station was sombre and looked established, almost old. I had not noticed it become so, any more than I had marked my own establishment in the ranks of the venerable. My eyes saw the town – through tears – as if for the first time. The broad King Billy planks of the platform felt buoyant as a jetty beneath my feet. I remember them as still sappy planks, creaking in the warm sun like old knees at a miners' picnic. I looked over the little flock of hats, up along the length of Orr Street to Mt Owen, gleaming in the sun above the town and felt I might float away into the sky, so dreamlike was my state. It was ending, finally.

All around me good people gathered to bid farewell, though it was goodbye. The long anticipation did nothing to dissipate the tragedy of the moment but for once I felt that I was living in that moment and not watching myself in it. I was Marion Oak Stage again, and I was going away now, forever and you would never know the truth of my time among you. I was leaving the place that had been my home for half my life but that I had never felt was home. And yet I cried, cried for the loss of the life we had lived and for the one we had forsaken. Dear Archie ushered me aboard the train, his hand cupping my elbow with an intimacy I could not resist and will never forget. He sat me in my seat, kissed my cheek, the whistle blew, steam filled the air, people waved, some cried. They may as well have played 'Nearer My God to Thee' again.

No looking back. Along the line south people had come out to wave. It was a kind thing to do. I made it past the cemetery, but only just.

thou hast shewed thy people hard things

21

17 August 1923

It is early morning; the sun is weak and milk-clouded. A bleak westerly is gathering force and there is a faint tang of salt on its cold breath. The clouds looming in the west behind the wind are dark and boisterous. There is serious weather afoot. It is cold, colder now than before dawn. Cold, as befits the occasion. It would never do to leave on a sunny day, like the day we buried Papa. With the warm wind off the endless prairie and the scent of summer in the horses' nostrils and our hair. This sombre weather is more fitting entirely for my departure from the only world I know. I give myself up henceforth to the black crow doctors and the stiff-backed nurses whose job it will be to see me out and pretend they can save me. I will charm them, of course, because I can and because it's what I do and because none of this is their fault.

if it were done when 'tis done, then 'twere well it were done quickly

We will run for Melbourne. It would be too obscure to die here. It would be untidy. We load my flotsam on to the dray. Or rather Bob and young Ethel do. Then Ethel's bags as well. She will go back to Queenstown from Burnie. I wonder how she will remember me?

We walk out the door and the squeaking hinge pipes the end as the door clunks shut with a thud like the fall of clay on a coffin. Bob gives it the extra shove it needs to close properly and locks the door. Against what I cannot say but he was always a careful boy.

I walk out through the rickety remains of the front gate that is unsupported by a fence. Bob helps me cover this daunting distance. He lifts me up onto the dray. Ethel climbs up behind, Bob flicks the reins and we set off up Henry St, past the empty ruins and the empty paddocks, and the ruined gardens, up to Alexander St and the cobbles. One last look around as we swing downhill – I shall not look back again. The mirror cracked when I left Penghana and I am tired of Balfour anyway. I turn my back for the last time on my six acres and two roods and the derelict garden of dreams on the red hill and the cold south light over the heath and the distant mountains full of metal. We set off across the muddy heath for the coast and Melbourne and the final act.

You don't think any of this will happen to you. Disease, dying, loss, decrepitude; I had so long defied the conventions of my family – three strong sons, fortune, love – I began to take the future for granted. I had reason enough to understand the fragility of life yet I was confident beyond good reason, and for a while it worked. There is no such thing as luck, of course. The wave that flung this pebble high is long since spent.

now I only hear its melancholy, long withdrawing roar

Most of the people I know and love – have known and loved – have been damaged and disappointed by life. We look around us at the compounding carnage of our broken families, the wreckage of our friends and wonder where God is, why Jesus redeems yet we still suffer and like dear Mama we imagine that all those who have been wrecked and taken too soon from us await us in Heaven. As though they've all conspired in a surprise party of celestial proportions.

Elvin, Gilmon, Samuel and Nancy,

Mary, Abigail, Annette,

Napoleon, Emma, Charlie and Louise

Sarah and Lizzie and Marion

I do not think redemption or reconciliation await me. I wish I could hear the footsteps of angels, but I am deaf. I made my bed and, uncomfortable as it has become, I will lie me down with a will and remember all the while the comfort of our bed and the great adventure we undertook across continents and oceans and I'll remember those good souls who lit my life and forgive those few who dimmed it. Most of them, at least. I hope I made some difference, that I shed some light of my own in the darkness. I hope my boys will be strong and happy. I will die wanting to live.

the author of all things watches over me

My father, dear Napoleon, whose strength and love and fairness I never truly understood, will die again with me. A man such as he, who departs your life at such an impressionable age, is simply what he is, a hero or a saint but not a person who ever had a choice to be something other than a paragon. I had to grow old to understand that courage is not reckless.

I am tired now and sleep so much that the boundaries between sleep and waking begin to blur. Our little life is bounded by a sleep and sleep seeps in around the frayed edges of my little life. I long for it yet fight it. It is weakness – but I am weak. I no longer fear it. It has been so long and I have been so tired. Sleepwalking through the final act, yet I would love to know what happens next.

Sometimes – more often as I have grown older and less wise – I sense something familiar on the edge of the wind – a shiver in the evening light,

———

a rustle in the long grass. I smell the sweet breath of childhood in the angle of light or the air caressing this face that is now a map, and something rolls through me like a breaking wave on a long, lonely beach – I am struck simultaneously by the strange wonder of living and by the rare knowledge that I am alone, that I cannot share this fleeting understanding ever, with anyone. Why try to describe what is quick as mercury and of little interest to others anyway? I know now that this is true of all experience. Heroic or ignorant, it matters little in the end – it is all foolishness.

Perhaps that is the truth of my life. That I have lived a foolish and often happy life in unique circumstances. I had no expectation of longevity. In my family threescore and ten is a dangerous conceit. In my family death sat at table.

'tis the wink of an eye, 'tis the draught of a breath,
from the blossom of health to the paleness of death

Leaving Balfour is symbolic but leaving Penghana was the end of our grand, mad dream. It was the place I should have loved more than I loved the past and leaving it was death. The rest is coda.

THE MERCURY

1st November 1923

The numerous friends of Mrs. Robert Sticht, widow of the late general manager of the Mt. Lyell mine, will regret to learn that she is lying in a critical condition in a private hospital in Melbourne. Her two sons, Robert and Hadmar, who have been living at Balfour, left Tasmania on Monday to go to her bedside.

22

21st January 1924

Queens Rd, Melbourne

I sense the dull rumble of the world outside as I drift in and out of sleep. Seagulls scratch their crooked song and in my mind I see them cork-screwing over the waves. I fancy I can hear the low thunder of the bay collapsing on the distant shore. The difference between waking and sleeping is so vague now I cannot tell if I am dreaming. I have no pain – can that be dreamt?

a dream has power to poison sleep

A cool wind now off the water billows the stark white curtains. They fill the room for a moment like a breath of mist on a cold morning. There was a hot northerly earlier... today? A year ago that hot northerly chased us over the blasted heath, from Whale's Head Inn to Marion's Last Stand. A year ago... to the day? I feel the salty breeze fan my sweated head...

I see a lily on thy brow, with anguish moist and fever dew and strain to hear the seagulls squawking, falling down the sky like Icarus. But there is silence now. I am nothing.

and no birds sing

Acknowledgements

Many good and generous people have lent their support to this project and shared information and ideas with me. There are too many to name them all but some cannot go without mention. They are, in no particular order:

In Queenstown: Raymond Arnold, who had faith in me and the book from the start; Helena Demczuk, whose passion for the stories of West Coast women is inspiring and who supplied many leads and ideas; and Peter Reid, who introduced me ten years ago to the real history of Queenstown.

In Balfour: Marty Laan, whose generosity in sharing his home and his great knowledge of Balfour, mining and geology was an enormous help.

In Hobart: Linda Forbes, whose great grandmother was Fanny Westmoreland (Miss Wissie); and Sue & Warwick Lee, who found Alice in a bookstore in Melbourne.

In Swansea: Sarah Buckley for her advice and proofreading.

In Melbourne: Heather Gaunt, whose landmark article on the Sticht Collection* first stirred my interest in this story and who shared her reseach with me; Beth Hemming, for organising the German translations; and Helen Dean, who found the ashes.

In Edgar Co Illinois: Joyce Brown and the good people at the Edgar Co Genealogy Society. It emerged that Joyce had once lived in the old Stage house at Bloomfield.

In California: Carrie Cohen, who has been researching George Beardsley for her Masters at UCLA; and Trish Richards at The University of the Pacific Library, who arranged access to the Hazelton letters.

In New York – Colleen Mallett, Registrar at Vassar College;

I should also like to thank Nic Haygarth, Bob Vincent, Lou Rae, Sally McGushin, Shirley Scolyer, Leonie Oakes, Ruth Johnston and Maureen and Bill Kerr at Penghana, for their contributions and encouragement.

To all the others, friends and family, who have given advice, listened and generally supported me through these five years, my sincere thanks. I hope you think it was worthwhile.

For more information on the life of Marion Oak Sticht (nee Stage) go to Brett Martin's blog at: https://marionoak.wordpress.com

* For an overview of the range, size and quality of the Sticht Collection, see Heather Gaunt's excellent article, 'The Library of Robert Carl Sticht', in the Latrobe Journal No 79, 2007, at: http://www.slv.vic.gov.au/latrobejournal/issue/latrobe-79/t1-g-t2.html

---

p152   Marion to Mrs Millar, 16th October 1906
        Courtesy of Linda Forbes.

p159   Robert Sticht to Dr E. D. Peters, 22nd October 1907
        Collection of the State Library of Tasmania

p160   Marion to Mrs Millar, 22nd August 1908
        Courtesy of Linda Forbes

p167   Robert Sticht to Ernst Sticht, c 1910
        Collection of the State Library of Tasmania

p168   Robert Sticht to Manager of the Republic Mines Corporation,
        3rd June 1911. Sticht letterbooks, cited by Heather Gaunt, Latrobe
        Journal no 79, Autumn 2007

p174   Robert Sticht to Sir Elliot Lewis (date unknown)
        Collection of the State Library of Tasmania

p189   Robert to Robert Jr, 26th April 1912
        Collection of State Library of Tasmania

p201   Marion to Mrs Millar, 24th November 1913
        Courtesy of Linda Forbes

p204   Robert Sticht to Mr Goode, 26th April 1912
        Collection of the State Library of Tasmania

p214   Robert Sticht to Mr Millar, 6th May 1915
        Courtesy of Linda Forbes

p231   Sarah Stage to Marion, c. 1882
        Holt-Atherton Special Collection, University of the Pacific, California

p237   Robert Sticht to Robert Jr, 15th January 1916
        Collection of the State Library of Tasmania

p239   Robert Carl Sticht to Marion, 17th January 1892
        Sticht Letterbooks, cited by Heather Gaunt, Latrobe Journal no. 79,
        Autumn 2007

p245   Robert Sticht to Luke Williams, 18th November 1918
        Collection of the State Library of Tasmania

p245   Robert Sticht to Robert Sticht Jr, 28th October 1918
        Collection of the State Library of Tasmania

p255   Robert Sticht to George (surname not given) 30th April 1920
        Collection of the State Library of Tasmania

Images

ROBERT EARL STICHT
1857-1922
MARION OAK STICHT
1865-1924

Brett Martin

Brett Martin was born in Devonport Tasmania in 1952, grew up on the Gold Coast and has lived in Hobart, Canberra, Wagga Wagga and Launceston. His working life was as a labourer and a librarian. It makes no sense to him either.

He now lives in Swansea, on Tasmania's East Coast, where he spends most of his time gardening, fishing and writing. He has published one other novel, *Fundamental Things* (2001), and is presently working on a memoir: *Hiroshima 21*.